TRIGGER YAPPY

Also by Diana Orgain

TRIGGER YAPPY

Diana Orgain

MINOTAUR BOOKS

A THOMAS DUNNE BOOK

NEW YORK

A THOMAS DUNNE BOOK FOR MINOTAUR BOOKS.
An imprint of St. Martin's Publishing Group.

TRIGGER YAPPY. Copyright © 2016 by Diana Orgain. All rights reserved. Printed in the United States of America. For information, address St. Martin's Press, 175 Fifth Avenue, New York, N.Y. 10010.

www.thomasdunnebooks.com
www.minotaurbooks.com

The Library of Congress Cataloging-in-Publication Data is available upon request.

ISBN 978-1-250-06912-2 (hardcover)
ISBN 978-1-4668-7793-1 (e-book)

Our books may be purchased in bulk for promotional, educational, or business use. Please contact your local bookseller or the Macmillan Corporate and Premium Sales Department at 1-800-221-7945, extension 5442, or by e-mail at MacmillanSpecialMarkets@macmillan.com.

First Edition: December 2016

10 9 8 7 6 5 4 3 2 1

For my loving family,
Tom Sr., Carmen,
Tommy, and Bobby

TRIGGER YAPPY

Chapter One

"The wine is smooth, right?" the stubbled face in front of me asked.

At the moment, it was difficult to discern any qualities the wine might have to offer. In a few days, I would report for my very first bookkeeper/purser assignment with Soleado Mexican Riviera Cruise Line. Last night had been my going away party and, regrettably, I'd over indulged. But this morning my sister, Rachel, owner of the Wine and Bark—a wine bar that catered to dog owners and their beloved beasts—had confessed that she had also indulged a bit too much. She wasn't even able to get out of bed.

She'd begged me to meet Hendrick, the proprietor of Verdant Vines, and select a few varieties to feature at the Wine and Bark. I suppose the feeling of guilt at abandoning my sister and Pacific Cove in favor of the Mexican Riviera was too much to bear, so I'd agreed to meet Hendrick and taste test.

I tapped on the laminated sheet of prices that lay between the wine vendor and myself. "I can't make any money at these prices."

Hendrick shrugged. "I can knock a dollar off for you."

I nearly gagged on the, admittedly getting smoother by the sip, Merlot. A dollar off would barely put a dent in the price.

Hendrick ignored my expression and carried on with his sales pitch. "We specialize in green energy. Verdant Vines owns a wind turbine that harnesses the power of the unique air currents that run through the Central Valley."

"Someone would need to be made of green to fork over the kind of cash you're asking," I said.

Before Hendrick could reply, the doors to the Wine and Bark flew open and Yolanda bustled in. She was the chief organizer of the Roundup Crew, a group that met every Friday on the beach to walk dogs and ultimately end up at Rachel's bar for "Yappy Hour." She wore her trademark skintight leather pants, strappy sandals, and an animal print halter top. Her hair was blown in Marilyn Monroe–style curls and she cradled her Yorkie, Beepo, in her arms.

Beepo gave a lukewarm yap at seeing me.

Beepo and I had a complicated relationship.

Yolanda held the door for another woman, one I'd never seen before. The woman was rail thin with dark, straight hair. She wore a severe expression, but on her head was a ridiculous hat; perched atop the hat was a chicken with one very long feather decidedly pointing to the east.

Good grief! What was the woman thinking?

The only thing I'd seen in recent history as ridiculous as that hat were Yolanda's "designer" chicken purses.

The woman took one look at Hendrick, who was leaning against the bar, and bristled. He jolted himself up straight, as if he'd been just been electrocuted. He turned away from her and locked eyes with me.

There was definitely a story there. But before I could probe, Yolanda rapped on the bar with her long painted nails and said,

"Maggie! What are you doing here? I would have thought you'd be home packing! Where's Rachel?"

"Unfortunately, she's in bed ill."

Yolanda waved a hand around dismissing Rachel's illness. "Probably a case of partying too hard." She put a possessive arm around the woman next to her. "Fran and I will take a table, we have some business to discuss." She eyed the open bottle between Hendrick and me. "Is that a new wine you're sampling for the bar?"

Fran shrugged Yolanda's arm from her shoulders and Hendrick took a sharp inhale as if readying himself for attack. Instead, Fran said, "The Merlot is the best anyone could offer. Take my word for it."

Hendrick relaxed. "That's kind of you to say."

The corners of Fran's mouth turned downward. "It's the truth. I may not miss you, but I do miss the wine."

A scowl passed over Hendrick's handsome features, but Fran turned quickly before she could see it.

Ouch!

Yolanda and Fran clacked over to a private table, and I resisted the urge to ask Hendrick about Fran. He leaned over and dug into his wine case, producing another bottle that he plunked down on the bar. "This is the best wine for your budget. And it's her favorite. Go ahead and serve them this one."

He uncorked the bottle with a flourish and poured out a taste for me in a clean glass. "It's a full-bodied wine with a velvet finish."

I sipped the wine and immediately wanted more. No wonder this was Fran's favorite.

Hendrick smiled at my reaction. "If you like fuller wines, I have some other samples—"

"Are we going to get some service here or what?" Fran yelled, twisting around in her chair to look at me.

Hendrick pushed a business card in my direction and closed his wine case. "I hope we can do business together soon, Maggie. Perhaps you can make it up to the winery tomorrow. I have tastings starting in the morning. You can sample anything you like."

There was no way with my full schedule that I could squeeze in a winery tour, but I didn't want to rude, so I smiled and said, "Thank you."

He nodded and then disappeared out the front without a glance back in Fran's direction, leaving me to wonder about the obvious bad blood between them. I grabbed two clean wineglasses and the bottle Hendrick had left and high-tailed it over to their table before Fran could bark at me again.

As I approached, Fran's phone buzzed from the depths of her purse. She hiked the purse onto her lap and began to sort through it. I placed the glasses on the table and poured the wine. Yolanda did her best to ignore me, but I was still able to catch her eye and quirk an eyebrow in Fran's direction giving her my best get-a-load-of-that-hat expression.

Yolanda frowned and Beepo growled.

I shrugged. There was no accounting for taste.

Fran produced the vibrating phone from her bag with such a flourish she knocked the freshly poured wine all over the table.

"Shoot!" she exclaimed. "Why did you put that so close to me? Is this the first table you've ever waited?"

I grabbed the towel hanging from my back pocket and took a deep breath, trying to hang on to my sanity. After all, the Mexican Riveria was beckoning. I wiped the table and offered her a sincere apology, even though it had been clearly her fault she'd spilled the wine. "My apologies, Fran. Please enjoy a round on the house."

She barely acknowledged me as she answered her phone. "Yes? What is it, Cornelia?" she demanded into the receiver.

I had barely escaped their table and reached the relative safety behind the bar when I spotted Gus DelVecchio making his way across the shared patio between the Wine and Bark and DelVecchio's restaurant. My hangover quickly dissipated. Dressed in tight blue jeans and a snug black shirt, he radiated his usual animal magnetism. My heart skipped a beat as he pushed open the door and entered. He flashed a warm smile and approached the bar.

"Hi, Maggie," he said.

For no good reason, I blushed. "Hi, Gus," I muttered shyly, like a schoolgirl overrun with hormones. Gus and I had only met a few weeks earlier, but we'd quickly struck up a friendship. Only problem was, I'd struck up an equally quick friendship with Officer Brad Brooks, and dating two men at the same time was not only completely foreign to me, it was also a bit treacherous.

After careful deliberation, I'd decided not to invite either to my going-away party. It had only been Rachel, myself, and our great-uncle Ernest, aka Grunkly.

Gus reached across the bar and grabbed my hand. "It's good to see you. Did you have a nice time last night with your family?"

Yolanda and Fran craned to see what was happening between Gus and me, although for all I knew they were checking out his backside. I mean, that's what I would have been doing if I had their vantage point.

"Stop being such a nervous Nellie, Cornelia!" Fran screamed into her phone.

Gus ignored them, leaning in closer toward me. "I missed you. I wanted to talk to you about something." He freed my hand and ran his fingers through his thick dark hair.

I poured him a glass of the Verdant Vines Merlot and watched him work his lower lip.

Uh-oh. He's nervous about something. Does he have bad news for me?

My stomach clenched at the thought.

"It's about the restaurant." He fixed his dark eyes on mine. "I think I need to keep it closed awhile . . . I need to . . . you know . . . figure things out."

I knew Gus had recently inherited one hundred percent of the restaurant from his partner and had some restructuring in mind, but I couldn't guess what was causing him such distress at the moment.

I pushed the glass of wine toward him, but he reached for my hand again instead of the glass. He laced his fingers through mine and said, "Maggie, I got an offer I want to discuss with you."

"That's not even close to a fair price!" Fran shouted at Yolanda.

Gus glanced over his shoulder at Yolanda and Fran's table. Fran had hung up the phone and she and Yolanda were now having an animated discussion. Yolanda looked insulted and Beepo yowled.

"Now is probably not a good time," Gus said.

I tugged on Gus's hand. "Come to the back. I should get started on the Arf d'oeuvres."

He laughed as he followed me to the makeshift kitchen. "Not the Arf d'oeuvres!"

I yanked open the freezer and pulled out a bag of frozen little hot dogs wrapped in mini-croissants. Gus made a face, as if merely watching the proceedings offended his palate, but since he was the best chef in town I forgave his food snobbery. In fact, I secretly wished he was getting ready to ask me to dinner.

I turned from him and put the dogs in a blanket onto a baking sheet. From behind me, he snaked an arm around my waist. He moved his lips close to my ear and asked, "Are you really going to take that purser job?"

His breath on my ear warmed my blood, and as I much as I wanted to say, "Forget the stupid job," I knew I couldn't. My failed stint as a financial advisor in New York had put a significant drain on my savings and now California rent was driving the nail in the coffin of what remained.

Not to mention, I'd wanted to travel, right? The Mexican Riviera, the Bahamas, the Florida Keys, they were practically shouting my name. And I'd be away from the dogs . . . away from the bar . . . away from Pacific Cove . . .

Gus's body heat drew me in and I leaned against him for a moment. "You're not making it easy," I grumbled.

"I'm glad to hear that," he whispered. "What time do you get off?"

I slipped out of his embrace and turned the oven on. "I'm not technically supposed to be working. Rachel promised she'd be here by Yappy Hour."

Gus and I both glanced at the oven clock at the same time. Five minutes till. So like Rachel to be late. She'd be milking my covering for her at the bar for as long as she could.

Gus smiled. "In that case, how about I . . ." He reached for my hip just as my phone rang from inside my pants pocket. He pulled his hand away, as if the ringing phone had given him a shock.

He bit his lip. "Do you need to get that?"

I didn't even want to look at my phone. Who was more important than Gus at this moment? Wasn't he about to suggest making me dinner? Or was I just daydreaming?

"No," I said.

He lowered his gaze. "It could be Officer Brooks."

That was a setup. I knew. He was prompting me to say he was more important than Brad, but that sort of talk wasn't going to get me anywhere. Instead, I said, "Probably Rachel telling me she's going to be late."

He watched me expectantly. My phone stopped ringing and even though I felt compelled to pull out my phone and check the missed-call log, I didn't. Instead, I said, "What did you want to tell me?"

He shifted his weight, and the oven, having reached its preheated temperature, beeped. Almost on instinct, he reached over and grabbed the cookie sheet and popped it in the oven.

I laughed. "I feel like I'm forcing you to cook Arf d'oeuvres against your will."

He smiled. "Cooking is in my blood. See, that's what I wanted to talk to you about. I received an opportunity that's hard to pass up."

"What is it?"

"I got a call from one of the producers of *Gourmet Games*. They want to fly me out to New York to audition."

I clapped a hand over my mouth and squealed. *Gourmet Games* was quickly becoming one of the top-rated cooking reality shows on television. "Oh my goodness! Gus, you have to take it! This could be the opportunity of a lifetime."

He smiled sadly at me and reached for my face. He cradled my chin in his hand and said, "I know. It's just that they want me to fly out right away . . . I don't . . ."

"I'm going to be on the cruise. You know that. This is perfect timing."

My phone rang again and he frowned.

"When do you leave?" I asked, ignoring my phone.

"I should go home and pack. There's a red-eye tonight out of SFO."

My throat suddenly became dry and I realized how much I'd miss him. I wrapped my arms around his neck and pressed my check against his.

"Tonight?" I asked.

"I know it's sudden, but—"

"No. No. You should go. You have to go. I'm just going to miss you, is all," I said.

"I'm going to miss you, too. But, if I don't get cast," he said. "I'll be back in town before your cruise is over."

"They'd be crazy not to cast you, Gus."

He shrugged. "I hope I can out cook the competition."

"You can out cook anyone!"

"The competition is going to be top rate. I have to bring my A-game. In fact—"

A terrible screeching from the bar cut off his words and we both rushed out to the bar toward the sound. Yolanda and Fran were standing, facing each other and screaming. Beepo was emitting a high-pitched bark and growl.

"What's going on?" I demanded.

"You're a fraud!" Yolanda said to Fran.

"I'm not selling!" Fran said, fixing her chicken hat so that the tail feather waved under Yolanda's nose.

Beepo dove out of Yolanda's arms and straight for the chicken on top of Fran's head.

Fran screamed. Gus hurried over to disentangle the dog from Fran's hat.

"Calm down!" I said.

Fran yanked her hat out of Gus's hand and stormed toward the front door. "You can forget about your *chicken empire,* Yolanda. That'll happen over my dead body!" She pulled open the front door and exited with bravado.

Beepo howled after her.

Gus turned to me and I shrugged. We both looked at Yolanda.

Yolanda affectionately stroked Beepo's triangle ears. "Hush now, Beep." She put Beepo down, then looked at Gus and said, "There's no talking to some people. I wanted to buy out her hat business, but she went cuckoo on me."

Gus smirked but didn't say a word.

My phone rang again from inside my pocket. Gus leaned in and kissed me. "I think you have your hands full here, Maggie."

I clutched at his arm. "Good luck! Let me know what happens, okay?"

He nodded. "I will." He waved at us and stepped toward the front door.

I pulled the phone and glanced at the caller ID: Rachel.
Of course.

Yolanda sipped what was left of her wine, but quirked an eyebrow at me to let me know she was waiting on me.

I answered the phone. "Hi, Rach."

Silence greeted me.

"Hello?"

A voice I didn't recognize came on the line. "Ms. Patterson?"

My stomach clenched. Who was this? Where was Rachel?

"This is Nurse Joan. Your sister asked me to phone you to let you know that's she's been admitted to the hospital."

"The hospital!"

Yolanda hurried over to me with a look of alarm on her face. "What's going on?" She pressed her ear close to my phone.

"She has a case of salmonella poisoning," Nurse Joan said. "Basically, she ate some bad chicken."

"There's no such thing as a bad chicken!" Yolanda squawked.

Chapter Two

"Salmonella?" I asked.

"Nonsense!" Yolanda shrieked. She had such an indignant look on her face that I pulled the phone away from her before she could burst into flames. "She's blaming her hangover on chicken? Ridiculous!"

"Tell her I'm on my way," I said to Nurse Joan.

Nurse Joan grumbled something into the phone I couldn't understand. Then there was a rustling sound and she said, "Hold on a minute."

"Maggie?" My sister's voice filled the line. She sounded as if she had rocks in her mouth.

"Rachel! How do you feel? What happened?"

Next to me, Yolanda angled her head toward the phone again, straining to hear.

"I kept throwing up and . . . uh . . ." She sighed and took a deep breath. "I'll tell you later, okay? I'm so tired . . . sleepy. It must be the pain medicine they gave me."

"I'll be right there."

"No, uh . . . Maggie, you have to do Yappy Hour. There's a woman . . . oh . . . I can't remember her name. She going to visit the bar tonight. You have to be open. She's the editor of *Doggie Day*—"

Yolanda let out a squeal. "*Doggie Day*!"

"Who's that?" Rachel asked.

"Yolanda," I said.

"Hi, Yo," Rachel said. "Let me talk to her."

"I'm not bartending while you're in the hospital!" I said. "I'm coming to see you—"

"I'm not dying, Maggie. You can check on me later. They're just holding me to monitor—"

"I'm on my way."

"No! Ugh . . . You're impossible. Let me talk to Yolanda," Rachel said.

Yolanda snatched the phone out of my hand and walked away from me so I couldn't eavesdrop on their conversation. Although I could clearly hear Yolanda's exaggerated gasps and whispers of, "*Doggie Day*? Oh my goodness gracious! They're coming here?"

Through the front window of the bar, I saw a crowd approaching. I glanced at my watch. Just like clockwork, the Roundup Crew was ready for Yappy Hour. My friends Abigail, Brenda, and Max were in the lead. Brenda and Max had started up a romance and were holding hands. Behind them, I could see Yolanda's nemesis, the infamous Geraldine, and next to her was a woman I hadn't seen before.

Each of them had a small dog attached to the end of a Wine and Bark Day-Glo green leashes. They had just come from their Friday afternoon walk on the beach, so most of them were wearing shorts and sunhats.

I took a deep breath to fortify myself; dealing with the dogs had never been my strong suit, especially as they never seemed particularly fond of me.

The door flung open, and Beepo eagerly ran to greet them, his tiny nails scratching along the terra-cotta floor. As the group streamed into the bar, the cacophony of yapping dogs reverberated off the walls.

Abigail rushed over to me. "Maggie! I didn't expect to see you here. I thought you'd be packing." Her dog, Missy, a white Shih Tzu wearing a rhinestone bow on the top of her head, sniffed around my ankles and barked accusingly. "Oh, can you give her a Bark Bite?" Abigail asked. "She was such a dear at the beach, I promised."

How can Missy know what Abigail promised? I wondered, but I didn't say anything out loud. Even though I'd only recently met all of these doggie aficionados, I knew them well enough not to ask.

The rest of the crew took up several tables in front of the bar and someone shouted, "Hey, Maggie! How about a round of Salty Dogs?"

Abigail and her dog, Missy, followed me to the bar. I went around to the back side and grabbed a Bark Bite from the bowl nestled near the cash register. As soon as I tossed the biscuit to Missy, the rest of the dogs scampered over.

"How about us humans? Any food around?" Abigail sniffed the air. "Is something burning?"

Ugh!

I raced to the back kitchen and pulled the Arf d'oeuvres out just in time. Only a few needed to be sacrificed, I turned to pitch them into the trash and stumbled over Beepo.

"Why are you always underfoot?" I asked.

Beepo looked up at me with watery sad eyes and I immediately felt guilty for scolding him. I scratched him between his tiny triangle ears and he padded away from me, contented for the moment.

Max peeked around the corner. "Because there's food around," he said. He strode over and picked a doggie in a blanket off the tray and popped it into his mouth. "Hot!"

"They just came out of the oven, genius."

Max smirked at me. He had a classic boy-next-door vibe about him and we'd quickly become friends.

"You need help behind the bar?" Max asked. "I can whip up the pitcher of Salties for you."

"Yes. You're a lifesaver."

I tossed the overly crisp Arf d'oeuvres to Beepo, who caught them midair in his mouth.

"Don't tell the others," I warned Beepo, "or I'll be overrun with begging canines."

Beepo's little tail wagged so hard, it shook his entire body.

Max and I went behind the bar where he immediately pulled a bottle of Stoli from the rack. "Where's Rachel?"

I salted the rims of the glasses while Max grabbed a pitcher of ice. "She's sick. Salmonella."

Max made a face. "Oh, no. That's awful. Where'd she get it from?"

I cringed. I hadn't had a moment to contemplate the question. Where had she gotten whatever made her sick? I shrugged. "Rachel and I had both had cheese and crackers last night for dinner. I didn't get sick."

Max poured the vodka over ice and then grabbed a bottle of grapefruit juice. As he finished preparing the pitcher, I pulled out a tray and, after placing the best-looking Arf d'oeuvres onto a plate, added the martini glasses. Max put the pitcher onto the tray and I walked it over to the table by the window.

Yolanda seemed to be holding court. She stood at the head of the table and towered over the ladies. She was mid speech. "I wanted to scratch her eyes out. She's so rude."

Brenda gave Yolanda a sympathetic look, while Geraldine scowled.

The woman I didn't know had long blond hair pulled through the back loop of a baseball cap. The image on the cap was the Verdant Vines logo. She said, "Fran? Oh, she's a nightmare. Don't even get me started."

Geraldine let out a low whistle and the poodle seated at her feet came to attention. "I don't want to hear any negative talk about Fran. She's been a good friend to me."

"Ladies," I said in greeting as I placed the tray in the middle of the table.

"I don't know her," Brenda said. "I've only seen her around town."

I carefully poured the drinks into each glass as they continued their gossip. I couldn't afford to spill drinks on any other patrons or Rachel would never let me live it down . . . On second thought . . . Maybe that was a way to get out of tending bar!

No. I was way too uptight to make mistakes on purpose. Lord knew they happened frequently enough on their own.

Geraldine leveled her gaze at the new woman. "You don't like Fran because she used to date Hendrick."

The woman self-consciously adjusted her cap. "That's not the reason. He's dated a lot of woman. It's that Fran is so snobby."

Geraldine harrumphed and said, "She is not."

Yolanda snickered and said, "Birds of a feather."

Geraldine cut Yolanda a mean glare, while I turned back to the bar as quickly as I could. Max joined the table, sitting close to Brenda with a hand on her knee as they giggled together.

Yolanda followed me back to the bar. "Rachel said not to worry about her. She'll likely get released from the hospital in the morning. I'll pick you up at nine o'clock and drive you."

As I didn't have a car, riding with Yolanda was the best option for me. "What about that editor that's supposed to show up? Am I supposed to do anything special?"

Yolanda shook her head. "Oh, the woman called while Rachel and I were on the phone. She can't make it tonight. She'll probably come by tomorrow."

Well, that was a relief. I didn't want to be responsible for the editor's impression of the bar. I shuddered to think about a review on the slightly crispy Arf d'oeuvres. I could see the title now "Yappy Hour's Bark Is Worse Than Its Bite!"

Yolanda fiddled with a coaster on the bar. "So what about your trip? Are you really leaving us?"

I wiped the counter and squinted at Yolanda. "You've known for a couple of weeks that I'm leaving. Don't give me any static now. Ten-day Mexican Riviera cruise: Baja, Cabo San Lucas, Puerto Vallarta, Mazatlan."

Yolanda tossed her full blond hair at me. "I'll miss you, Mags. And you'll miss us, too. You just don't realize how much. Until you're on that boat, way far away from us, with nothing to do."

"Except shop in the Mexican stores, lie on the beaches, and drink margaritas."

"*Pfft.*" Yolanda waved a hand around. "Who needs margaritas when you can have a Muttgarita?"

I studied her. "Is that what you'd like now?"

She shrugged her shoulders. "What I'd like is for you to stay."

I ignored her comment and began to mix up a Muttgarita for her. A steady stream of patrons were starting to arrive, so after I fixed the Muttgarita, and put it in front of Yolanda, I got busy pouring drafts and opening various wines. The table near the window was getting increasingly louder and both Yolanda and I glanced over. It seemed like Geraldine and the woman with the ball cap were having a heated discussion.

Yolanda turned back to me. "I don't know what it's going to take, but I'll get you to stay."

I said nothing.

"Do you know how seasick those cruise people can get?" she asked.

I laughed.

"Plus, if you leave, you'll miss out on all the gossip." Yolanda glanced over her shoulder at the table by the window.

It looked like Geraldine and the woman with the Verdant Vines cap on were about to come to blows. Both stood at the same time and were glaring at each other. Their respective dogs had come to attention and were barking at each other.

I raced from behind the bar toward the table, Yolanda on my heels. "Is everything all right here, ladies?"

"You can tell Fran, if I ever see her near Hendrick again I'll strangle her little chicken neck!" the woman with the cap said.

"And you can leave right now!" Geraldine said, pointing to the door.

"Wait! You can't kick her out!" Yolanda said. "If you don't like what she's got to say, then you leave!"

"Now, everyone calm down," I said in my best diplomatic voice.

The woman turned on a heel. "No, I'll leave. I have plans with Hendrick tonight." She marched toward the front door, her Maltipoo trailing behind her. Once she reached the door, she yanked it open and, with a dramatic gesture said, "You should serve some of his wine here. It would class the place up!"

As soon as the door closed, Geraldine said, "I think that woman is a mole!"

"A mole? What do you mean?" Brenda asked.

"In our Roundup Crew," Geraldine said. "I think she just joined us so she could try and sell her boyfriend's wine here."

"Oh, Geraldine," Max waved a hand around. "I hardly think someone would target the group to—"

"Really?" Geraldine screeched, cutting him off. "I know some people who even faked owning a dog to be part of our group." Geraldine's coiffed show poodle howled on cue, showing the maximum disdain for anyone posing as a dog owner.

Max reddened. Only a few weeks earlier, he had borrowed a dog in order to get close to Brenda.

Brenda laughed. "Gerry! You can't be serious."

Abigail sat a little straighter and sipped her cocktail. "I know Gerry doesn't like anyone talking bad about Fran, but I certainly have a bone to pick with her."

Yolanda took the open seat across from Geraldine. Despite her feud with Geraldine, the gossip draw was just too much for her to resist. "Do tell," she prompted Abigail.

"Well, my cousin Ronnie, the poultry farmer—"

"Sexy cousin Ronnie?" Brenda interrupted. Max pulled his hand off her knee and she said, "I mean sexy in a farmer way. Suspenders and stuff." She wrinkled her nose at him and said coquettishly, "Not like you." Max smiled shyly and replaced his hand. Brenda turned to Abigail. "You should introduce him to Yolanda."

Yolanda waved an impatient hand around. "I don't do suspenders." The table laughed, but Yolanda prompted, "What about him, anyway?"

"He has a prize chicken," Abigail said. "And the little girl artist, Coral, at Meat and Greet, well, she did up a very nice watercolor rendition of it. Then Fran just *stole* the image for the logo she uses for her shop."

The table gasped in unison.

"That's illegal!" Brenda said. Ever the attorney, she added, "We can sue."

Geraldine's face contorted and she let out a little whimper as if in pain.

"I love her logo," Yolanda said. Then she stroked her cheek thoughtfully. "Would a suit put her out of business?"

"You just want to see her close up shop!" Geraldine said, in an accusing tone.

Yolanda thrust out her chin defiantly. "I love her shop. In fact, I offered to buy her out, and she ridiculed me."

Due to the tension between Geraldine and Yolanda, I began to clear the table of drinks. No good would come from fanning tempers with more alcohol.

"She should!" Geraldine fired back. "You happen to be ridiculous!"

Yolanda took a sharp inhale of breath, but before she could reply, I said, "Well, y'all certainly know how to take the *happy* out of Yappy Hour."

"I don't think Ronnie wants to sue," Abigail said. "He's pretty happy on his farm. He just wants to grow his business. I think he had a meeting with Rachel to sell her some chicken. She is going to use his chicken dogs in the Arf d'oeuvres."

Panic suddenly overwhelmed me. Chicken in the Arf d'oeuvres? *Rachel is in the hospital with salmonella poisoning!*

Did it have anything to do with Ronnie's chicken? Alarm coursed through my veins as I watched Geraldine pick up one of the Arf d'oeuvres.

"I was wondering why these taste different. Quite yummy!" Geraldine raised her hand to her mouth and I slapped the Arf d'oeuvres out of it.

She recoiled in shock, her poodle barking ferociously at me.

"Rachel's in the hospital with salmonella," I said.

Geraldine frowned, but Abigail jumped up. "You're not blaming Ronnie, are you?"

"No, no. I don't know." I rushed to clear away the tray of Arf d'oeuvres. "Maybe they sat out on the counter before Rach froze them or something. I just don't want anyone to get sick. Better safe than sorry."

I bused the tray to the back of the bar, as Brenda called out, "You can't get salmonella from vodka, right? Maybe we should have another round of Salty Dogs."

Chapter Three

The following morning, Yolanda turned up at my apartment right on time. She drove a flashy red convertible and, as was her habit, she leaned on the horn until I came out.

I rushed around my apartment ensuring all lights were off and all doors were locked, before racing downstairs to meet her.

"Stop honking," I said. "I'm here. You're going to wake the neighborhood!"

She let off the horn and glanced at her slim gold bracelet watch. "It's nine A.M. The neighborhood should be up. What's wrong with these people?"

I laughed as I opened the passenger side. Beepo, who seemed permanently housed on the passenger-side seat, growled at me. "Beach town, I guess," I said, ignoring Beepo, who barked madly at being upended.

"Hush now, Beepo!" Yolanda scowled, scooping him onto her lap.

"When I lived in New York, I was always up at the crack of dawn, but it seems like everyone in Pacific Cove sleeps in."

"Do you think it's the sea air?" Yolanda asked.

I shrugged. "Well, New York has sea air, right?"

She wrinkled her delicate nose. "It's not the same."

I laughed. She was right. New York City and Pacific Cove had zero in common. One of the reasons I'd recently relocated to Pacific Cove was to escape the never-ending hustle and bustle that pulsed through New York, especially when I was a financial advisor.

Thinking of New York brought Gus to mind, and a little pang pricked my heart. I imagined him already settling into a fine hotel in New York, getting ready for *Gourmet Games* audition. New York definitely had big opportunities to offer.

Yolanda put the convertible in reverse and gunned it out of my apartment house driveway. The wind bellowed through her blond hair fanning it around her face. "I'd like to make a little pit stop on the way to the hospital, if you don't mind."

From the way Yolanda narrowed her eyes at me, I could tell that I clearly *should* mind. What kind of pit stop was she contemplating?

"Where?" I asked.

She pressed her full, glossy red lips together and glanced at her own reflection in the rearview mirror.

"Have you talked to Rachel this morning?" I asked. "When I called, the nurse told me she was still asleep. She said I'd have to talk to the doctor about discharge, but he wasn't going to do his rounds until eleven or so."

"I haven't talked to her." Yolanda said. She gave a sidelong glance. "I want to stop at Chic Chickie on the way."

I frowned. "Where's that?"

"It's on the way."

"What is it? A shop?"

She nodded eagerly. Almost too eagerly . . . Beepo yowled in agreement.

"I don't think we have time for shopping," I said. "I kinda want to get straight to the hospital."

"You said yourself she won't be discharged until eleven. We have plenty of time," Yolanda said.

I sighed.

"It'll only take us a few minutes and it's such a cute shop!" Yolanda pressed. "You're going to love it."

I laughed. Yolanda and I had completely different taste in fashion. She favored stilettos, halter tops, and skintight pants and skirts, while I was conservative by nature. Blame it on my accounting degree, but this morning I was decked out in tan chinos and a sky-blue sweater set.

"Please, Maggie," Yolanda whined, while Beepo simpered alongside her.

"If it's on the way, I suppose it's fine."

She clapped her hands loudly and then flung the car around in a U-turn. It was such a sharp turn that Beepo, frightened for his life, sprang into my lap.

"Whoa! I thought you said it was on the way."

She waved a hand around nonchalantly. "It is."

A few minutes later we pulled off the main road onto a side street. Yolanda parked the convertible and set the alarm with her key fob. In front of us was a small boutique shop featuring some very dramatic chicken hats in the window.

Oh, no!

"Wait a minute!" I said in an octave altogether too high. "Is this Fran's store?"

Yolanda flashed me her best, most-charming smile. "Well . . ."

"Well, what! Why didn't you tell me?

"Because I knew you wouldn't want to stop. And I have unfinished business with that woman!"

"I'm not going in there, just to witness another catfight," I said. Beepo let out a mean howl at the word *cat*. "See, even Beepo agrees, don't ya, boy?"

"Oh, stop," Yolanda straightened her fuchsia skirt and checked her reflection in the store window. "You two are both overreacting. Look. I'd really like to buy the business from Fran, and I offered her a fair price yesterday. It's just that she doesn't realize yet how generous I'm being. Now that she's had a chance to sleep on it, I think she'll be much more reasonable." She placed a hand on the doorknob. "You don't even have to be involved. You can peruse the merchandise. Don't you need a fashionable sunhat for Mexico?"

I glanced at an outrageous hat in the center display of the arched front bay window. It featured a rooster tail feather and had a red brim that resembled a gobble.

"I wouldn't be caught dead in that," I said.

Yolanda tsked, shaking her head at what she considered my obvious bad taste. She pranced over to the parking meter in front of the store and wrapped Beepo's leash around it. He gave a howl of disagreement. "Hush now. You know I can't take you in, Beep. You remember the last time?"

I knew from experience that Beepo was not of fan of Yolanda's bright yellow-and-orange faux chicken, so-called *designer* purses.

Yolanda pushed open the door and an overhead bell chimed as we stepped into the shop.

The store featured cathedral-style ceilings, wide wood-planked floors, and the walls boasted a fresh coat of paint in robin's-egg blue. Along the far wall was a mind-boggling display of mounted birds.

"Hellllloooo?" Yolanda singsonged.

An eerie silence greeted us.

The south side of the shop was covered with wraps of all sizes, the unifying theme was that they all appeared to be made of chicken feathers.

"Oh my God, is this even legal?" I asked.

Yolanda looked alarmed. "What do you mean?

I pointed at a large black-and-white stole. "How many chickens had to die to make that wrap?"

"No, no, no," Yolanda squealed. "No chickens died! They molt!" Yolanda's hand fluttered to her heart as if my accusation was about to give her a cardiac arrest. "Anyway, these are synthetic! Do you think we would kill a chicken for fashion?"

I hid my smile. "I think these feathers are ostrich anyway."

Yolanda's expression became even more severe. "They are not!"

"What about those chickens?" I motioned to the far wall of mounts.

Yolanda gripped my wrist. "Hush now. Some people like that sort of thing!"

I stared up at the marble eyes of the taxidermy birds and said, "I feel like we're being watched."

Yolanda gave my wrist a firm shake. "I can see bringing you here was a mistake. You're much more of a liability than I'd imagined." She leaned in close to me and whispered, "Fran's probably in the back. I don't want her to overhear you dissing the merchandise."

"Why not? It may help your negotiating position. Let her know not everybody is crazy about chickens."

How could this stuff be popular?

I'm not totally alone on this one, right?

Was there an entire chicken fashion movement taking the country by storm and I was the only one not hip to it? It wouldn't be the first time I was totally out of the loop. After all, there had to be enough of a clientele to keep a high-end store like this one in the black.

"Is that a pot holder?" I pointed to a table that housed various chicken-theme items from pot holders to salt and pepper shakers. "Where are your handbags?"

Yolanda stiffened.

A thought suddenly struck me. "She's not carrying your bags?" I whispered. Yolanda sniffed the air as if looking for a reason not to answer me. "Why isn't she carrying your bags? They're perfect for this place."

Yolanda nodded. "Thank you, Maggie. I know you love my designs. You're a true friend."

Love her designs?

That was a bit of stretch, but, still, I couldn't imagine a store more apropos than this to feature them.

Yolanda clacked over to the back of the store, where a creamy canary-yellow curtain hung, presumably separating the front of the store from the back. Yolanda stood gingerly in front of the curtain and cleared her throat. "Umm . . . Fran? Hello?"

When no answer came, Yolanda glanced nervously at me and made a face. "I can't imagine where she could be. Do you think she stepped out to grab a cup of coffee or something and forgot to lock the door?"

"Uh . . . Why don't you try her cell phone?" I asked. I realized the store lights were off. It didn't mean anything, of course, the store was still well lit from the sunshine pouring through the bay window. But didn't most store owners put the lights on anyway? Wasn't that the first thing they did when opening up the shop?

A feeling of unease began to snake through my belly.

And what kind of store owner bopped out to get a cup of coffee and left the store unlocked?

Perhaps an assistant has the morning shift? An assistant who forgot to lock the shop?

"Maybe she's in the back and she just hasn't heard us," I ventured.

Yolanda nodded and called loudly, "Yoo-hoo, Fran!" When no response came, Yolanda said, "Maybe we should just go."

But now I was like a dog with a bone, unable to let go. "Call her on her cell phone." I insisted. After all, if someone had found the bar unlocked and unattended Rachel would definitely want to know. "If she's not in the neighborhood, she can tell us how to lock up—"

"Are you kidding?" Yolanda's hand fluttered to her chest and fiddled nervously with her necklace chain. "If anything is missing or disrupted or anything she'll blame me. The woman is a nightmare."

"Then why are we here?"

Yolanda looked at me like I was idiot. "Because I want to buy the place." She flung her arms out wide, as if to encompass the store. "Look at it. It's beautiful. Absolutely beautiful."

"Except that it's missing your designer bags."

"Right," Yolanda said. "I said beautiful, not perfect."

I laughed and headed toward the curtain.

"Where are you going?" Yolanda demanded, her voice suddenly shrill.

"I'm going to see if she's in the back."

Yolanda blocked my path "No, don't go back there. Let's just go. I told you if anything is missing or—"

"Come on, Yo. What if she fell off a ladder and hit her head or something. I can't leave without—"

"Please don't, Maggie. I got a bad feeling," Yolanda whispered.

I looked straight into her eyes. "I got the same bad feeling."

Yolanda swallowed hard and nodded.

"I can't leave without checking the back," I said.

She took a deep breath and squared her shoulders. "I know. I know how you are, Maggie, and that's why I love you."

Together Yolanda and I both pushed open the yellow curtain, part of me feeling ridiculous, as if I was getting ready to expose the Wizard of Oz, the other part of me trying fiercely to ignore the anxiety in my chest.

The curtain opened up to a narrow passageway. There were three doors. One on the right and two on the left.

"Fran?" Yolanda called out.

The first doorway on the right was open, revealing a small office, the size of a large closet. There were several file cabinets and tidy little desk. Yolanda let out a noisy exhale of breath.

"Oh, thank God! I thought for sure we were going to find her shot dead at her desk!" Yolanda said.

Yes, the same awful thought had also occurred to me.

"What else is back here?" I asked.

Yolanda shrugged. "I've never been back here. A bathroom, I suppose, and . . ."

I turned down the hallway and tried the knob to the first door on the left. It turned and opened to an empty bathroom. Yolanda let out another exaggerated sigh of relief.

"Would you stop with the deep breathing, you're driving me nuts!" I said.

Yolanda flashed me her most offended expression, one I was getting quite familiar with. "Well, you're the one insisting on all this poking around. I told you we should just leave."

I ignored her and the warning system vibrating throughout my entire body and tried the last door on the left. It opened to small stockroom. It was overcrowded with boxes and a strange metallic smell filled the room . . .

The air felt different in this room, charged with electricity or malice or . . . "Uh . . . I don't like this," I said.

Yolanda gripped my arm, digging her nails into my flesh. "What? What?" She shrieked. "You don't like what?"

I shook free of her arm and crept farther into the room. Behind a large cardboard box I spied some thick, red goo on the floor. "That," I said, pointing.

Yolanda's expression froze, but she began to slowly back out of the room. "Is that paint?" she asked feebly.

Although I wanted to slink right out of the room alongside

Yolanda, I forced myself forward, leaning my whole upper body farther into the room, so I could peek around the large cardboard box.

The metallic smell was stronger now and an involuntary gasp escaped me as I saw Fran lying still on the floor in a pool of blood.

Chapter Four

"Oh my goodness! Oh my goodness, Fran! Fran!" Yolanda screamed. She'd somehow managed to wiggle herself right up to my ear and howled like a lunatic. "Fran! Is she okay? Is she going to be okay, Maggie?"

"Don't touch anything. Don't touch anything!" I repeated, sounding just as hysterical as Yolanda.

Yolanda threw her hands in the air and shouted, "I'm not touching anything!"

We fled the storage room as if being chased. I pushed back the yellow curtain that separated the back room from the front and we returned to the relative safety of the store. Outside the large front window, Beepo spotted us and strained at his leash in an attempt to get to Yolanda. He began to bark and howl wildly.

"We have to call Brad!" I said. "He'll know what to do."

Yolanda nodded. "Call him. No use calling 9-1-1, they can't do anything for Fran now." She suddenly turned white and grabbed the counter.

"You're not going to pass out, are you?" I asked.

Yolanda and I had already been through the trauma of finding another body and, oddly, that time, I was the one who had a panic attack. Now, it seemed the shoe was on the other foot.

Why is Yolanda having such an emotional response?

"So much blood . . ." Yolanda mumbled.

Beepo barked loudly and jumped up and down trying to free himself from the parking meter.

"Yeah," I soothed. "It's awful. Why don't you go outside and keep Beepo company?"

Yolanda took a deep breath. "I'm fine. Go ahead and call Brad." I pulled my cell phone out of my hip pocket as Yolanda carried on. "What do you think happened? Cousin Ronnie get fed up with her using his logo or what? He walks in here and shoots her?"

I shrugged. "I don't know. Why do you say that? Was she shot?"

Yolanda's eyes widened in alarm. "I don't know! I figured she was shot. Why else would there be all the blood?" She fanned her face.

A chill crept up my spine as I thought of everyone at the bar the night before. Fran had not been well liked. Almost everyone at the table had expressed some animus toward Fran. Yolanda certainly had motive. Of course, so did the woman with the Verdant Vines baseball cap. She'd been extremely jealous of Fran. I couldn't imagine Hendrick was too fond of Fran, either.

Or could Fran have killed herself? Or perhaps something all together different, a robbery gone bad?

While I cataloged my thoughts, Beepo continued to raise a ruckus outside.

"The poor dear," Yolanda said. "You call. I'll see to Beep." She skirted out the front door to join Beepo.

I dialed Brad.

He picked up on the first ring, his baritone voice filled the line.

My knees felt weak at the sound of his voice and my brain turned to mush. An image of his sexy square jaw and electric blue eyes clouded my vision and I blushed, even though I knew he couldn't see me.

I opened my mouth to speak, but no sound came out.

What an idiot! Maggie, focus! This is no time to be thinking about your complicated love life.

"I shouldn't have come inside," I stuttered into the phone.

"Maggie?" Brad's voice sounded alarmed. "Where are you? What's happened? Are you okay?"

"I let Yolanda talk me into stopping at Chic Chickie . . . Fran, the owner, she's dead."

"Slow down. Where are you?"

"Chic Chickie," I repeated.

"Where's that?"

"Oh! Let me see." I fumbled around the front counter and discovered a handful of frequent-shopper cards, the kind that gets a stamp every time a customer purchases an item. The address was printed by the logo, which I gave to Brad.

"I'm on my way. Stay put and don't touch anything."

"I know."

We hung up and I suddenly realized I'd just rummaged around the counter, touching everything in sight. Oh, well, the counter probably wasn't part the crime scene, was it?

I made a mental note to tell Brad when he arrived, just in case. Then, in order not to sully anything further, I decided it would be better to wait outside. I joined Yolanda and Beepo on the curb. Yolanda had released Beepo from the parking meter and was cradling him in her arms. He growled at me as if I was the source of Yolanda's stress.

She stroked his triangle ears. "I should have listened to Beepo. I knew he didn't like that store, but I thought he was being silly."

I shook off the impulse to tell Yolanda he was just a dog, because I knew she wouldn't listen to reason.

"How well did you know Fran?" I asked.

"Not that well," Yolanda confessed. "We had a couple of run-ins actually. The last time I saw her was at The Show. She made a huge splash with her hats and everyone, it seems, went from my booth to hers or vice versa."

The Show—Las Vegas was the largest accessory show in the West. Yolanda had been over the moon to be invited to participate in it. But if her purses and Fran's hats were the talk of the show, I made a silent promise to myself to make sure I never got dragged to it.

"I thought combining our businesses would be a great idea," Yolanda said. "But Fran didn't see it that way."

"What way did she see it?"

Yolanda shrugged.

There was more to the story, but I'd have to pry later because a woman, holding a steaming paper cup, rounded the corner. When she spotted us, she hurried over. "Are you waiting for the store to open? I'm so sorry to keep you waiting! I thought Fran was scheduled."

"Do you work here?" I asked.

"Yes," the woman said, pulling a key from her pocket.

Yolanda scurried over to block the door. "No. Don't go in there."

Beepo yapped at the woman and she looked offended. "Excuse me?" she demanded.

Brad's police cruiser appeared down the street. The woman looked momentarily confused, then gasped. Her hand flew to touch the base of her throat, in a classic self-protection gesture. "Oh, my! Has something happened?" She stared at the front window of the shop. "A break-in?"

When neither Yolanda nor I answered, the woman's eyes grew wide and she asked. "Fran's not hurt, is she? Was she here during the hold-up?"

Brad's vehicle pulled up to the curb and my shoulders immediately relaxed.

When the car door swung open, Beepo barked happily in greeting. As Brad exited the car and I glimpsed his tall, confident posture, I had to fight the urge to rush into his arms.

Not that he looked ready to receive me.

His expression was sober as he took in Yolanda, the woman, and myself. "Ladies, I'm going to ask you to wait outside here for my partner, Officer Ellington, who should be along in just a few moments. He'll take your statements."

The woman nearly jumped out of her skin. "Statement? What statement. For God's sake, someone tell me what's happened."

Brad frowned at her.

"She's only just arrived," I said. "She works here."

"She was supposed to open the store," Yolanda piped in.

"No, I wasn't!" the woman said. "I wasn't supposed to open. I wasn't even on the schedule! It was Fran who was opening the store. I only came by to—"

"Sorry," Yolanda said. "I didn't mean to imply—"

Brad held up a hand to stop them from bickering; at the same time, Beepo barked at the woman. The woman scowled at Beepo, and Beepo let out a frightful growl.

The woman pointed a finger at him. "Wait a minute! Are you the little dog who ruined our inventory the other day?"

Brad stepped between Yolanda and the woman. "Ladies, ladies. I'm going to have to ask you to stop right here."

Another police cruiser came into view and Brad's face revealed the relief he felt at his backup arriving. At the very least, he wouldn't be required to referee a catfight.

"Ah, Officer Ellington is here," he said. "I'm sure he'll be able to sort the whole thing out."

Officer Ellington stepped out of his car and nodded a greeting toward Brad. He quickly assessed the scene, and I swear I felt a breeze of cold air when his gaze landed on me. Ever since the night he'd escorted me into an interrogation room, I've never gotten a warm-and-fuzzy vibe from Ellington.

Brad mumbled a bunch of codes to Ellington, who grunted an "Alright," in response. The radio on Ellington's shoulder beeped and then a rapid series of squawks followed.

"Crime scene team's been dispatched," Ellington said. "They'll be here momentarily."

Brad nodded. "Okay, I'll wait for them here. You can take the ladies down to the station."

"Crime scene team?" The woman next to me gripped my arm. "Is Fran . . . What's happened?"

Brad shot a warning look in my direction and I bit my lip. I knew the drill. Brad would have to notify the next of kin, and he wouldn't want word leaking out beforehand.

"Ma'am, if you wouldn't mind," he said, gesturing toward Ellington's police car. "Officer Ellington will take good care of you."

The coffee cup the woman had been holding slipped from her grasp and spilled onto the pavement. Everyone took an involuntary step back and for a mad moment, I envisioned the woman turning and running, but instead she mumbled, "I'm sorry, I'm so sorry. But down to the station? I don't understand. Am I being arrested?"

"No, no, no," Ellington soothed, in a much warmer and reassuring tone than I'd ever gotten from him. "Of course not, miss. I just need to ask you a few questions. Same as these ladies." He jutted a chin in my direction.

"I see," the woman said, although she looked altogether unconvinced.

My heart went out to her; she looked as frightened as a little girl. I knew she was playing out the worst-case scenario in her mind and the horrible part of it was that the reality was probably worse than she could imagine.

Officer Ellington turned on a heel, and opened the back door of the cruiser for the woman.

"I'll drive Maggie and myself to the station," Yolanda said.

Ellington made a face. "Good. I can't have that dog in a police vehicle."

Yolanda inhaled sharply, a look of the indignation on her face. Beepo howled alongside her. Out of the corner of my eye, I caught Brad stifling a laugh.

Yolanda crushed Beepo to her breast and said, "Oh, believe me, Officer Ellington, I know where you and your cold, cold heart stands when it comes to our canine friends."

Ellington ignored Yolanda and turned his attention back to the woman. She looked up at him, as she climbed into the backseat of the cruiser and batted her eyelashes, saying. "I'm Cornelia."

Yolanda huffed over to her car and I seized the moment alone with Brad. "It's awful, Brad. Very bloody. I feel horrible for Fran."

He put a warm hand on my shoulder. "I'm sorry you had to find her, Maggie."

I gripped at his hand for support. "We were on the way to the hospital. I wish we'd never come here." But as soon as I'd said it, I knew it was wrong. If Yolanda and I hadn't beat Cornelia there, she would have been the one to find her friend. That would have been worse. At least, we'd spared her that nightmare.

Brad frowned and asked. "Hospital? Is Grunkly okay?"

A few months back, my great uncle Grunkly had suffered a mild heart attack. He'd been hospitalized and on the verge of what he called "the great beyond" but he'd battled back.

"He's fine. It's Rachel. She has salmonella poisoning."

"Salmonella? Geez! It's not serious, is it?"

"I hope not. Can I go see her first, then go to the station?"

Brad glanced over at Officer Ellington, who was practically skipping over to the driver's side. "Sure. I'm going to be held up here for a couple hours with the tech team. I can come to your place as soon as I'm done and you can give me your statement."

A realization struck me. My cruise to the Mexican Riviera was leaving tomorrow morning. There was a check-in scheduled for staff this afternoon at 4:00 P.M. I was supposed to report to the ship for my list of purser duties and a bit of training.

"I . . . um . . . I have to leave my apartment by three-thirty. You'll be able to stop by before then, right?"

Brad glanced at his wristwatch. "Yes. Of course. It's still early." His hand left my shoulder and reached for the knob on the front door of Chic Chickie. "If all goes as expected, we have plenty of time."

My stomach dropped as he disappeared into the store.

Finding someone dead on the day you start a new job—well, heck, on any day—was *not* things going as expected. . . .

Chapter Five

Yolanda and Beepo waited for me in the convertible. I yanked open the passenger-side door and displaced Beepo, who'd been content to rest his eyes while I had chatted with Brad.

"Let's go to the hospital. Brad's going to check in with me later," I said.

"What about me?" Yolanda asked.

"What about you?"

Yolanda quirked an eyebrow. "Who's going to check in with me? Take my statement? You're going to get me in trouble with Crankpot Ellington!"

"Brad said it was fine," I assured her.

Yolanda chewed on the inside of her cheek. "I dunno. Ellington gets mad about that sort of thing." She revved the engine, and pulled out of the parking spot. "But I'm not too eager to run into Sergeant Gottlieb over at the station, so—"

It was my turn to quirk an eyebrow. "Oh? Trouble in paradise?"

Yolanda scoffed at me. "What do you mean? It's not like we're dating or anything."

"I thought you liked him?"

"I do," she said.

"So? What's the problem then?" I asked.

"There's no problem. He just hasn't asked me out, yet." She glanced over at me. "And I have no intention of asking him, so don't even say it."

"He probably thinks you're out of his league," I said.

Yolanda bristled. "Why would he think that? He's a sergeant!"

"You look like Marilyn Monroe and he's bald with bushy eyebrows—"

"Oh! You're so superficial. I happen to think he's very handsome!" Yolanda scolded me.

"I'm not being superficial. I think Sergeant Gottlieb is a very nice man. I'm simply saying that he's likely intimidated by your beauty."

Yolanda let out a low disapproving snort, which Beepo copied. We all got quiet as we took the exit for Pacific Cove General Hospital. Yolanda fiddled with the radio, hunting for anything but static. I found myself hoping for a news story, something that might give us more information about Fran, until I realized Brad wouldn't have let the story leak yet.

Beepo yelped at the static coming from the speakers, and then buried his head under his paws. Yolanda flipped the radio off.

"What did you make of Cornelia?" I asked.

"What do you mean?" Yolanda asked. "She seemed shocked, poor thing. What else should I think about her?"

"Did you believe her story about not being scheduled to open the store?"

Yolanda glanced at me, confused. "Sure, why not?"

"If she wasn't on the schedule, what was she doing going by the store?" I asked.

"Well, you make a good point." Yolanda pulled into the hospital parking lot. "Last night, when we were at the Wine and Bark, Cornelia called Fran. It seemed to me that they had an argument of some sort."

"What were they arguing about?" I asked.

"I couldn't say. Inventory or something? I'm not sure. Fran just kept telling her to calm down. I think Fran was probably pretty difficult to work with." She shrugged. "No people skills."

I laughed despite myself.

She glanced over at me. "What?"

"If anyone knows people skills it's you."

Yolanda dismissed my remark and parked. She secured Beepo's leash to the steering wheel. He whimpered and begged, turning his big sad eyes toward her. "Hush now, Beep. You know you can't go into the hospital! You be a good boy here."

We tumbled out of the car and walked toward the main hospital doors.

"I saw the logo," I said.

"What logo?" Yolanda asked.

"The one Coral did. The watercolor rendition of Cousin Ronnie's prize chicken."

"Oh, yes!" Yolanda said. "It's stunning right?"

Actually, it was stunning. I amazed myself by agreeing with her. *Are chickens growing on me?*

"I can understand why Ronnie felt ripped off."

Yolanda nodded. "I'd feel the same way."

We stopped at the nurses' station where a woman in a white coat was typing notes in a computer. She looked up as we approached.

"Hello. We're here to see my sister, Rachel Patterson. Can you tell us what room she's in?"

"Down the hall, room 209, on the right side," the nurse said.

Yolanda and I ducked down the corridor toward Rachel's room. In the narrow passageway, we saw a man leaving her room.

I grabbed Yolanda's wrist. "Who's that?"

The man was tall, wearing a thick brown Carhartt work coat, dark jeans, and black boots. His expression was serious, but that did nothing to detract from his handsomeness. He spotted us, squared his shoulders, and put his hands on his hips. The gesture opened his coat a bit and revealed something underneath.

"Suspenders!" Yolanda whispered to me.

Was the hunk of a man in front of us Abigail's cousin Ronnie? *The poultry farmer?*

"Maybe you can get over your thing about suspenders," I whispered to Yolanda. "He's hot."

Yolanda made a face. "Not my type."

As we neared, the man stuck out a hand. "Are you Rachel's sister? I'm Ronnie."

What is he doing here?

I shook his hand. "I didn't know you were so close to my sister."

Ronnie nodded. "We haven't know each other that long, but when I heard—"

"Was it your chicken?" Yolanda demanded.

Ronnie paled. "My chicken? No! No. No way. Definitely not. Mine are free-range, farm-raised. I have impeccable sterilization and hygienic sanitation."

While he protested, I pushed open the door to Rachel's room and peeked in. She was asleep with her arms folded across her chest, an IV attached to her left hand. She looked pale and drawn, her hair matted against her forehead. My heart lurched to see my baby sister looking so fragile.

I rushed toward her bedside.

Ronnie leaned in and said, "She sleeping now. The nurse came in a while ago and gave her some meds."

"What are you doing here visiting Rachel?" Yolanda pressed.

Ronnie looked defiant. "I was with her yesterday. I heard she was in the hospital and I wanted to visit."

"Who told you she was in the hospital?" Yolanda asked.

"My cousin Abigail," Ronnie said.

Rachel stirred and I grabbed her hand. "Rach. It's me, Maggie. I'm here now. How do you feel?"

Rachel's lips twitched, but said nothing. Guilt bore down on me. *I should have come to my sister last night.*

I'd had no idea how bad off she was. She looked drawn and thin, like she had dropped about ten pounds since yesterday and she didn't have much to lose in the first place.

My stomach clenched, full of nervous knots as I glanced at Yolanda for support.

She patted Rachel's foot. "I'm here, too, honey. We'll break you out of this place in no time. Soon as the nurse gives us the go-ahead."

Rachel moaned and pitched to the right, away from us. Her hand shot out searching for something. "Ugh . . . Get the nurse . . . uh . . . Where's my . . ."

Ronnie, who'd obviously seen this earlier, grabbed a pan from the wheeled cart next to Rachel's bedside and handed it to her. "Here you go, babe. Take it is easy. You can't have much left to throw up."

Rachel went through a series of frightful dry heaves and moans before she collapsed back onto the bed. Ronnie took the pan out of her hands and placed it back on the wheeled cart. A vase of fresh flowers sat next to the TV, and I realized with a start Ronnie must have brought them. So either he was feeling guilty about serving Rachel bad chicken . . . or . . . what?

Were they dating?

No! Rachel would have told me if that was the case.

Yolanda pulled the green upholstered chair that was nestled

against the windowsill and pushed it toward the bed. She put a hand on my shoulder urging me to take the seat. I did.

I leaned in. "Have you been this bad all night, Rach? You should have called me again!"

Rachel shook her head, her eyelids getting heavy. "I slept a lot."

Ronnie nodded. "She's been kind of in and out all morning."

All of sudden, Rachel's face looked peaceful again and she seemed to drift off to sleep.

A vibrating sound emanated from Ronnie's hip and his hand shot out to cover it. "Excuse me, ladies." He glanced down at the phone attached to his belt loop and said, "I have to take this one." He moved toward the door and said, "Yeah . . . it's me . . . Is the job done? I don't want a repeat of last night."

Yolanda shot a me a look that I couldn't quite make out.

"Well, has the problem been eliminated or not?" Ronnie said into the phone, his voice rising a notch. He yanked the door open and exited.

"What's that about, do you think?" Yolanda hissed.

I shrugged. "How would I know?"

She shuddered. "Gave me the creeps is all. What problem do you think he's talking about?"

"Could be anything," I said.

"I wonder where he was last night . . ." Yolanda said.

The hair on the back of my neck stood at attention. What had Ronnie been talking about? Problem eliminated?

Could he have meant . . . ?

No. It was ridiculous. He seemed like a really nice guy. He'd just handed my sister a pan to vomit in, he'd brought flowers. People like that didn't kill someone over the illegal use of their prize chicken logo.

Goodness, what was happening to my logic?

I needed to get out of Pacific Cove and get some fresh air. I checked my watch. It was noon already. I had to get back to my apartment and intersect Brad.

"Where's the nurse?" I asked. "We need to get Rachel discharged."

As if on cue, the door cracked open and a woman in a blue nurse's uniform carrying a tray stepped in. "Good afternoon. I brought her some fresh ice chips. No solids yet, I'm afraid. Doctor's orders."

I stood. "I'm Maggie. Rachel's sister. I was under the impression she was going to be discharged today. Can you help—"

"Discharged?" the nurse said. "Oh, no, I don't think so. She hasn't been able to keep anything down. It's going to be at least another few days."

The surprise jolted through my system. "'Another few days'?" I whined, immediately regretting it. Of course Rachel needed to be in hospital. She looked like the walking dead.

My new job!

Who was going to take care of Rachel if I was onboard the Soleado Mexican Riviera Cruise Line?

Yolanda squinted at me. "Right about now, I think you're probably considering giving up your new gig, am I right?"

I sighed.

"As much I want you to stay, Mags, you have to go," Yolanda said. "You'll be back soon enough. I can take care of Rachel."

At this Rachel's eyes popped open. "Maggie, don't go!" Her hand lurched for my shirt and she said, *Doggie Day*! Maggie, what happened with the editor? Did you land the spread?"

I untangled her fingers from my shirt and held her hand in mine. "Rach, the editor never showed up—"

"She's supposed to come today," Yolanda said.

Despair rumbled through my tummy.

Oh God! They are going to trap me here.

Between Rachel's salmonella, The *Doggie Day* editorial spread, Ronnie's mysterious grumblings, not to mention Fran . . .

The nurse snapped to attention. "Do you need to sit down? You look pale."

"I . . . um . . ." I seated myself. What could I say?

"The editor's coming today?" Rachel asked.

Yolanda nodded. Rachel moaned then pointed at the pan. Yolanda passed her the pan, while the nurse scribbled something on Rachel's chart.

Rachel proceeded to battle with another bout of dry heaves, while we all looked on.

The nurse said, "I let the doctor know her condition isn't improving. He may need to change her dosage." After mopping Rachel up and taking her blood pressure, the nurse scurried out of the room.

Rachel grabbed my wrist. "Mags, you'll be there for Yappy Hour, right? Promise?"

I knew I had to be onboard for training at 4:00 P.M. I had no idea how long the training would take though. "I'll call Max. He can open for us and I'll be there as soon as my orientation on the ship is over, okay? I promise."

Rachel's eyes squeezed shut and she looked miserable.

Guilt pressed against my shoulders, weighing me down.

How can I consider abandoning my baby sister at a time like this?

I hadn't even had a chance to fill her in on Fran.

I glanced at Yolanda. She gave me a reassuring nod and placed a cool hand on my sister's forehead. "Don't you worry, darling. Beepo and I will be there to greet the editor. I'll make sure it all goes smoothly."

Rachel moaned and motioned for the pan again. "Thank you, Yolanda. Thanks, Maggie. What would I do without you guys?" Before I could respond, Rachel said, "Whatever you all do tonight at Yappy Hour . . ." She gripped the pan and, between dry heaves, said, "Don't serve the chicken Arf d'oeuvres!"

Chapter Six

Beepo's tail wagged maniacally at seeing us approach the convertible. I opened the passenger-side door and jumped in, running my list of to-dos through my head: rush to the apartment and finishing packing, call Max and ask him to cover opening for Yappy Hour, give my statement to Brad.

Poor Fran.

I must have made a noise because Yolanda patted my knee as she revved the engine.

"Rachel is going to be fine," she said.

I nodded. "Yes. She'll recover. I should get over to Grunkly's and let him know."

Yolanda tsked. "Don't worry him. She'll probably be discharged tomorrow."

I leveled a gaze at her. "I'll be on a cruise tomorrow." Even as I said it, doubt overcame me, tying my stomach in knots.

"Sure, sure. Of course," Yolanda soothed. "I'll take care of Rachel.

If, for some reason, she has to stay another day at the hospital. I'll call your great uncle."

I picked at the knob of the glove compartment in front of me. "No. I better go see him. Tell him myself. I don't want him to get nervous. You can just drop me off at his place."

"You have to pack!" Yolanda said.

I shrugged. "You're right. I guess you can take me to my place. I'll pack fast and then walk to Grunkly's." I glanced down at my tan chinos. "My entire wardrobe mixes and matches, anyway. I just have to pull a few things from my closet and shove them into a bag."

Yolanda flinched as if my bland wardrobe was a personal assault. "You're not bringing those pants with you to Mexico, are you?" Her chin jutted out, indicating the khakis I was wearing.

I grinned. "You don't like my pants? They go with everything, you know."

"So does animal print," Yolanda said. We giggled as she turned down the street to my apartment. "Do you want me to go in with you?"

"No, I'm fine," I said.

She nodded. "Okay, I think I'll go over to Abigail's and have her do my hair." She ran her fingers through her perfectly coiffed blond mane. "Get ready for tonight, you know."

I frowned. "What do you mean? What's so important about tonight?"

Yolanda gave me a frightful and very disappointed look. "The editor from *Doggie Day*! Maggie, we need to impress! How else is the Wine and Bark going to score a spread in the magazine?"

"Why's it so important to you?" I asked.

Yolanda gasped. "*Doggie Day*! Do you know what kind of readership they get?"

I was afraid to admit I didn't. Dogs had always been more Rachel's thing than my own. I'd never been bitten or anything that spooks most people about dogs, but I'd also never owned one or fallen in love like the clientele at the Wine and Bark had.

"Right, right," I muttered. "Sorry. I . . ."

Yolanda waved a hand around. "You have a lot on your mind. I'll call Max to make sure he can open the bar on time. But you have to get there as soon as your orientation is over. He can't run the bar alone all night." She gave me a meaningful glance. "Not if we want to make an impression."

I got out of the car in front of the Casa Ensenada Apartments and ran all the way up the stairs to my front door. I jammed the key into the lock and ran around dumping a few favorite items into my duffel bag. Glancing at the hall clock, I realized with a jolt that I only had two hours left to pack, give my statement to Brad, and get over to Grunkly's.

I hadn't eaten all morning and my stomach growled as I raced around the room collecting my belongings. Hopefully the kitchen would serve appetizers during the staff orientation. At the very least some chips and salsa to get us in the Cabo San Lucas frame of mind!

I focused on clothes, figuring any cosmetic items I forgot to pack could likely be purchased onboard.

When I finished packing, it dawned on me that instead of waiting around for Brad to give him my statement, I should leave him a note and head out to Grunkly's right away. Otherwise, I'd never make it to the orientation.

I sent a text to Brad's mobile, but when he didn't immediately confirm receipt I scribbled out a note and taped it to my front door.

I walked along the beach toward Grunkly's house, fretting about Fran and Rachel until it felt like my blood pressure was high enough to make blood ooze out of my ears. In the distance, a man in uniform approached. My heart skipped a beat anticipating Brad, but then I noticed that the man's gait was wrong. No. It wasn't Brad.

My shoulders tightened and a sense of doom descended upon me as I realized the man was Officer Ellington.

As soon as he was within earshot he called out, "Miss Patterson, if I may have a word." The look on his face was stern and even over the hum of the surf, I could hear the anger in his voice. I felt as if I'd suddenly been called to the principal's office.

"Of course, Officer," I said, as brightly as I could muster.

"I was expecting you at the station. I thought you were coming in to give your statement. Then when I stopped by your apartment, I saw the note. You're heading out of town?"

He looked incredulous and I found myself inexplicably nervous. "I . . . oh . . . I was going to head to the police station, but then Officer Brooks told me that he would come by my apartment, but it was getting late and I . . ." *Uh-oh, this is sounding all wrong.* "My sister's in the hospital," I sputtered. "I had to check in on her."

He snarled and indicated our surrounding. The water lapped the sand in a mocking reminder of how opposite the beach was to the hospital. "Right," he muttered.

Anger flared inside me, and my blood buzzed in my ears.

What the heck was he insinuating? That I'd used my sister's illness to get out of giving a statement?

"Look, I'm not avoiding you or avoiding giving my statement. I start a new job in a few—"

"A job? On that silly cruise ship? You think that's more important than a murder investigation?"

His words were so full of venom, they winded me.

"I didn't say it was more important, only that—"

"I know, I know," he said, cutting me off. "All the girls of your generation are the same, only concerned with themselves."

I didn't reply. Ellington was the same generation as I was. He was baiting me, but I refused to bite.

"I found Fran this morning, dead in a pool of her own blood. I can't tell you much more than that. I didn't know her, I have no idea—"

"You didn't know her?" Ellington interjected. "You fought with her just last night."

"What? That's not right."

Ellington glared at me. "Isn't it? You and she fought at the Wine and Bark. You threw a drink at her."

My stomach burned and I was suddenly glad I hadn't eaten for fear I'd retch right on Ellington's department-issued steel-toed tactical boots.

"No!" I said. "That's not what happened. I didn't throw a drink on her. Fran spilled her wine. It was an accident."

Ellington made a face, barely refraining from rolling his eyes. He removed a notepad from his breast pocket and said, "Recount for me exactly what happened."

I told him about the wine tasting with Hendrick, how Yolanda and Fran had come into the bar and Hendrick had sent over a bottle of Fran's favorite wine.

Ellington frowned. "Hendrick is the ex-boyfriend, huh?"

I nodded. "I suppose."

"That's a bit of a coincidence, isn't it? Are you dating him?"

"What? No! Of course not. I only met him yesterday because Rachel's in the hospital with salmonella."

"Fran comes into the bar, sees you with her old beau, and you fight. You throw a drink at her. You realize Hendrick is still in love with her and she's an obstacle. So you decide to take matters into your own hands. Kill the competition, is that it, Miss Patterson?"

"You're being ridiculous!" I pushed past him. "I'll give my statement to Officer Brooks. He doesn't put words into my mouth."

Ellington grabbed my arm as I passed. "I'll put out a warrant for your arrest if you don't cooperate."

Rage burned my lungs and I cried out, "I am cooperating!"

He released my arm, but not without a snicker. "Running off on a cruise in the middle of a murder investigation is *not* cooperating."

As soon as he said it, I knew it was true.

What had I been hoping? That I could present myself to my new job, ignore the fact that I'd found a woman murdered just this morning? Ignore the fact that my sister was in the hospital and needed me? Ignore everyone else's needs and just satisfy myself?

Ellington was right.

I was being selfish.

Regret scorched my throat and I found it difficult to speak. "I want to help," I squawked.

Ellington turned away from me and looked out toward the ocean. "Why were you working at the bar instead of your sister?"

"She's in the hospital," I said. "I told you that. Salmonella poisoning."

Ellington chewed on his lip. "When did she set up the wine tasting with Verdant Vines? Who knew about it?"

"Wait a minute! Do you think Rachel was poisoned on purpose?"

Ellington sighed and rubbed at his face as if he was suddenly tired. "I don't know. I'm going to get to the bottom of it, though. Fran was my friend."

<> <> <>

Although, Ellington's aggressive behavior was now understandable, his admission had shocked me.

We'd parted, his words echoing in my head.

Farther down the beach, I spotted a couple walking two small dogs. The dogs were bouncing in and out of the surf as the man tossed a ball at them. I recognized the dogs first, which actually gave me a jolt.

What was happening to me? Since when did I notice dogs before people?

The couple was Max and Brenda. I hurried toward them, waving and calling out.

Brenda's Chihuahua, Pee Wee, ran toward me, quickly followed by Buster, the beagle that Max walked. The dogs jumped to greet me, covering my khakis with mud.

"Get down," Brenda admonished.

"It's fine," I said.

Max quirked an eyebrow and grinned. "Ah, they're growing on you, huh, Mags?"

I buried my head in my hands. "I guess I have other things to worry about."

Brenda put an arm around my shoulder. "What is it? What's wrong?"

"Hey," Max said. "Aren't you supposed to be on that boat now? We saw a big group heading over, just a few minutes ago. It's the opening party, or something, right?"

"It's staff orientation. I can't go, though. I have to stay in Pacific Cove . . . it's . . ." Emotion overwhelmed me and I found I couldn't finish the sentence.

Brenda rubbed my arm. "It's okay, honey. You can talk to us. What's wrong?" She paused. "Is Rachel alright?"

I brought them up to speed on my morning as we walked toward Grunkly's house.

"I can't believe it. Fran's dead?" Max said.

"Well." Brenda shrugged. "She really didn't have that many friends, did she? Think about last night. Everyone seemed to have a reason to dislike her."

"Disliking someone is not the same as murdering someone," Max said.

"Abigail's cousin Ronnie was at the hospital, visiting Rachel. Officer Ellington sort of suggested that perhaps Rachel was poisoned on purpose."

Brenda's eyes grew wide. "Oh my God. You've got to be kidding! Ronnie wouldn't hurt a fly!"

Max's body language changed: His shoulders squared and his chest puffed out. I remembered the flash of jealousy he'd had the night before when Brenda mentioned how cute she thought Ronnie was.

"You said yourself that Ronnie had a grudge against Fran," Max said. "Because of the stolen logo, right?"

Brenda shuffled self-consciously. "That doesn't mean he would kill her, or poison Rachel!"

"How well do you guys know Cornelia?" I asked.

"Who's that?" Max asked. "I don't know a Cornelia."

Brenda's eyes shifted toward the ocean and I noticed she didn't answer me.

"Cornelia was Fran's assistant, I think. Or rather, she worked at the store, Chic Chickie."

Max shrugged. "I don't know her." He turned to Brenda. "Do you know her, honey?"

Brenda stooped to pick up the ball that Pee Wee had deposited at her feet, and avoided eye contact with us. "I know her." She tossed the ball into the water. Pee Wee and Buster flew into the surf to retrieve it.

"I think she told Ellington that Fran and I had a fight last night," I said.

"Why would she say that?" Brenda asked.

"I don't know, but Ellington told me that's what he heard and I think the only person he's spoken to so far is Cornelia."

"What about Yolanda?" Max asked. "She was with you when you found Fran, right?"

"Yes, but I don't think she's talked to him yet." I shrugged. "I'm sure she's hoping to give her statement to Sergeant Gottlieb."

Brenda giggled. "I don't blame her. Ellington can be such a cold fish."

"I guess Ellington was friends with Fran," I said.

Brenda made a face. "'Friends'? I don't think so. I heard he asked her out and she turned him down flat. But that was when she and Hendrick were together."

"Ah, Hendrick, the scorned lover. What happened between them?" I asked.

Brenda shrugged. "You'll have to ask Geraldine. She knows all the sordid details much better than I do."

"So how do you know Cornelia?" I probed.

Brenda grimaced. "She's come to see me about some business. I'm sorry, Maggie, but I can't say any more than that."

Brenda had her own law practice in town, Bradford and Blahnik. During the recession, she'd had to get creative and began selling designer shoes in order to keep her practice open.

"Don't tell me she had a chicken slipper idea or something equally awful to sell you."

Max snorted, but Brenda only shook her head.

"Did she come to see you for legal advice?" I asked.

Brenda pressed her lips together, which pretty much told me all I needed to know.

Chapter Seven

I walked the rest of the way to Grunkly's in a complete state of agitation, fretting over Rachel and the fact that I'd have to skip out on my new job. Just how was I supposed to pay my rent? I still had a little savings, but without a regular income, the money would be gone fast.

I knocked on Grunkly's door and waited the requisite time before pulling out my phone and dialing him. He never opened the door, so at this point I didn't even know why I bothered knocking.

He picked up on the first ring. "Is that you at the door, Magpie?" Grunkly asked.

"Yes, it's me. Are you all right? Can you get to the door?" I asked.

"Sure, but there's a key under the mat," he said. "Why don't you just let yourself in."

I hung up and dug the key out from under the mat. A surge of protectiveness overwhelmed me. Had someone poisoned Rachel on purpose? If so, was there any sense in Grunkly leaving his key under the front doormat? It didn't seem the prudent thing to do.

I let myself inside and found my octogenarian great uncle in the living room, seated in his favorite easy chair with a Sudoku puzzle book in his lap. Surprisingly the TV was off. Grunkly was a racehorse owner and was addicted to races. I'd become accustomed to vying for his attention every time I came to visit.

I glanced at the black screen. "No race on?"

Grunkly shook his head. "McMann's horse is racing, and he and I don't speak ever since he cheated me on that stall fee."

I climbed over the mountain of discarded electronics that Grunkly kept, *just in case,* and settled myself on the sofa. I never bothered ask him in case of what. I was sure he had detailed and individual reasons for retaining each and every item, but right now I didn't have the time or the energy to try and talk him into decluttering.

"I have bad news, Grunkly. Rachel is in the hospital."

My poor Grunkly paled and looked stricken, I immediately regretted blurting it out.

"She's going to be fine. Don't worry. I'm sure she'll be fine, but she got salmonella poisoning and she's over at Pacific Cove General."

"Oh, my poor darling!" He threw off his old ball cap and rustled his fingers through his thick white hair. "Let me comb my hair and we can get right over there for a visit."

"No, no. I just came from there. She's fine."

"You just came from there?" Grunkly looked indignant. "Why didn't you call me? I would have gone with you."

"I'm sorry," I said. "I didn't think. I thought she was being discharged."

Grunkly was taking the news about Rachel rather hard and I hesitated to tell him more. If I told him about finding Fran or hinted about the idea that perhaps the salmonella poisoning could have been intentional, I feared it would put him into cardiac arrest.

"I have some good news," I said, trying to brighten the mood. Grunkly perked up. "Oh? What's that?"

"I won't be going on the cruise. I decided not to take the job."

Grunkly squinted at me. "This is good news?"

"Uh . . . yes . . . I mean that . . . Well, I can come over and take care of you and stuff, because I won't be gone."

Grunkly wasn't falling for it. "Why aren't you going on the cruise? You need the job, Magpie. That's what you told me. You were excited about it." He studied me for a moment saying nothing.

"I need to keep the Wine and Bark open while Rachel's in the hospital. She's got some magazine editor ready to do a story and—"

Grunkly waved a hand around. "Let the editor come back next week, when Rachel's out of the hospital."

"I know. It's just that—"

"You think Rachel's stuff is more important than your own?" he asked.

"It's not that."

"You told me you needed the job, to make rent money," he said. "Even though, you know, you can always come live with me. Great big bedroom in the back with an ocean view all for you!"

It seemed I'd had this same conversation with Grunkly almost every time I came to visit, the only problem was the thought of living in his cluttered home gave me palpitations.

I took a deep breath.

He frowned. "Does it have to do with that DelVecchio fellow?" Grunkly glanced around the room as if Gus was hiding somewhere between the stacks of papers and broken electronics.

"No—"

"Where is he today?" Grunkly asked. "Maybe you can bring him over again. That guy sure can cook. He was very nice, Maggie." He paused and smiled. "And I think he liked you . . ."

Not too long ago Gus had come with to me to visit Grunkly and wound up making us an exquisite steak dinner. My mouth watered just thinking about it.

"Gus is in New York. He left last night on a red-eye. He went there to audition for one of those cooking shows."

Grunkly suddenly looked crestfallen and despite myself my stomach rumbled. "I see," Grunkly said. "Well, he'll be back right, Maggie?"

"Yeah. Sure. He's coming back."

"Then you should definitely go on your cruise." Grunkly shrugged. "We'll see him when he gets back."

I nodded and bit my lip. "It's not about Gus . . . I . . ." I sighed.

"You told me you wanted to travel. This was a perfect job for you, you said." Grunkly looked me over seriously with his sage eyes boring into mine, challenging me. When I remained stoic, he motioned for me to continue, "Spill it," he said.

In one long ramble, I told him about finding Fran, about Officer Ellington, about my conversation with Max and Brenda. I told him everything before I could stop myself, even my suspicions about Rachel's poisoning, ending with: "Don't leave your key under the mat!"

Grunkly closed the Sudoku puzzle book on his lap, removed his glasses and proceeded to wipe them clean with the corner of his shirt. He said nothing.

"Well?" I asked.

He glanced over at me, distracted. "Well what?"

Frustration overcame me. Hadn't he been listening at all?

"You see now why I can't go on the cruise?" I prompted.

He shook his head. "Not at all. What does all that have to do with the cruise?"

I stood. "I can't just go off during a murder investigation. There will be questions, there'll be—"

"You think you can help the police? Like you did last time?"

There it was, hitting me square in the face. Some part of me wasn't going to let me move on until I knew what had happened to Fran.

I shrugged. "I guess I have to help. I can't leave it alone, Grunkly. I won't be able to rest until I know Rachel is alright and Fran has justice."

Grunkly nodded. "Maggie, you're like my favorite horse, Miss Boom Boom. Did I ever tell you about her? That little filly never gives up. If she makes the course, she's tough."

I laughed. "And if she doesn't make the course?"

He grinned at me. "Well, then she's like the rest of us."

<><><>

I polished a few glasses behind the bar as I waited for the impending hustle and bustle of Yappy Hour. After leaving Grunkly's, I'd called my boss, Jan, over at the Soleado Cruise Line and explained that, due to a family medical emergency, I wouldn't be able to make the orientation or the cruise. Jan took the news well and assured me that I could pick up the next cruise out of Pacific Cove next month.

Through the front window of the bar, I saw a uniformed man make his way across the courtyard. Oh, no, not Officer Ellington again! I glanced around for a quick exit, while at the same time admonishing myself. I'd done nothing wrong. I didn't have to hide from Ellington.

As the man drew closer, I recognized his gait and I happily crossed the bar to unlock the door for Brad.

As soon as the door was open, he grabbed my hands. "Maggie, I'm so sorry I couldn't come to see you earlier. It's been a long day. I heard from Ellington that he read you the riot act."

"You could say that. Come in. I'm just preparing for Yappy Hour." Brad followed me into the bar. "Are you still on duty? Or can I pour you a draft?"

He shook his head. "Better not. How about a Coke?"

I nodded and filled a pint glass with soda for him.

When I handed it to him, he asked. "Why aren't you at the orientation?"

I sort of gave a half grunt, stalling for time. Admitting to him that I thought I'd better stay around Pacific Cove and "help" him with *his* investigation wasn't going to go over well. When I said nothing, Brad asked, "How is Rachel? It's not serious, right?"

"She should be released soon. I think."

Brad leveled a gaze at me, his eyes still silently asking why I wasn't on the cruise ship.

"I couldn't leave with her in the hospital," I said simply. "Do you think it's all related?"

"Rachel's salmonella and Fran's death?" he asked.

I nodded.

He shook his head. "Salmonella poisoning would be a dumb way to try to kill someone. How could the murderer even get a controlled dose? Unless, they worked in a lab or something." He shrugged. "And Fran was shot. I hardly think they're connected."

"I guess I'm just worried about Rachel," I said.

He nodded his understanding and sipped his Coke, his blue eyes never leaving mine. "I'm sorry you are going to miss your cruise, but does it leave you free for dinner tomorrow?"

Warmth spread through my chest. "Yes, definitely. I'd love to have dinner with you tomorrow."

He smiled. "Good. Now." He pulled his notebook out of his pocket. "I know you spoke to Ellington already, but if you don't mind, I have a few more questions for you."

Tension quickly replaced the warmth I'd just felt as I suddenly became alert. I blinked at him to clear away my fuzzy daydreamy thoughts of our date. "Okay, go ahead."

He took a seat at the bar and asked, "Where were you last night?"

A nagging sensation filled my gut.

What? Am I a suspect?

When I didn't answer, Brad said, "Don't look at me like that, Maggie. I just need to get everything down for the report."

"I was here at the Wine and Bark."

"Fran and Yolanda were here too, right?" Brad probed.

"Yes, they were here, so was Abigail, Brenda, Max, Geraldine, and another woman. I don't know her name, but she didn't like Fran much."

"What makes you say that?" Brad asked.

"She said she'd strangle her if she ever saw her with Hendrick again."

Brad flipped through the pages of his notebook. "Hendrick is Fran's ex, right?"

"Yeah."

"Was the woman the current girlfriend?"

"I think so."

Brad tapped his pen against his notebook. "Darla. Was it Darla?"

"I don't know her name. Geraldine will though." I glanced at the clock. Yappy Hour was only a few minutes away. "The crew will be here soon. Why don't you ask her?"

Brad nodded absently. "Maggie, why did you and Yolanda go to see Fran this morning?"

I explained to him about Yolanda being interested in buying Chic Chickie from Fran.

Brad held his pen in midair. "Yolanda offered to buy Fran out?"

I nodded.

"How did Fran react to that?" he asked.

I swallowed back the panic building in my throat. Fran had reacting badly. She and Yolanda had fought. Fran had screamed at Yolanda that she'd hadn't offered a fair price and then told her to forget about her chicken empire.

But if I told Brad that, it wouldn't reflect very well on Yolanda. "Uh . . ." I stalled. "What do you mean?"

He squinted at me. "Did they make a deal or what? Did Fran accept the offer?"

I picked up a rag and nervously wiped down the bar, evading his eyes. "Uh . . . no. No deal. That's why we went over to the shop this morning. Yolanda wanted to try her luck again."

Brad was silent for a moment and finally I looked up from my busywork of cleaning the bar.

His eyes were on me when he asked slowly, "What are you not telling me?"

I shrugged. "It's nothing. Nothing really. It's just that Fran got upset. She said no to Yolanda's offer."

"How serious was Yolanda about the offer?" Brad asked.

"I don't know. She hadn't talked to me beforehand. I didn't even know about it until after it happened," I said.

"Well, I know this: If Yolanda wants something she stops at nothing until she gets it." He made a note in his notebook.

I strained to see what he wrote, but he quickly closed the little book and stuffed it into his breast pocket.

I hung the bar towel on the hook behind the bar and tried to look nonchalant as I asked, "What was that last little thing you made a note on?"

Brad rubbed at his temple. "I wrote down to check out Yolanda's whereabouts last night."

Anxiety twisted through my belly. I hated to think of the people who frequented the bar as suspects of any kind, especially not the ones I considered friends.

"You can't seriously think Yolanda had anything to do with Fran's murder. She doesn't have a mean bone in her body."

Brad laughed. "She doesn't?"

"Well, mean maybe, but not murderous!"

Brad shrugged and finished his soda. "Don't get upset, Maggie. I'm just doing my job. You know that. I have to look at everything." He reached out and grabbed my hand, gently tapping on my knuckles with his forefinger and fixing his dark blue eyes on me. "You're not mad, right?"

Under his sexy gaze, my bravado seemed to melt. "I'm not mad," I said cautiously. "I just know Yolanda didn't have anything to do with Fran's murder."

Brad released my hand and stood. "I'm sure you're right."

A thought struck me and I blurted out, "It was murder, wasn't it, Brad? I mean Fran didn't kill herself."

He shook his head. "It doesn't seem self-inflicted."

"She was shot, right? A gun. Do you know what kind?"

He narrowed his eyes at me. "You know I'm not supposed to give out information, Maggie."

I took the empty glass from him and gave him a refill. "Well, I'm planning on going to Verdant Vines tomorrow and I'll share whatever information—"

"Verdant Vines? That's Hendrick's winery, right?"

I nodded. "Yeah. He was here yesterday and the wine is—"

Brad squared his shoulders. "You're not intending to go there to ask him a bunch of questions about Fran, are you?"

I squared my shoulders back at him and we did a silent little squared-off battle until I changed tactics and batted my eyelashes. "I have legitimate business with Verdant Vines. Do you want to come along for wine tasting?"

Before Brad could answer, Yolanda popped into the bar. Her hair was styled with big soft curls that framed her face. She wore a vintage polka-dot dress that flared at the bottom, accessorized with big red earrings and high heels that featured a sexy ankle strap. But the prize accessory by far, was Beepo. He was cradled in her arms, sporting a red beret. He growled when he saw me, as if daring me to snicker at his hat.

I remained silent, but Brad made the mistake of chuckling. Beepo launched himself into a full-fledged barking fit.

"Maggie! What are you doing here? Did you already finish with the orientation?"

I waved her off. "Long story."

"Where's Max?" Yolanda squeaked. "I asked him to get here early! Why aren't the tables set up?"

I glanced around the room. "The tables are set up like they're normally set up."

Yolanda released Beepo, who darted down the corridor toward the restrooms, apparently eager to be away from us to tear the ridiculous beret off his head.

"Not like this!" Yolanda whined. "*Doggie Day* is coming! We can't be *normal*! We have to be special! We have to be *sensational*! Quick, Officer Brawn"—she smacked Brad's arm—"get to the back room and pull down the Mardi Gras boxes."

"Hello to you, too, Yolanda," Brad said. Despite not liking to be told what to do, I noticed that he hopped to do her bidding. He gave me a sidelong glance as he headed to the back room and mouthed, *I'm doing this for you.*

From the courtyard came the sound of a crowd approaching.

"Everyone is right on time," I said.

Yolanda glanced at her wristwatch. "Well, I hope we still have a little time before the editor shows up. Everyone will just have to pitch in."

The door burst open with most of the usual crowd: Abigail, Brenda, Max, and all of their canine friends. As they filled the room, Beepo eagerly scampered back down the hallway to join them.

Abigail rushed over to me. "Maggie! What are you doing here? I thought you'd be at the orientation."

Yolanda waved her off. "Oh, she's not going anywhere. I told you so. She can't leave us!"

Abigail frowned and looked to me for an explanation; at that same moment, Brad reappeared holding two large cardboard boxes. "Where do I put these?"

Yolanda punched Max's arm. "You! You're late! Help him set up the décor."

Brad stiffened. "I'm not doing décor."

Max took a box from him and upturned the contents onto the table; multicolored candles, party hats, streamers, and beads tumbled out.

Brad backed away from the decorations as the ladies took over the table, each grabbing tablecloths or garlands and getting to work. He turned to Yolanda. "May I have a word?"

Yolanda looked alarmed. "Not now! We have work to do!"

"I have work to do, too. I need to get your statement—"

Abigail held up a roll of teal streamers. "This one?" She asked Yolanda.

"Oh! Not the teal!" Yolanda said, horrified. As she rushed over to rummage through the second box, she called to Brad over her shoulder, "I've already spoken to Gottlieb." With that she stuck her nose in the box and made exaggerated noises about the items inside. The squeals and gasps erupting from her seemed to alternate between good and bad.

Brad seemed about to protest, but realized that, while Yolanda was absorbed with the task of decorating, he wouldn't be able to tear her away.

I leaned in close to him. "I think we can let you off the hook now that you carried in those heavy boxes for us." Then into his ear, I whispered, "You big hunk of man, you."

He laughed despite himself and said, "I know it's about to get crazy in here, so I'll let you whip up the Mutt-tinis and party. Don't forget about dinner tomorrow."

"I won't."

As I walked him to the door, he put a hand on my shoulder and suddenly his expression was serious. "Maggie, about Verdant Vines, please give us a chance to look into a few things first. Don't go up there tomorrow. It could be dangerous."

Chapter Eight

"Where's Geraldine?" I asked, smoothing down the teal tablecloth as Abigail placed a candle in the center of the table.

"She didn't want to come out tonight. She's terribly upset about Fran," Abigail said.

"I can understand that. Were they very close?"

Abigail lit the candle. "Yeah. As much as other people couldn't stand Fran, Geraldine always defended her. But, you know, Geraldine can be a bit difficult, too, so I guess they had that in common."

Max found his way behind the bar and the sound of a blender interrupted us as he called out, "Show of hands for Muttgaritas."

While Max took a silent count, I said to Abigail, "I met your cousin today. He was at the hospital visiting Rachel. He brought her flowers."

"Isn't he so sweet! He's got a mad crush on her."

"Abigail, I know this is a weird question and don't take it the wrong way, but do you know where Ronnie was last night?"

She frowned. "Last night? I don't really know. At the farm, I suppose. He didn't used to come into town much. Although, ever since I introduced him to Rachel a couple of weeks ago, I think he's been in town every day."

It was curious. Rachel hadn't mentioned him to me at all, but sometimes she was secretive about who she dated.

Abigail fidgeted with the tablecloth. "You don't think Ronnie is the reason she's in the hospital, do you? He's got really high standards for his chickens—"

"Abigail!" Yolanda barked. "Do you have the Howling Hounds on speed dial? We need to liven this place up ASAP!"

My breath caught. "Not the Howling Hounds," I said. The last time they'd played at the bar had been a fiasco.

Yolanda sashayed over to us and patted my arm. "Don't worry, Maggie, Bishop is in charge now. There won't be any trouble."

Abigail obediently pulled out her cell phone and dialed the guitar player. She began to chat amicably to him. I turned to Yolanda. "What happened with Gottlieb today?"

Yolanda glanced around to make sure no one was listening. She nodded discreetly and then motioned me to the restroom. We walked down the corridor past the framed photos of Gidget (the Taco Bell Chihuahua) and Rin Tin Tin. Yolanda pushed open the door to the ladies' room and ushered me in.

"Pinkie-promise secrecy, right?" she asked.

"Of course."

"You can't even tell Officer McHottie, or Sergeant Gottlieb will never ever ever tell me anything again."

I nodded.

Suddenly from outside the door, Beepo whined.

Yolanda opened the door to let him and double-checked the corridor. "Okay, here's what I know. Ellington had a mad crush on Fran—"

"Yeah."

"You knew?" Yolanda looked disappointed.

"Sort of. Ellington mentioned she was a friend and then Brenda told me he'd asked her out."

Yolanda turned toward the sink and ran the tap water. "She was killed by a Beretta handgun. The technicians were able to pick up a man's footprint in the blood, size twelve, workman-style boots."

"Are you sure? Gottlieb told you this?"

Yolanda pursed her lips. "I snuck a peek at his file while he took a phone call."

There was a sharp rap on the bathroom door and Abigail peeked in. "I wondered where you both made off to. Howling Hounds are on their way. Max is setting up the sound system for them now and, other than that, I think we're ready."

Yolanda and I slipped out of the restroom and followed Abigail into the main bar area. In a short time, the Roundup Crew had transformed the Wine and Bark into a magical place. The tables were festive with multicolored Mardi Gras beads strewn about, and the candle centerpieces gave the room a warm, cozy glow.

"It looks fabulous!" I said.

A crowd was starting to gather around the bar, so I hustled over to serve drinks. Soon, Max appeared by side.

"Sound system is ready to go. I heard the band will be here soon," Max said.

"Thank you, Max, for you all your help. I think we got this editorial spread in the bag."

"I hope so," Max said, gracing me with one of his boy-next-door smiles and taking over the blender.

"Pitcher of Muttgaritas for table seven," I said. "And table eight wants a pitcher of Pomeranians."

"Got it," Max said.

The door opened again, and I spotted Bishop and Smasher from the Howling Hounds. They gave me a semi-salute and took the stage. Within a few minutes the bar was in full festive mode.

"Man, they are rocking it!" Max said, excitedly.

Before I could match his enthusiasm, the door flew open and the woman with the Verdant Vines baseball cap from the day before entered. A rush of cold air seemed to swirl around the bar as she made a beeline toward me. This evening instead of a ball cap, her long blond hair was smoothly pinned into a low ponytail, she wore tight black jeans, a moss-colored tank top, and large military-style combat boots. Her brown Maltipoo trailed behind her, barely interested in the other dogs.

"What's that woman's name?" I whispered to Max.

He looked and nodded a greeting to her. "Darla, good to see you."

"Glass of Pinot, please, Max. Tonight I'm celebrating," she said.

I uncorked a bottle and quirked an eyebrow at her. "Congratulations. What are you celebrating?" I took a red wineglass from the overhead shelf and began to pour.

She quirked an eyebrow back at me. "Well, of anyone, you should know. 'Ding-dong the witch is dead.'"

My blood rushed into my head and I felt a little faint as I realized she was talking about Fran. "It was awful . . ." I stuttered. The glass suddenly slipped from my fingers and shattered across the terra-cotta.

Max grabbed my elbow. "I got it," he said, whipping out his bar towel and picking up the shards of glass from the floor.

Darla waved a hand around dismissing my shock. "Don't feel bad about it. She was awful. A truly warped individual. She had a way of making everyone feel miserable, and cheated, and just downright depressed. I'm glad she's gone. And I'll be honest with you, I'm even happier to see that Hendrick doesn't seem in the least bit upset!"

Max straightened and poured another glass of wine for her.

"Still," he said, handing her the glass. "She's dead, Darla. You really shouldn't be making light of it."

Darla pursed her lips. "It's bad taste, is that right?" She sipped the wine. "You really should carry Verdant Vines here, this wine is too bitter."

Oh God. I had to get this woman out of here before the editor from *Doggie Day* showed up. It wouldn't do any good to have her complaining about the wine in front of the editor.

"I'd like that," I said. "I was thinking of going to visit the winery tomorrow."

Darla perked up. "Oh, do! Hendrick would love that. He loves giving tours and he's been trying to win this account since forever."

Brenda saddled up to the bar. "I'm starving. Any Arf d'oeuvres?"

Max nodded. "I'll get some in the oven."

I grabbed his arm. "No! Don't!"

Brenda, Max, and I silently exchanged glances as Darla watched on. Yolanda sashayed over to us.

"Maggie!" Yolanda screeched. "Everything is divine. Smashing. I just got a text from Vrishali. She'll be here in a few, but I think we've got it handled." At her feet, Beepo let out a string of half barks as if to agree with her.

"Who's Vrishali?" Brenda asked.

"The editor," Yolanda hissed.

"The editor of what?" Darla asked.

"The editor from *Doggie Day*," Yolanda said, her eyes nearly popping out of her skull. "What do you think we're jumping through all these hoops for! You twit!"

"Yolanda!" I said. I turned to Max. "Cut her off."

"I'm not drunk!" Yolanda said. "It's the stress." She grabbed Darla's wrist. "I'm sorry. I'm so sorry. I get little bursts of Tourette's when I'm stressed. I found a woman this morning . . ." Beepo hovered around Darla and growled. "Hush now, Beep."

Darla's Maltipoo sniffed at Beepo, and Beepo let out a yap.

"Beepo!" Yolanda admonisted, just as the door to the bar swung open.

A tall, slender woman, dressed in a fuchsia-colored sari stood in the doorway.

"That must be Vrishali," Brenda breathed.

Vrishali was indeed breathtaking. The entire bar seemed to pause mid-conversation to take her in. Of course, it wasn't every day someone sauntered into the Wine and Bark in full Indian garb, but when they did, man, the bar wanted to welcome her. The Howling Hounds concluded their song and took a break, and Yolanda suddenly found her feet and flew to the door to greet the woman.

Vrishali took a moment to survey the bar and my heart lurched when her expression turned sour.

What is wrong?

The woman turned on a heel and pushed her way back out the door. Yolanda trailed her and Beepo scampered out before the door *whoosh*ed shut.

"Max, cover for me!" I dashed out of the bar after them.

The evening was surprisingly cool, the coastal breezes whipping my hair into my face. I caught up with Yolanda and Vrishali on the patio and introduced myself. Vrishali's face was set in a serious mask.

"I'm afraid it's not what we were looking for," Vrishali said.

"Whoa, whoa, wait a minute," I said. "What's the problem?"

"It's so rowdy," Vrishali said. "I thought it was a quiet wine bar."

"It is," Yolanda and I said in unison.

"There's a band!" Vrishali said.

"We called the band because we wanted to impress you. Usually there's no band, just on special occasions," Yolanda said.

Vrishali seemed to soften. "I didn't want anyone to make a fuss. I just wanted to get an impression—"

"Right, right," Yolanda cooed.

Beepo barked at Vrishali, seeming to echo Yolanda's comments. She looked down at him. "What a dear." She bent down and scooped him into her arms. "Do you like the Wine and Bark?" Vrishali stroked Beepo's chin and looked into his dark eyes.

I was suddenly wildly happy that Beepo had freed himself of the ridiculous red beret. He seemed much less over the top without it, even as he practically purred in Vrishali's arms.

"You do like that little bar, don't you?" Vrishali asked. Beepo's tail wagged at a frenzied pace as if he was attention starved, instead of a coddled rascal.

Yolanda and I exchanged glances.

"Why don't you come by tomorrow?" Yolanda asked.

I grimaced. The Wine and Bark was usually closed on Sundays, not to mention I'd wanted to take a little tour of Verdant Vines and see what I could dig up on Hendrick and Darla.

"We're closed tomorrow," I said. "How about Tuesday. Rachel should be out of the hospital by then."

Vrishali's eyes grew wide. "She's in the hospital? What's happened?"

I glared at Yolanda, willing her to keep quiet. The last thing we needed was for Vrishali to get a whiff of the salmonella. I couldn't imagine it would be good for business for the Wine and Bark—especially not if people thought she got it there.

"It's nothing," I said quickly. "Will Tuesday work?"

Vrishali handed Beepo back to Yolanda and pulled out her cell phone. "I'd like to make it work. I really need a feature. Would you be open to a few changes?"

"Like what?" I said as Yolanda said, "Of course we would!"

Vrishali scrolled through her appointment calendar. "Maybe a sofa. It would soften the place up. Make it look more like a doggie lounge. Paint, curtains . . . Let's see, Tuesday did you say?" She made a face as she looked at her appointments.

I flashed Yolanda a frantic look, trying to communicate telepathically with her.

Paint! Curtains! A sofa!

That would add up to major dollars, dollars I know Rachel didn't have. Who cared about *Doggie Day*, anyway?

Yolanda ignored me, practically stepping on my toes with her high heels as she positioned herself next to Vrishali and blocked any protest coming from me.

"Yes, Tuesday, does that work?" Yolanda asked sweetly.

"Yes," Vrishali said. "I can make it work. The only other thing I have on my calendar that day is to check out the new Kitty Corner that's opening soon. *Doggie Day* is not just about dogs these days."

"Kitty Corner?" I stuttered. My stomach dropped, and by the look on Yolanda's face I gathered she felt the same way. A Kitty Corner opening nearby could ruin our business. Then in true canine fashion, Beepo let out ghastly bellow that summed up my feelings.

Chapter Nine

Even though I slept poorly, I awoke on Sunday with a new sense of purpose. Today I would visit Verdant Vines and try to get traction on Fran's murder. But before I could make my morning tea, my phone rang.

"How did it go last night?" Rachel's voice was groggy but strident.

I groaned inwardly. How to tell her that the *Doggie Day* interview had been a flop?

"Well, the good news is Vrishali is going to come on Tuesday. You'll be out by then, right? Are you ready to come home now?" I asked hopefully.

She moaned. "I had a terrible night. The nurses kept coming in and waking me. I hope I get to go home today. Why is she coming back on Tuesday?"

"It was pretty rowdy last night. I think she was looking for something more low-key. Yolanda suggested she come back."

"More low-key? What do you mean? I don't get it," Rachel said.

I didn't dare mention the Kitty Corner, not until Rachel had her strength back.

"Uh . . ." I struggled to switch the subject. "Listen, I have a date with Brad tonight. How about I come see you this afternoon?"

"That'd be nice," Rachel said. "Can you stop by my apartment and bring me my laptop?"

My door buzzer sounded. "I will, Rachel. I gotta go now. I'll see you later, okay?"

We hung up and I yanked open my door to greet Yolanda. She held a steaming take-out cup in one hand and Beepo in the other.

"Ready, sugar?" she asked. "I've been honking, but you never showed up."

I gestured for her to come in. "I didn't hear you. I was on the phone with Rachel."

I brought Yolanda up to speed on Rachel as I put the teakettle on to boil and pulled out my travel mug.

Yolanda sat on my kitchen stool and stroked Beepo's triangle-shaped ears. Late last night, I'd managed to convince her to drive me to Verdant Vines this morning, but now she said, "I'm not sure we should go poking around that winery today, Maggie. I got a bad feeling."

"You have a bad feeling because of yesterday, but that doesn't mean we shouldn't go. We can help Brad and Gottlieb figure this out. Plus, I need to make sure that no one's out to hurt Rachel. So after the winery we're checking out Cousin Ronnie's farm. It's not that far from Verdant Vines."

Yolanda looked down at her outfit. "I'm not really decked out for a farm."

She wore white capri pants and Saucony walking shoes. Her feet were so petite I absently wondered if she had to special order her shoes.

"Oh, stop," I said, pouring the hot water over my tea bag. "Think about Rachel stuck in the hospital instead of your outfit."

Yolanda made a noise in throat as if I hadn't one iota of fashion sense, which I probably didn't. Beepo mimicked her noise. Ignoring them, I snapped down the lid to my travel mug and motioned to the front door.

◇◇◇

Verdant Vines was located on a hilltop outside of Pacific Cove. It had a spectacular view of the ocean on the west side and acres of rolling green farmland on the east side. On the north side, however, the view was somewhat obstructed by dozens upon dozens of wind turbines.

"What in the world?" Yolanda asked.

"Verdant Vines is 'green,'" I said. "Supposedly the entire winery is powered by those things."

Yolanda pulled her convertible into the parking lot, which was full of car-charging stations. "Pretty nifty, these things," she said. "If only gas wasn't so cheap, I'd considering going green."

"You're supposed to *want* to be green," I said. "Reduce your carbon footprint. This is California, after all."

Yolanda made a face. "I'm green. I recycle." She pressed the lock button on her key fob and the convertible chirped in response. "Anyway, I could be even more green and get rid of my car, but then who would drive you around?"

The parking lot was deserted, so I asked, "Do you think they're even open?"

Yolanda shrugged and headed toward the tasting room. Beepo followed her obediently, but I called out, "Maybe we should leave him in the car?"

Beepo growled at me and darted up ahead.

How does he understand me?

The old farmhouse that held the tasting room oozed charm. It had a white façade with green trim and exposed wooden beams. Yolanda twisted the knob to the front door and a little bell rang out overhead as we entered.

There was a small bar with a mirror behind it and several tables and chairs. No one seemed to be working. We exchanged glances and hovered near the door.

"Hello?" Yolanda called out. When no answer came she turned and hissed at me, "I told you I had a bad feeling."

"Stop it. It's early. Look," I pointed to the sign near the lower left-hand side of the mirror that stated the hours. "Wine tastings start at ten-thirty."

Beepo, who hovered near our feet, suddenly let out a small bark.

Yolanda's eyes grew wide. "What it is? What do you hear, boy?"

Beepo barked louder, adding a snarl for good emphasis. Yolanda jumped and a chill zipped up my spine.

"We better get out of here," Yolanda said, yanking on the front door, the bell overhead ringing again.

Then a man's voice called out, "Uh . . . hello?"

"Yes, hello!" I called out.

"I'll be right there," the voice called.

I turned to Yolanda. "You see, everything is fine. Stop over-reacting. You're freaking me out!"

Yolanda scowled at me, but said nothing. Beepo lost interest in us and padded along to sniff behind the bar. After a few seconds Hendrick appeared. He crossed to us, his eyes were red-rimmed and his handsome face looked tired.

"I'm so sorry. I was . . . I didn't . . . ." His voice drifted off and he shook his head. "I had some terrible news yesterday and I thought I'd cancel the tours today . . ." He covered his mouth with his hand and seemed to collect his thoughts. "But I'm happy you're here. Did you want come to place an order for the Wine and Bark?"

Now I felt super awkward. I couldn't very well grill him about his relationship with Fran and not place an order for the Wine and Bark, could I?

I absently wondered what Rachel's budget was.

"Yes," I said. "We need a shipment in for Tuesday. Will that be possible?"

Hendrick nodded. "I'm sure we can manage something. Let me give you a tour."

We followed Hendrick out through a small tasting room with sliding-glass doors. The doors opened to a wooden deck with a view of straight rows of wine grape vines. The sun was beginning to peek over the hilltop to warm the day. It felt as if we'd been transported to the South of France.

Yolanda gasped. "This is lovely!"

We strolled quietly down the trail, then Beepo dashed out from the deck and raised his hind leg to go on one of the grape vines. As Beepo marked it, Hendrick howled, "What the devil!"

Yolanda giggled. "I'm so sorry."

Hendrick's face looked ashen. "I don't normally allow dogs on the tour." He glanced at me and said, "I suppose I can make an exception for the clientele of the Wine and Bark." He looked about as miserable at having a dog on the tour as I did.

We proceeded down the trail in silence until Hendrick stopped at the bottom and gestured to a bush. "These are the Pinot Noir grapes we use." He plucked a bundle of large black grapes from the vine and handed them to Yolanda and me.

"Yes, lovely," Yolanda said. "But I thought we were going to taste the wine."

I stifled a laugh, but Hendrick frowned and took the grapes back from Yolanda.

"I like to give all my guests a sense of what goes into the wine." He waved around at the vineyard. "I usually talk about our wind power . . . and . . . I'm sorry, I suppose I'm not a very good host today."

"I'm very sorry about Fran," I said.

Yolanda echoed me. "Me, too. I was with Maggie. It was awful. We're so sorry for your loss."

Hendrick sighed. "We were together for a long time, Fran and I. Even though our relationship ended a while ago, I loved her very much. It's still a shock to me."

Yolanda glanced at me while Hendrick spoke, motioning toward his boots. Hendrick wore heavy work boots, like those prints at the crime scene. I gave Yolanda a disapproving look.

Hendrick's grief seemed real to me. He looked like he'd spent the night crying. I wondered about Darla.

"You have a new woman in your life," I said.

"Yes," Hendrick said. "Darla. She's lovely. In fact, losing Fran in such an abrupt manner has made me realize that I have to take life by the horns. I'm going to propose to Darla."

My breath caught and a warm sensation filled me. Out of loss could come something wonderful. Yolanda on the other hand made a strange face I couldn't interpret.

"Where's Darla now?" Yolanda asked.

Hendrick looked around, distracted, as if he'd misplaced her in a pocket. "Oh, I don't know. She was at the Wine and Bark last night, right? She called me to say good night. She doesn't live here at the winery with me, like Fran did . . ." His voice trailed off as if he were trying to reconcile with himself why he was telling us about his personal life.

"Let's head back to the tasting room," Yolanda suggested.

Hendrick nodded absently and we strolled together toward the farmhouse.

"Have you spoken with the police, Hendrick?" I asked.

"Yes. Officers Ellington and Brooks came to see me yesterday.

Told me the news. Asked me lots of questions about my relationship with Fran." He shuffled his feet and looked uncomfortable. "I suppose the ex is always the first suspect in something like this."

Yolanda shook her head. "No. Not the ex. It's usually the current lover. Isn't that right, Maggie?"

How am I supposed to know?

"Uh . . . I wouldn't know." I stuttered.

"Who was Fran dating most recently? Did she have another boyfriend?" Yolanda asked.

Hendrick took a deep breath. "Last I heard, she was going out with that fellow."

"What fellow?" I asked.

"Officer Ellington," Hendrick said, his face turning red. He squeezed the bundle of grapes in his hand. The juice spit out and, like a heat-seeking missile, splattered against Yolanda's white pants.

Yolanda stopped in her tracks and, God help me, the only image that ran through my head were Ellington's steel-toe boots.

Chapter Ten

Ronnie's farm turned out to be a short drive from Verdant Vines, but it didn't matter. Yolanda complained the entire time.

"Tell me again why I let you talk me into this?"

"You want to know what happened to Fran as much as I do," I said.

"But I didn't know that involved farms and vineyards." She quirked an eyebrow at me and then glared at her tailored white capri pants, now ruined by the stain from the grapes.

I winced, but before I could deny culpability, Yolanda added, "Anyway, we don't need to talk to Ronnie. It's clear Hendrick murdered Fran."

"You can't be serious. How is it clear?"

"You saw his honking monster boots. Those are obviously a size twelve."

"You don't know that! And even if he wears size twelve it's hardly enough evidence to convict a man. Darla was wearing big work boots last night at the Wine and Bark."

Yolanda scoffed at me. "Darla doesn't wear a man's size twelve boots. Anyway, Fran was shot. Isn't that a man's choice of weapon, a gun?"

Now it was my turn to scoff. "No! What do you think, that if she was killed by a woman she'd have been strangled with an apron?"

Yolanda shook her head at me. "You're hopeless as an investigator."

"It's a good thing you're not a suspect then," I said. "Any men's size twelve boots in your closest?"

Yolanda glanced at me. "I'm not telling you about any skeletons in my closet." She turned onto a dirt road that meandered up a hillside. At the top was a small yellow farmhouse.

"Is this the right place?" Yolanda asked.

I double-checked Ronnie's address on my phone. "Yeah."

Yolanda wrinkled her nose. "Where are all the chickens?"

She was right. The land in front of us was eerily quiet with not a chicken coop in sight. In fact, instead of chickens, two small boys sat on the front porch, next to them was a large Golden Retriever. They watched as we parked the car. As soon as we stepped out of the car, the boys ran to greet us. They were darlings, with matching crew cuts, blue jeans, and suspenders. Spitting images of Ronnie.

Please tell me Rachel's not dating a married man, I silently prayed.

One of the boys squirmed, but the other boy stuck his hand out. "I'm Dougie and this is my brother, Danny," he said.

Beepo yapped madly to be let out of the car. The Golden Retriever seemingly more interested in sniffing Yolanda's shoes than proving anything to Beepo.

"I'm Maggie and this is my friend Yolanda. Is your dad here?"

"He's down at the barn," Dougie said, pointing in the distance. At the end of the dirt trail was an old farmhouse. "I can get him."

Dougie ran toward a three-wheeler parked next to a white F-150

Ford truck. His brother raced behind with the dog in tow. "Me, too," he said.

Together the boys and the dog piled into the all-terrain vehicle and tore off.

"Is that legal?" I asked.

Yolanda shrugged. "They probably should wear helmets. Darling though, huh?"

As they raced down the dirt trail, Yolanda pulled me toward the farmhouse. "Do you think there's time to snoop inside the house?"

"No!" I said. "The last thing we need is to get caught rummaging through Ronnie's closet!"

We waited the requisite time before the three-wheeler appeared again, this time heading in our direction with Ronnie at the wheel and the boys and dog nowhere in sight.

Alarm was written all over his face when he saw me. "Is Rachel alright?" he called out, killing the motor on the ATV.

"Yes. Yes, I spoke with her this morning. She may have another night at the hospital but she's recovering."

Ronnie rubbed at the back of his head and nodded. "I'll clean up and go see her this afternoon."

I noted his attire. He was in jeans, suspenders, and, of course, wore men's work boots. Yolanda seemed to note the same thing because she flashed me a meaningful glance.

"Your sons," Yolanda said. "They're adorable."

"My nephews," Ronnie clarified. "They may be cute, but they're a handful. My brother came by to help me out today, but they're a package deal. I don't know what's worse, not having help or having to babysit the help." He motioned toward the front porch. "Would you ladies like an iced tea?"

The vision of Rachel cramped up in the hospital bed with salmonella poisoning played in my mind and I politely declined. Yolanda, on the other hand, accepted. As Ronnie walked past us and into the farm house, I mouthed to Yolanda, *Salmonella!*

She waved at hand at me, ignoring me. I followed Ronnie to the kitchen, but Yolanda made a detour down the hallway calling out, "Is the ladies' room this way?"

"Yeah," Ronnie called, "Just down the hall."

I turned in time to see Yolanda avoid the restroom and make a beeline toward a bedroom. Beepo trotted after her.

In the kitchen, Ronnie opened the refrigerator and pulled out an iced tea pitcher. I noted that his kitchen was spotless. There were two tea towels hanging from the oven door, each with a picture of a rooster. The same one as on the logo of Chic Chickie.

"Is that the infamous prize rooster?" I asked.

Ronnie pulled out three pint glasses and filled them with iced tea. "Is Henry infamous?" Ronnie asked.

"I heard that Fran stole his image illegally for use on her logo."

Ronnie scratched at the stumble on his chin. "Oh, that. What a piece of work that woman was."

"No love lost, huh?" I asked.

"I'm sorry she's dead," he said suddenly. "But you can't go around stealing and cheating your way through life and expect it to all turn out well in the end."

"Did she steal and cheat?" I asked.

"She stole my image," he said. "But that's not all. She had a reputation for just taking what she wanted. You should talk to your sister about her. She knows."

"Rachel knew Fran? She never mentioned her to me."

Ronnie shrugged. "Did she mention me?"

The look on my face must have told him everything, because he pressed his lips together and lowered his eyes.

Before coming to Pacific Cove, I'd imagined that Rachel and I'd been close, but since arriving in town, it was becoming increasingly obvious that Rachel led a separate life from the one she'd shared with me. Along the way, I'd lost her trust somehow. She no longer confided any secrets to me.

My heart seemed to hollow out and a sadness descended upon me.

Ronnie pushed a glass of iced tea in my direction. "She's told me a lot about you."

Our eyes met as I took the iced tea from him, and I found solace and friendship in him that I hadn't seen before.

Yolanda joined us in the kitchen. She glanced from me to Ronnie and then said, "Out with it, Ronnie, where were you Friday night?"

Ronnie looked momentarily confused. "What?"

"The night Fran was killed. You have a huge gun safe in your bedroom and you wear size twelve boots."

Ronnie leaned against his counter and smiled. "Why don't you ask Rachel?"

◇◇◇

On the car ride to Rachel's apartment to pick up her laptop, Yolanda said, "If Ronnie has an alibi, then I think it's Hendrick. He's shifty-eyed."

"He was red-eyed is what he was," I said.

Yolanda shrugged. "I'm not buying that. It's almost as if he wanted us to think he was up all night crying about Fran."

"Probably because he was," I replied.

"No." Yolanda shook her head. "If he's all brokenhearted over Fran, why would he tell us in the next breath that he was going to propose to Darla?"

She had a point. I fiddled with the radio buying some thinking time. "It comes down to motive doesn't it?" I asked.

"He's guilty," Yolanda countered.

"Because he wears boots?" I asked. "Darla wears boots, too, and so does Ronnie for that matter."

"Darla doesn't wear a man's size twelve," Yolanda said.

That much is true.

"Who benefits the most from Fran's murder?" I asked. "Darla gets to marry Hendrick, which is clearly what she wants."

Yolanda made a face. "I don't know why anybody would want to marry *him*. I get a strange, creepy vibe from him."

"I don't get that. He seems very nice. I believed his grief. You should have seen his face when you walked into the Wine and Bark the other day with Fran. I think he still loves her."

Yolanda looked about as indifferent as she could get. "He makes good wine. I'll give him that."

"Further," I said, "he doesn't benefit from Fran's death."

Yolanda quirked an eyebrow. "What about common-law marriage? If they lived together for seven years, he could be entitled to half of everything. Does he get her business?"

Hmm. I'll have to investigate how long they were together.

"Good question," I said. "Maybe I can ask Brad over dinner."

"Are you crazy? You can't ask Brad!"

"Why not?" I asked.

"He'll hate that we're poking around. Don't ask him." We stopped at a red light and she turned to stare at me. "And if you happen to lose your mind in a hot moment of passion and it slips out, don't mention I went with you!"

I laughed. "Well, we're not quite at the hot-moment-of-passion stage yet. But point taken, I'll leave you out of it."

Yolanda tapped her long red lacquered nails against the steering wheel. "I should have asked Hendrick directly. If he gets the business maybe I can buy it from him."

"If he gets the business, I'm sure you could. He doesn't exactly strike me as the type that would want to run the Chicken Shop."

Yolanda laughed. "'The Chicken Shop,' I like that."

"Or maybe he was an insurance beneficiary?" I said. A thought occurred to me. If we suspected Hendrick of bumping off Fran due to a business or insurance benefit, wouldn't the same have been true of Fran? She could have been searching for a different type of business benefit, by blackmailing Hendrick, looking for a way to get a payout from him. "I wonder how well the winery does," I said.

We turned onto Rachel's street and then pulled into the parking lot in front of her apartment. Yolanda parked the car in the lot. "The winery must do great. Look how much you just paid per case!"

She was right, of course. I'd felt terrible about Hendrick looking so teary eyed and sad, so I overbought his wine by a few dozen cases. I tried to tell myself that his wine was exactly what the editor of *Doggie Day* would love and the investment would pay off.

"Anyway," Yolanda said. "What do we care how well the winery does?"

"It was just a thought, but maybe Fran was blackmailing Hendrick or threatening him in some way."

"Anything is possible," Yolanda said. "Especially after what Ronnie said. It sounds like Fran didn't have that many friends."

"Did she have a business partner?" I asked.

Yolanda shook her head. "No. She was in it alone, as far as I know. Sole proprietor."

I opened the car door. "You and Beepo stay put. I'll be right back."

Yolanda nodded and Beepo barked after me and jumped into Yolanda's lap, as if he'd understood me.

How does he do that?

I climbed up the wooden stairs to the main door of the apartment building and pushed open the front door. Rachel lived in two-story stone building built in the early 1900s. Supposedly, the stones had been gathered from Pismo Beach. It was a beautiful building with huge wraparound windows in each apartment on the west side, affording a luxurious view of the Pacific Ocean.

Unfortunately, Rachel's apartment was a tiny, cramped one-bedroom on the east side. It was probably a good thing, otherwise, I might have been tempted to move in with her. I sprinted up the interior staircase to the second floor. A little pang tickled my heart as I passed Gus DelVecchio's apartment.

How is his audition for the food show going?

I dug out Rachel's key from my pocket and stuck it into the door. I was immediately reminded why I was so glad to have my own place. Across the floor were piles of laundry. Rachel took after Grunkly's non-housekeeping tendencies.

I beelined toward her bedroom, thinking she could benefit from Ronnie's influence. His place had been spotless. In her room, there was a small desk that held her laptop computer and a printer. Papers were strewn across the floor and I realized she must have printed something without securing the tray that held the printed sheets in place. I fixed the tray and stooped to pick up the paper.

Glancing through the sheets, I saw that Rachel had printed an e-mail conversation between herself and Cornelia Hayden.

Cornelia?

She was Fran's assistant.

I quickly scanned the e-mails. It appeared that Cornelia was applying for a job at the Wine and Bark. As I turned to the second page and read, one of the notes in the e-mail chain made the hair on the back of my neck bristle.

"I've got to get out of here—working for this woman is driving me nuts! I feel like I'm going to snap and do something crazy."

Chapter Eleven

So Cornelia and her boss, Fran, were at odds. Cornelia felt like she might snap!

What did that mean? Could she have gone over the edge and done the unthinkable?

My heart raced as I shoved the printed pages along with Rachel's laptop into my bag. I rushed out of her apartment and down the two flights of steps, outside toward the convertible.

Yolanda was on the phone, happily chatting to someone to pass the time. I jumped into the car, upending Beepo, and said, "You're not going to believe this!"

Beepo barked at me, excited and ready to receive my shocking news. Yolanda, on the other hand, waved her fingers at me signaling for me to be quiet. I dug out the e-mail chain from my bag and shoved the papers under her nose. "Look at this!" I hissed.

"Tonight?" Yolanda asked coquettishly into the phone. "Oh, I suppose I could break free."

I bit my lip, waiting for her to finish making her plans.

"Ooooh . . . I'd love to," she said into the phone. After a moment, she singsonged, "Sounds great. See you tonight." She hung up the phone, turned to me, and squealed, "That was Officer Gottlieb! He asked me out for dinner tonight!"

"That's great," I said, shoving the papers back at her. "Look what I found in Rachel's apartment."

"What am I going to wear?" she asked. "Should I wear my black dress with the A-line skirt or the polka-dot—"

"Yeah. That'll look great," I said, cutting her off, fearing that if she launched into a litany of her wardrobe we might be stuck in the car until the middle of next week.

She looked pleased. "Yes, I'll wear the black dress with my rhinestone heels."

"Right," I agreed. Then I abruptly changed the subject back to the e-mails. "Cornelia was fed up with Fran."

Yolanda looked confused. "What?"

I indicated the e-mails. "Read these."

Yolanda scanned the papers and, giving off a tone of dismissal, she said, "This doesn't mean anything. Everyone hates their boss."

Before I could protest, Yolanda added, "Anyway, if she was really going to kill her, she certainly wouldn't put something like that in writing."

Disappointment weighed me down. Yolanda was probably right. I hadn't stumbled onto a smoking gun. "I guess you're right," I mumbled.

"And we know the killer is a man," Yolanda added.

"That's true," I said. But something wasn't quite right. I still didn't like the tone of Cornelia's note. I'd have to ask Rachel about it.

Since Yolanda was in a hurry to rush home and get gussied up for Gottlieb, we agreed that she'd drop me off at the hospital and I'd grab a cab home.

She turned over the engine and we headed toward the freeway. While she chatted happily about what accessories would go best with the bedazzled heels, I noticed an ominous black van in the side rearview mirror. It seemed to be barreling down on us.

"Hey, Yo! Watch out for the van!"

Yolanda glanced into her mirror and yelped. "Why do people tailgate?"

"It's too close," I said, whipping around to look at the driver.

The van suddenly lurched into the right lane. I strained to catch a glimpse of the driver as the van speed off. The driver was small, like a woman. The only feature I could make out was a pair of aviator sunglasses and baseball cap with a logo on it.

Could that have been Darla?

<><><>

When I arrived at the hospital, I was pleasantly surprised to find Rachel awake. The curtains in her room had been opened and with the sunlight washing her face, she seemed almost recovered.

She smiled to see me. "Maggie! I'm so glad you're here. I'm bored out of my mind."

I laughed. "I can imagine. How are you feeling?" I pulled the green upholstered chair from underneath the window and pushed it toward her bed.

"I'm feeling a lot better. I hope they'll let me go home today."

I knew that was doubtful. Usually hospitals release patients in the morning and it was already mid-afternoon, but I didn't want to ruin her mood. Instead, I said, "I brought your laptop."

"Thank you," she said, then all of a sudden her face clouded over. "Maggie! Your cruise!"

"Yeah, it left this morning."

Rachel's face tightened and her eyes welled up with tears. "I'm so sorry. I feel like I keep messing things up for you."

I squeezed her hand. "It's okay, Rach. I spoke with the hiring manager. There's a cruise next month that I can start on."

Rachel's face brightened. "I'm so glad!"

I thought of Ronnie and the fact that Rachel hadn't exactly been forthcoming with me about her love life. Just recently, she'd run off with a man I'd never met before to Vegas to elope, but things hadn't worked out for them. I wanted my sister to trust me, to feel she could confide in me about anything.

"I saw Ronnie today. He's very nice," I said.

Rachel smiled shyly. "Isn't he? Where did you see him?"

"Yolanda and I drove out to his farm."

Confusion splashed across Rachel's delicate features, a small line creasing her otherwise smooth forehead. "Why?"

"How do you think you got the salmonella poisoning?" I asked.

"Not from Ronnie!" Rachel suddenly became defensive. "The nurse thinks I got it from a frozen dinner that got contaminated."

"Is that so? I didn't think you could get it like that."

That would definitely put Ronnie and his chicken farm in the clear.

Which was a good thing, Ronnie was a much better match for Rachel than the last guy she'd dated.

"Rachel, there's something we need to talk about," I said.

"I'm sorry I didn't tell you about him sooner," she said in a rush. "I didn't know if it was serious or not. We've only gone out on a couple dates, you know, but I think he's super."

"It's not about Ronnie," I said. "Although, I'm glad you're not ready to sneak off and elope!"

Rachel smiled. "Not yet."

I pushed on her shoulder. "You better not even think about it. When you're ready to get hitched we'll have a big shindig for you at the Wine and Bark."

Rachel giggled. "I don't know that dogs and chickens get along."

"Some do," I said. We laughed for a moment, but then I turned serious enough that Rachel grabbed my hand.

I told her about Fran and Rachel gasped, then covered her mouth with her hand.

"Murdered?" she asked.

"Yes. She was shot and killed on Friday night or Saturday morning anyway . . . Yolanda and I found her at her store yesterday. Brad and Ellington are investigating," I said.

"I can't believe it!" Rachel said. "I just saw her the other day. She was going on and on about a huge fight she'd had."

"Fight? Fight with who? Cornelia?" I asked.

Rachel shook her head. "No. Geraldine."

"Geraldine? Weren't they good friends?"

Rachel nodded. "As far as I know they were, but I know Geraldine was very upset with her."

"What did they fight about?" I asked.

Rachel shrugged. "I don't know. You should ask Geraldine."

"I will," I said. "What about Cornelia? She seems too desperate to get a job somewhere else." I dug into my bag and pulled out Rachel's laptop along with the printed e-mail chain.

Rachel stroked the laptop longingly. "Uh . . . I don't think I have the energy for this now. Can you put it over there?" She motioned to the top of a counter that ran alongside the wall. Then Rachel laid back on the bed and pulled the sheet up under her chin. "Yeah, Cornelia and Fran hadn't been getting along lately, either. But I think it was just one of those things. Cornelia had a lot of ideas and Fran wasn't ready to let her run with them. Or worse, she took them and then never gave Cornelia any credit."

"What about Ronnie?" I asked.

Rachel squinted at me. "What about him? He's not a murderer, if that's what you're thinking."

"You're his alibi?" I asked.

Rachel half shrugged. "Let's just say his whereabouts are accounted for."

"What about Hendrick?" I asked.

"I only know they went out for a long time, years." Rachel said. "He seems very nice. Did you do the wine tasting?"

"I did. I also bought several cases for the Wine and Bark."

Rachel clapped her hands together in childlike delight. "I'm so glad. His winery is the next up-and-coming thing. Plus, I think the editor of *Doggie Day* will really dig their wine, being that the vineyard is wind powered and all. She's really into eco-friendly businesses."

I tried not to cringe. I knew what was coming next.

"So about the meeting with the editor: Why is she coming back on Tuesday?"

Nerves fluttered through my stomach, telling her about the flop with Vrishali was going to be harder than telling her about Fran and even worse would be telling her about the Kitty Corner opening up down the street. Rachel's face darkened as she watched me.

"Well . . ." I hedged. "She is going to come back. Give us another opportunity."

Rachel's face brightened, but only for a moment. "That's great. I'm sure I'll be out of the hospital soon. I really want to meet her. Put the Wine and Bark on the map."

I nodded. "Right. There's a few things we need to take care of before then. Curtains, a couch . . ."

Rachel's mouth twisted in concern. "Curtains and a couch? We can't have that sort of stuff. The couch would be full of dog hair in a minute! And draperies! They can be pricey. The dogs would ruin them . . ." She shook her head. "I don't think we could even get them installed in time." Rachel's face paled, and she added, "Can you pass me the tub over there? I think I'm going to be sick."

Chapter Twelve

I caught a cab from the hospital and found myself repeatedly looking out the back window for that ominous black van.

Was it Darla following Yolanda and me in that black van? If so, why?

I'd wanted to take a quick nap before heading out to meet Brad, but one glance at my watch told me I'd have to shower quickly and get ready post-haste if I had any chance of being on time.

I ran up the stairs and shoved my key into the door. Racing through my apartment, I mentally inventoried my wardrobe. Brad was taking me to The Best Catch, which was the fancy local seafood restaurant. Did I have anything swanky enough for The Best Catch?

Fingering the dresses in my closet, I decided on my white-and-navy embroidered dress. It had an ornate neckline that was decorated with intricate lace, and a full, tulle-lined skirt. It seemed perfect for dinner this evening. Elegant yet modern and playful enough that hopefully Brad wouldn't consider me too stuffy.

I wandering over to the bathroom and started the hot water. Just then, I thought I heard a scratching or rasping at the front door. I turned off the water and padded down my hallway, calling, "Coming!"

I opened the door, but no one was there. A chill zipped up my spine.

Did I imagine a noise?

I shrugged off the chill and beelined to the bathroom. If I didn't get a move on, Brad would be waiting. I quickly turned on the hot water again, stripped, and dove into the shower. I shampooed and threw in a little cream rinse for good measure. Suddenly a loud bang shook the apartment. What the heck was going on?

Were the hot water pipes about to burst?

I moved out of the way of the stream of the shower and turned off the hot water. The pipes shuddered loudly. Then, as soon as the hot water dwindled to a tepid stream, the pipes were silenced. I strained to listen and heard no further noise, but my hair was full of deep conditioner that needed to be rinsed. I'd rather suffer the dreadful noise than be victim of a cold water rinse. I fearlessly turned the hot water back on and quickly finished my hair.

The pipes rattled so loudly that I was relieved to turn off the water, only to realize the noise persisted. My throat went dry and my heart hammered in chest. There was a shuffling sound coming from my bedroom.

Someone is in my apartment!

I grabbed a towel and wrapped it around my body. My cell phone was in my bedroom. What was I supposed to do?

In a panic, I yelled out, "Brad? Is that you, Officer? You're right on time, I'm sorry I'm running late!"

Whoever was in my bedroom kicked it into overdrive. It sounded as if a raccoon had been let loose in the hallway as they dashed out my front door.

I tore out of the bathroom and scrambled for my phone, preparing to give chase. I stopped cold when I saw the note on my bed. In big, loopy handwriting were the words: *STOP asking questions or you'll end up like Fran.*

I took a deep breath, hoping to slow my racing heart. Jamming my arms into the sleeves of my robe I sprinted over to the window, catching a glimpse of my street. There were a few people walking, a couple arm-in-arm, a mother pushing a stroller, and a man rushing toward the corner.

Could that have been the man in my house?

I looked again at the note. The handwriting seemed like it belonged to a woman to me, but it could have been a man. It could have been from a man wearing size twelve work boots.

I glanced out the window again, but the man was gone. What footwear had he had on?

I hadn't noticed. Some detective I was.

I checked the rest of my apartment. My front door was open, and a few pillows had been tossed around and the books from my bookcase were upended. Other than that, nothing seemed to be missing. He'd been looking for something? What?

I paced up and down my small hallway racking my brain. Who could have left me that note?

Fran's murderer?

What did I know about the killer? A man, who wore size twelve work boots, at least according to Yolanda. Could it have be Ronnie or Hendrick? What about her current boyfriend? Out of habit, I reached for my journal, to jot down some notes. My heart constricted as I realized the nightstand next to my bed was empty.

My journal is gone!

Whoever had just been in my apartment had taken my journal. Nausea threatened. I'd been keeping a journal since I was a child.

In there, I'd recorded my dreams, my fears, my worries, anything that occurred to me really. I either wrote it down or sketched it out.

Ever since I'd started getting panic attacks in New York, I'd been more regular about writing or sketching and it seemed to quell my fears. Now, anxiety crept under my skin, like an insidious creature that had been waiting for an opportune moment. I'd been using the Moleskine journal that'd been taken for a few months. It was almost complete, but now it was gone.

In the hands of a stranger or, worse, a killer.

I felt violated. It was the thought of someone else reading my notes and seeing my doodles, which weren't meant for sharing, that made my stomach feel as if I'd eaten a ton of bricks.

I sat heavily on the bed and rubbed at my temples. Competing priorities filled my head. I had to get ready for dinner, but at the same time I had to figure out who could have done this. I know for certain I shouldn't tell Brad. He'd be angry to know I'd gone against his instructions and had been looking for answers to a crime he was supposed to solve.

My phone buzzed in the palm of my hand and without thinking I pressed the green answer button.

"Hey there, beautiful," Gus's voice filled the line. "I didn't think I'd get you live. Where are you? First port yet? What it is, San Diego?"

My shoulders relaxed just hearing his voice. "Hi, Gus! How are your auditions going?"

"I made the first round."

"Woo-hoo! I knew you would. I'm so proud of you."

He laughed and I could feel his energy through the phone. "We're going to tape show number one tomorrow, but the judging round will be live on Tuesday. Viewers call in and save the chef of their choice if they're in the crisper."

"I'm sure you don't have to worry about that," I said.

"I don't know. The competition is pretty stiff. They only give you a few ingredients. You have to barter and stuff to get spices," he paused. "You have to be a real people person, I think. You know, it's not all about cooking."

It was my turn to laugh. "You *are* a people person, Gus. You're going to do fine."

"If I land in the crisper, do you think you can call in, Maggie? Tuesday at five P.M. your time. I don't know where you'll be. Will you guys be at a port? Will you have reception?"

Anxiety replied through me. "I'm not on the cruise, Gus."

"What?" he asked. "What happened?"

"Long story. But part of it is, Rachel's in the hospital with salmonella poisoning."

"Oh, no!" he said. "How'd she get it?"

"We don't know yet. She started dating this guy, Ronnie, he's a poultry farmer—"

"I know Ronnie," Gus interrupted. "Nice guy. You don't think he's responsible, right?"

"I don't know—"

"Nah," Gus said. "There's no way. I buy all my poultry from him. His farm is tops on sanitation. Anyway, it's not likely he was feeding her any raw chicken or eggs or anything. I bet she most likely got it from a commercial product that's been recalled."

"Hmm," I said. "Good to know you trust Ronnie."

"I do," Gus said. "Tell Rachel I hope she recovers fast."

"I will," I said. "So about Tuesday—yes, absolutely. I'll be at the Wine and Bark on Tuesday. We'll all watch. I'll have the whole crew call in and save you, Gus. If it comes down to it."

"Ah, Mags, you're . . . you're the best." He sighed loudly, then his voice came back lower and thick. "I miss you, Maggie."

My blood fizzed and before I could stop myself, I whispered. "I miss you, too, Gus."

And I did. I suddenly missed him so bad it hurt. I wanted to tell him about Fran, about someone nearly running us off the road earlier, about someone breaking into my apartment.

I glanced at the clock. I was late. I knew I should hang up and get ready, but instead, I squeaked out. "Something's happened, Gus. I found that terrible woman Fran dead."

"Fran? The chicken hat lady?" he asked.

"Yeah," I said.

"Oh my God! That's awful. Are you alright?" he asked.

"I'm alright," I said.

"I guess Geraldine finally snapped, huh?"

Shock buzzed through me. Rachel had said they'd recently had a fight, but how would Gus know about that? "Why would you think it was Geraldine? I thought they were besties."

Gus was silent for a moment. "They had a feud going way back. It was around the time one of Geraldine's show poodles chewed through some of Fran's chicken hat merchandise, or something like that. Anyway, they told everyone they buried the hatchet, but Geraldine carries grudges. Just ask Yolanda."

◇◇◇

My navy-and-white embroidered dress fit like a dream, for which I was grateful, considering I was about to have another panic attack. The Best Catch was walking distance from my house. Most things in downtown Pacific Cove were. I clicked along the cobblestone path, around the fountain in the center of the town square, and toward the restaurant, with thoughts of murder and break-ins on my mind.

I vowed not to share any of the day's adventures with Brad. Tonight would be just about him and me getting to know each other better. He was a very nice man, and so far seemed interested in dating me. And while I'd never dated two men at the same time before, I didn't want to say or do anything that would jeopardize Brad's affection.

Standing at attention at the front door of The Best Catch was a doorman. He nodded at me as he held the door open. I walked into the lobby fighting the jitters that the butterflies in my tummy were causing. Then, I noticed something odd. Standing in front of me at the hostess podium was Sergeant Gottlieb.

Uh-oh!

Were Yolanda and the sergeant having dinner at the same restaurant as Brad and me?

Sergeant Gottlieb smiled warmly at me. "Hello, Maggie. I think you and I are the first to arrive."

First to arrive?

"Although," he continued, "it's not entirely surprising. I'm sure Yolanda takes her time getting ready."

I was dumbfounded. What did he mean "first to arrive"? Was this a double date? How had I not realized that?

He took my elbow and guided me over to the bar. "We can wait here. You look lovely, by the way. What would you like to drink?"

My tongue was suddenly thick and I found it difficult to speak. "Chardonnay," I finally squeaked.

He motioned over the bartender, just as the front door flew open and Brad stepped in. He was dressed in a blue suit that almost took my breath away. A teasing smile played on his face as he joined us. "Maggie!" He kissed both my cheeks. "You look beautiful." Before I could speak he gave a resounding thump to Gottlieb's shoulder. "Sarge!"

The bartender placed two bottles of beer in front of us and poured my Chardonnay. Gottlieb handed Brad a beer and said, "I think Yolanda may be a while."

Brad nodded his understanding and took a swig of beer. "How was your day, Mags? Quiet?" He flashed me a look that I couldn't quite read, but if I was a wagering soul, like my Grunkly, I'd bet he was warning me not to discuss Fran's murder.

Gottlieb was his superior, after all, and Brad wasn't supposed to discuss official matters with civilians.

"I went to visit Rachel in the hospital," I said. "I don't know that's she getting any better, though. She was pretty sick when I left."

"I'm sorry to hear that," Gottlieb said. He punctuated the sentence by pursing his lips, which made his bushy mustache wiggle. For some insane reason I found it hard not to laugh, and I choked on my wine.

Brad rubbed my back. "Hey, hey, easy there."

Suddenly everything seemed funny. The fact that no one had mentioned the double date. The fact that Gottlieb had such a shiny bald head and ridiculous-looking eyebrows and mustache. And mostly the fact that they seemed to treating me as if they were running an intervention against crime-solving busybodies.

The wine burned down my throat and threatened to come out through my nose.

Oh God, I am cracking up.

The front door opened and Yolanda breezed in. She wore a simple black dress that was accessorized with shimmering beads. In her hair and on her feet were the same glittery beads, giving off the impression that she was slick with moisture, as if she just stepped out of the ocean. The effect was stunning. Conversations stopped, Gottlieb's jaw dropped and indeed it seemed as if every man in the restaurant had paused to appreciate the siren beauty who had graced them with her presence.

She smiled knowingly at Gottlieb, but her face fell when she spotted Brad and me.

I wiggled my fingers at her and I swore her face sagged in disappointment for a split second, although I may have been the only one to notice.

She floated over to us. "Good evening, y'all," she drawled.

Gottlieb heartily kissed her cheeks in greeting and put a possessive arm around her shoulder. "Yolanda! You are stunning! What an amazing dress!" Gottlieb beamed as if he'd won the lottery.

Brad smiled at Yolanda. "Good evening," he soothed warmly. He must have noticed the same look I'd seen. He was talking to her like she was a wounded bird.

"Hi there, honey," I said.

Before she could reply, Gottlieb asked, "Would you like a glass of wine, Yolanda?"

Yolanda nodded pleasantly. "That would be very nice. If you don't mind, I'm just off to powder my nose, while you order." She clutched fiercely at my wrist, cutting off the blood flow. "You'll come along won't you, darling?"

Chapter Thirteen

Once in the ladies' room, Yolanda hissed, "What are you doing crashing my date?"

"I'm not crashing your date," I said. "I had no idea they planned this."

Yolanda turned on the water at the bathroom sink and wet her fingertips. She pressed them gently to her temples. "Let's not ruin our date with your murder talk, okay, Maggie?"

"My 'murder talk'? What do you mean? This afternoon *you* wanted to find out what happened to Fran as bad as I did."

"They don't want us investigating! Don't you see?" Yolanda asked. "This thing. This whole fake date thing—"

"It's not a fake date," I protested.

She waved a hand at me. "It's so that they can make sure we're not meddling."

"Someone broke into my apartment," I said.

Yolanda's eyes grew wide. "What?"

I recounted the break-in at my apartment for her.

She wrapped her arms around me in a fierce hug. "Oh my goodness, Maggie! You could have been killed!"

"No. That's the thing. He wasn't after me, was he? I mean he broke into my apartment while I was in the shower! He could easily have killed me, right? Bonked me on the head or whatever. But as soon as I called out he, or she, ran."

"She?" Yolanda asked.

I shrugged. "Well, that's the thing. I'm not convinced it was a man." I pulled the note out of my handbag and showed Yolanda the loopy handwriting. "It looks like a lady's writing, doesn't it?"

Yolanda made a face. "It could be a man trying to disguise the writing."

I sighed. "I know, but I think it was Darla in the van this afternoon."

Yolanda pressed her lips together. After a moment of deliberation she whispered, "Maggie, I saw the van again this afternoon. After I dropped you off. The driver cut me off at a red light."

My breath caught. "Was it Darla driving?"

Yolanda shook her head. "I really couldn't tell. But I'm scared. I could have been killed." She tsked. "I'm going to have to trade in my convertible for one of those awful SUVs."

I snickered despite myself.

Yolanda slapped my hand. "Don't laugh. This is a serious matter!" I tried to compose myself and her attention returned to the note she was now clutching. "Do you think Brad or Gottlieb could pull fingerprints off the note?"

I pulled the note out of her hands. "We're not showing this to them!"

Yolanda expression turned serious. "Maggie! This isn't a game! Someone is threatening us!"

"No, no, no. Don't say anything. Brad will kill me if finds out we've been asking questions."

◇◇◇

Since I couldn't decide between the Crispy Alaskan Cod covered in jalapeño tartar, served with a side of sesame slaw and spicy fries, or the Spiced Rubbed Mahi Mahi served with avocado-tomatillo salsa, Brad did me the favor of ordering the cod and offering me half.

I ate with abandon, as did Brad and Sergeant Gottlieb. Yolanda on the other hand, only daintily picked at her BBQ grilled salmon with chipotle sauce. Every time she got a chance she gave me a meaningful glance.

To avoid any talk about Fran or the break-in, I chatted about the food and alternatively queried Gottlieb about the kitchen renovations he was contemplating. In the middle of a discussion about the merits of tile verses terra-cotta, Yolanda burst out with, "I think you should tell them, Maggie. I'm scared."

Gottlieb was startled and put down his glass of Zinfandel. Brad, on the other hand, found his glass and drank with renewed energy, as if fortifying himself for the news.

I turned to Gottlieb and said, "Go with the terra-cotta. Yolanda is scared the tile could crack."

Yolanda glared at me. "You know perfectly well what I'm talking about."

I motioned to her plate. "She doesn't like the salmon and is scared she might have an allergic reaction. Blow up like a balloon!"

Yolanda's jaw clenched. "I'm not allergic to seafood."

Gottlieb examined her plate, his bushy eyebrows furrowing together so that it looked momentarily like a rodent had over run his face. "Well!" he said. "You've barely touched your food. Don't you like it?" He looked over shoulder for a waiter. "I'll send it back."

Brad put down his glass, his fingers drumming out a staccato rhythm as he studied me.

"It's not the salmon," Yolanda soothed. "The salmon is lovely. It's that—"

"She thought you two were going to have a hot and heavy date, and now she's mad at Brad and me for tagging along," I said.

Yolanda flushed scarlet, but Gottlieb perked up as if that was the best news he'd ever heard. He placed one of his enormous hands on top of Yolanda's delicate little fingers and said, "Ah now. Don't be disappointed. I'll take you out next week. Just the two of us."

Brad's tapping ceased and he gave me a look that said he saw straight through me. "How's the wine?" he asked pointedly.

I reached for my glass. "Delicious."

"As good as Verdant Vines?" he asked.

Yolanda seized the moment. "We went up there today to get some wine for the Wine and Bark and someone nearly ran us off the road. Maggie thinks it was Hendrick's girlfriend, Darla. And then someone—"

"You went up there after I asked you not to?" Brad asked.

"We had to," Yolanda interjected. "We have to make an impression on Vrishali because of the Kitty Corner opening up."

"What?" Gottlieb asked. His forehead creased and he looked as if we'd lost him several questions back. But with a wiggle of his eyebrows he was back in the saddle.

"Long story," I murmured, then took a sip of wine.

A tuxedo waiter approached our table. "How's everything tonight, folks?"

Brad smiled disarmingly. "It's just about to get interesting."

The waiter laughed. "I'll leave you to it then. Let me know if there is anything else I can bring you folks, before the dessert menu, of course." He turned on his heel and left.

Brad fixed his sexy blue eyes on me. "Maggie? You were saying?"

"I don't know that it was Darla. But it was definitely a woman driving and she wore a cap with a logo. I've seen Darla wearing a ball cap with the Verdant Vines logo—"

Gottlieb tsked. "Now, ladies. Detective work is more than just deducing who wears a cap or not. Someone could have been impersonating Darla to make you think just that. You really have to leave the police work up to Officer Brooks and myself."

Annoyance burned inside me. I knew Yolanda liked Gottlieb and overall he seemed like a very nice man, but I couldn't take the patronizing. "Leave the detective work to you? What about Officer Ellington? Do you know about his prior relationship with the victim? What about the fact that he fits the profile of the killer?"

Brad squinted at me. "What profile?"

"Man, size twelve work boots," Yolanda said.

Gottlieb and Brad stared at her and she suddenly clasped a hand over her mouth.

"And you know this how?" Gottlieb asked.

His eyebrows seemed to stand at attention, but Yolanda simply rolled her shoulders back and said, "I pay attention."

Gottlieb murmured and Brad pinched the bridge of his nose.

"Just so we are clear. Officer Ellington is *not* a suspect," Brad said.

"Why not?" I demanded.

"No, no. We're not going to do this. We're not going to discuss the ins and out of an ongoing investigation," Gottlieb said. "I'm sure you ladies understand."

Before we could protest, our waiter materialized at the table, asking, "May I clear some plates here?"

Brad leaned back to give the waiter access. The waiter silently cleared our plates and somehow magically presented a dessert menu to each of us.

Brad ordered the chocolate mousse for us to split and Yolanda and Gottlieb ordered the Macadamia Nut Brownie Sundae.

When the waiter retreated, Gottlieb asked, "What's this about a Kitty Corner? I do love little kittens."

Yolanda paled.

Gottlieb a cat lover?

Yolanda would never shut up about it. This date was going from bad to worse.

Brad seemed to pick up on the tension because he said, "Dogs, too. The sarge loves all animals."

Gottlieb's mustache twisted violently as if he was swallowing back a protest, but then he laughed a little too robustly. "Yes. Yes. I like all sorts of creatures."

Our waiter returned and meticulously placed the desserts between each couple.

Brad's hand brushed against mine as he picked up his spoon on the side of the saucer holding the mousse cup. He caught my eye and winked wickedly at me.

I dipped into the dessert and enjoyed the creamy decadence in my mouth for only a moment before I noticed Yolanda across the table, wringing her napkin.

"What about your apartment, though, Maggie. I think you should tell them," she said.

Ire bubbled up inside me. Wasn't I ever allowed one moment of peace before the next catastrophe assaulted me?

Brad put down his spoon and squinted at me. "What about your aparment?"

"It's nothing," I said.

Gottlieb cleared his throat. "If it's nothing, then tell us and let us judge."

"Someone broke into Maggie's apartment—," Yolanda said, her voice shrill and panicky.

"It's alright, Yolanda," I soothed. "Nothing is going to happen—"

"I don't want Maggie to end up like Fran," Yolanda sniveled, her eyes welling up with tears.

Brad slammed a fist down on the table. "Dammit, Maggie! Didn't I tell you not to get involved? To not go to the vineyard? This isn't a game. Fran is dead!"

Anxiety burned my throat. Suddenly I was the bad guy. Brad was angry, Yolanda was crying, and Gottlieb looked as if he wanted to choke me.

"I didn't mean for . . ." My voice sounded distant and the room tilted to the right. I pressed one hand to my forehead and the other on the table to steady myself. My vision blurred and then I had no peripheral vision. I sucked in a deep breath.

Oh Lord.

I knew this feeling all too well.

Things are closing in on me.

Brad stood and swiftly helped me out of my chair. "Let's get you some air."

My legs felt so wobbly that I feared I'd land facedown in a dessert plate, but Brad expertly guided me out of the restaurant. Once outside, a blast of fresh ocean air whipped my senses back in order and my wooziness subsided a bit.

"Panic attack," I whimpered. "I get them sometimes in moments of severe distress."

Brad's hands were on my arms, still supporting me. He leaned his face close to mine. " 'Severe distress,' huh? What the hell do you think you are causing me?"

"I dunno," I said lamely, wishing my balance would return.

Brad slipped a hand to the crook of my neck. "Repeat after me," he whispered. "No more investigating."

"Mmm," I mumbled.

He leaned in close until our foreheads were touching. "No more investigating. I mean it," he said again.

The low register in his voice made my tummy quiver.

"I agree with you," I said, barely able process the thought.

"I'm not trying to be an ogre here. I care about you, Maggie." His mouth was so close to mine, I could feel his breath on my lips. "I want you to be safe. Do you understand?"

I wrapped my arms around his back and squeezed my body into his. "I understand," I said.

"Say it," he said, pulling his body away from mine, but leaving his lips close.

Teasing me, toying with me.

Well, two can play at that game.

"No more investigating," I lied.

Chapter Fourteen

An obnoxious buzzing jarred me out of sleep. I'd been dreaming about Brad and how sweet his protective nature was. I fumbled for my alarm clock, then realized the buzzing was my phone.

Rubbing the sleep out of my eyes, I reached for the phone, hoping it was Rachel being released from the hospital.

"Hello?"

"Maggie!" It was Yolanda, her voice sounded hoarse and in pain.

I jolted up in bed. "What is it? What wrong?" I was suddenly disoriented. It was pitch black outside. Still night. Why was Yolanda calling me in the middle in the night? Had her and Gottlieb's date ended poorly?

"It's Beepo!" she wailed.

"Beepo? What do you mean?"

"He's . . . he's . . ." Her breath caught in a jagged way. She let out a huge sob. "He's gone, Maggie! I think he's . . ."

"Gone? Slow down, honey. Take a deep breath," I said. "Do you want me to come over?"

"I think someone took him. My place looks ransacked—"

"Okay, call Gottlieb, I'm on my way."

"No, no," she wailed. "I can't call him."

"What? Why not?"

"I . . . please. You come over. Can you call Brad?"

"I'll call him right now. Give us a couple of minutes."

I hung up and speed-dialed Brad. He picked up on the third ring, his voice groggy and thick with sleep. "Maggie? Is everything okay?"

"I'm sorry to wake you," I said. "I just got off the phone with Yolanda. She says her place has been broken into and Beepo's gone."

"She's just got in now?"

I glanced at the clock. It was 4:30 A.M. "I guess so," I answered.

"Hot damn, Sarge," he said.

"Get your mind out of the gutter. She's super distressed. You know how she loves that little dog."

Brad laughed. "Okay, okay, I'm just trying to wake myself up. I'll jump in the shower and head over to her place in a few minutes. Tell her not to touch anything."

"I will. But pick me up on your way. I want to go with you."

"Maggie. You promised no more investigating."

"This isn't investigating," I said, jumping out of bed and pulling on a pair of jeans. "This is being there for a friend."

He snorted.

"Besides, you know how I feel about Beepo."

This time Brad laughed out loud. "Yeah, you hate him."

I snickered. "*Hate* is such a strong word."

"I'll see you in a few minutes," he said, hanging up.

I rushed into the bathroom to brush my teeth and do something about the rings under my eyes and my tangled mess of hair. A girl is just not her best at 4:30 A.M.

Fortunately, Brad took long enough it that it gave me a chance to reset my hair and completely redo my makeup. When he knocked on my door, I opened it to find him fresh faced and shaved with damp hair and a bright smile. He wore blue jeans and snug T-shirt that outlined his pecs. It was all I could do to not pull him into my apartment there and then.

He leaned one arm on my door frame and said, "So you just wake up beautiful?"

I grabbed my purse off the couch. "No. I work at it, but apparently you don't."

He ran a hand through his hair self-consciously and shook his head. "Me? Beautiful? Yeah right. You're lying."

I pulled out my keys to lock the door and said, "I only lie about big stuff."

He snickered at my comment, but stopped my hand from locking the door. "Hold up." He fingered the lock. "You said someone broke in yesterday. How'd they get in? Did you leave the door unlocked?"

"I don't think so."

"There are no marks or scratches." He smoothed his palm across the doorjamb. "Did you leave your key anywhere? Or do you hide a spare?"

An uneasiness fluttered in my chest. "There's only one copy of my apartment key."

Brad looked at me expectantly. "Where it is?"

"At the Wine and Bark."

He groaned. "That means anyone could have swiped it, right?"

I locked my door and we headed down the hallway.

He slipped an arm around my waist and said, "Make me a list of everyone who was there on Saturday night, okay? And call a locksmith. I want you to have a new lock put in."

◇◇◇

Yolanda lived in a small cottage next to the ocean. Her space truly exemplified her personality. It was a historic cottage that Yolanda had made bright and modern. On the street side there was a wrap-around garden filled with hydrangea, alstroemeria, and poppies. The serene feeling was broken only by the sounds of seagulls and the distant barks of harbor seals.

I followed Brad up the walkway toward her front door. Yolanda had already seen us approach and was standing in the doorway in a cream tank top, capri-style teal pajamas bottoms, and bare feet. Her hair was pulled back in a ponytail and her face was washed clean of any makeup residue. If possible, she looked even more beautiful without her usual makeup.

She ushered us into the living room, where the hardwood floors gleamed and the skylights revealed that not a speck of dust covered a single surface. On the marble coffee table, Yolanda had set out a tea service for Brad and me, complete with tea, scones, and fruit. She motioned for us to help ourselves, then unceremoniously plunked herself down on her brocade fainting couch and buried her face in her hands.

"My poor little Beep-Beep!" she wailed.

I sat on the couch next to her and rubbed her back. "There, there, honey. Don't fret. We're going to find him."

"How could anyone by so cruel. Killing Fran is one thing. She was mean. She had enemies! But Beepo? He didn't have a mean bone in his tiny little terrier body!"

Brad leveled a gaze a Yolanda. "Were you and Fran enemies?"

Yolanda jolted herself upright and wiped her eyes. "What do you mean? I hardly knew her. I just wanted to buy her chicken hat business."

Brad looked around the immaculate cottage. "Did you say your place was ransacked?"

Yolanda followed his gaze around the room, a confused expression on her face. "Yes." She rose and led us down the hall into one of the bedrooms she used as her office. Along the windowsill was a marble countertop she used as a work surface. Atop the surface were several of Yolanda's handmade animal bags: frogs, owls, and even a pig, in various stages of completion.

Brad and I searched around the room. He turned to me with a confused expression on his face that must have mirrored mine.

"Uh," he said. "What exactly was ransacked?"

Yolanda looked aghast. "The place is a mess!"

I laughed. "Where?"

She pointed to a box that was tucked under the countertop in the corner. The box appeared to have been upended, with various pieces of materials tossed about.

"It looks like Beepo got into it," I said.

Yolanda did her best not to look insulted, but the way she stiffened I knew I'd hit a nerve. "He never goes in here!" she said. "I always close the door. He's never in here because, you know." She leaned toward Brad and whispered confidentially, "Because of *that thing* he does."

I tried not to laugh. I knew Beepo had a tendency to attack Yolanda's chicken bags and mark them.

"When I arrived home after our date, the door to my office was open and the box had been riffled through. Don't you see, someone's been in here trying to steal my designs!"

"It seems to me, perhaps you left the door open," Brad said. "Beepo took advantage of the opportunity and got in here. Could it be?"

"Absolutely not!" Yolanda exclaimed.

"Was your front door broken into?" Brad asked.

"No," Yolanda answered.

"Could Beepo have run away?" I asked.

Yolanda glared at us as if we were crazy. "No! He's gone! He's been taken. He would never run away!" Her eyes glazed over and she looked ready to burst into tears.

I wrapped an arm around her and directed her back toward the living room. "Let's have some tea and think about this."

"Anything else different from when you left last night?" Brad asked.

"No." Yolanda sat heavily onto the fainting couch. "That's it. The office door open, the box overturned, and Beepo gone. Isn't that enough?" she demanded.

"What about your front door? Did you lock it?" he asked, as he paced through the house looking at all the windows.

"Of course I locked my door," Yolanda said.

"You're on the ground floor here, did you lock all the windows?" he asked.

"Yes," she said.

He returned to stand in front of us with his hands on his hips. "Okay. Let's start from the beginning. You left last evening to meet us at what time?"

"Seven P.M.," Yolanda said.

Brad pulled out a leather notebook from his back pocket and jotted a note. "Alright. You returned to find your cottage door locked when you came home, correct?"

"Yes, that's right," Yolanda said. She sat with her hands folded in her lap like an obedient schoolgirl as she answered Brad's questions.

"There's no sign of forced entry," Brad said. "Who has a key to your place?"

"No one," Yolanda said. "Except for my neighbor Mrs. Blumenthal, who occasionally comes to water the plants and feed Beepo."

Brad nodded.

"And, of course, Mrs. Mezner," Yolanda continued. "She has Mrs. Blumenthal's keys and mine, you know, just in case."

Brad flashed me a look. "Okay."

"And Mrs. Murphy, too."

Brad tapped his pen against his notebook. "Uh-huh."

"And Mr. Conners. He's so sweet. He comes over every other morning to bring me the latest news from his niece, she's traveling in Australia and when—"

"So you're telling me the whole bloody neighborhood has a copy of your key."

Yolanda's eyelashes blinked in rapid succession. "They're my neighbors! They've had copies of my key for years. Not one of them ever came in without my permission, and I'm certain none of them dognapped Beepo!"

Brad took a deep breath. "Okay. Is that it then?"

Yolanda licked her lips hesitantly and flashed me a look, then mumbled half under her breath. "And the Roundup Crew."

"The whole crew?" I asked.

She shrugged. "Why not? They're my friends."

"I don't have a key!" I said, trying not to sound as offended as I felt.

Yolanda put a hand on my knee. "Oh, honey, I'm so sorry. Do you want a key?"

"No!" Brad barked.

Yolanda looked surprised. "Why ever not?"

"You can't go handing out your key to everyone in Pacific Cove and then call the police saying your place has been broken into, when clearly it hasn't!" Brad said.

"What do you mean?" Yolanda said. "My dog is missing. Someone stole my dog! Beepo is . . . gone!" All of sudden, she began to hyperventilate and Brad looked pained.

"I'm sorry," he said. "That was unprofessional of me. I'll put in a report. We'll call the pound and see if Beepo got picked up."

Yolanda sniffled, but said nothing.

I rubbed her knee. "We'll find him, sweetie. Don't worry."

We sat in silence for a moment, before I asked. "What about Geraldine?"

"What about her?" Yolanda asked.

I recalled the fight between Geraldine and Fran. A pit began to form in my tummy. "Does she have a key to your place?"

Yolanda nodded.

"I thought you and she were nemeses," I said.

"Well, that doesn't mean I don't trust her," she said.

Brad appeared as perplexed as I felt.

"Would Geraldine have come while we were out to dinner last night and snatched Beepo?" he asked.

"Of course not," Yolanda said. "Why would she do that?"

He shrugged. "Why does anybody do anything?" he said, sitting on the couch next to me. He popped a scone into his mouth and waited for a response from us.

Both Yolanda and I were silent.

Someone had broken into my apartment, left a note, and taken my journal. Was that the same person who'd taken Beepo?

What did all of it have to do with Geraldine?

It was time for answers.

Chapter Fifteen

After Brad left, I stayed with Yolanda to brainstorm about Beepo's whereabouts.

"I think we should call an emergency Roundup Crew meeting," I stated emphatically. "They can help us find Beepo, figure out who killed Fran, and prep the Wine and Bark for Vrishali's return tomorrow."

Yolanda slumped on the couch. "Yeah," she mumbled. "That's a good idea."

I ignored her lackluster attitude and pulled out my phone. I hit Max, Brenda, and Abigail with a group text message.

> Beepo is missing. Yolanda in urgent need of TLC. Meet at Wine and Bark ASAP. I'll provide coffee and doughnuts.

I hesitated to invite Geraldine. Even though I was dying to grill her about her fight with Fran, I knew Yolanda wouldn't want her there. I decided I'd pay Geraldine a visit later in the day.

Yolanda eyes were fixated on Beepo's empty doggie bed, which was parked in a corner of the living room. I poked her. "Put on some shoes, sister. We're going scouting for your little friend."

Yolanda gave me a weary look. "What if we don't find him?"

"Don't say that. We're going to find him." I sprang up and yanked on her arm. "Get up before I have to spatula you off the couch."

Yolanda trotted off to her bedroom and I followed. Her room was decorated in pink and creams. Her bedspread was neatly tucked. "So how did it end last night with Gottlieb?" I asked.

Yolanda opened her mirrored closet door and selected a pair of strappy walking sandals. She sat primly on the corner of her bed and put them on. "It was great, Maggie. He is such a sweet man. After you and Brad left the restaurant, we finished dessert and then he took me to his boat for a nightcap."

"His boat?"

"Yeah, he has a little schooner he keeps in the bay. We took it out for a bit. Very romantic." Her breath caught and she sniffled. "I can't believe I was out gallivanting while Beepo was being snatched! I'll never forgive myself!"

"Oh, come on. Don't be so melodramatic. He's going to turn up!"

Yolanda finished tying her sandals and stood. "Oh, we were wrong about the man's work boots."

"What?"

"Last night, I confessed to Gottlieb that I peeked in his file. After giving me a very stern reprimand, mind you, he told me I'd misread it." She wiggled her eyebrows at me to insinuate something about the scolding.

I held up a hand. "TMI."

She giggled. "You are such a prude. Anyway, he told me I was wrong. The shoe print was from the crime scene tech. That's why it was in the file. To annotate that he'd stepped in the blood."

"So no false assumption would be made?" I asked.

"Exactly," Yolanda said.

I felt foolish. Why had I ever believed we could figure this out? All we'd done was manage to get our homes burglarized and Beepo snatched.

◇◇◇

Inside the Wine and Bark, a pink pastry box sat between Brenda, Abigail, Yolanda, and me. Max hustled about filling our coffee mugs.

Abigail's white Shih Tzu, Missy, sat at her feet, while Brenda's Chihuahua, Pee Wee, nestled close by. Both dogs seemed curiously sad and subdued, as if they were missing Beepo, too.

Yolanda and I had filled everyone in on the break-ins and the black van close-calls. Now, we sat munching on old-fashioned chocolate-covered donuts with a few overturned coasters and a slew of colored markers, trying to figure out whodunit.

"Who are your top suspects?" Abigail asked. Even at this ungodly hour in the morning, Abigail's hair was fixed in her trademark elegant French braid—and somehow she'd managed to put lipstick on herself and a rhinestone bow on Missy's head.

"The men are Ronnie, Hendrick, and Ellington," I said, writing each name on a different coaster with a red marker as I said it.

"You can forget about my cousin Ronnie," Abigail said, picking up his coaster and tossing it across the bar like a Frisbee. "He's as gentle as a mouse, *plus* he was with Rachel that night."

"Hendrick is my top suspect," Yolanda chimed in. "He has beady eyes, and I think there's something funny about the way he and Fran broke up."

Brenda made a face. "He doesn't have beady eyes. He's quite handsome."

Max, who had been about to refill Brenda's coffee, prickled and reached over the table to refill my cup instead.

Brenda laughed. "I mean handsome in a German kind of way."

We all chuckled.

"Organized and prompt and stuff," Brenda continued. She winked at Max. "Not like you, honey."

"I'm not prompt?" he asked.

She stroked his arm. "You're so cute when you're jealous."

Max smiled shyly and refilled her coffee mug.

"I still think there's something fishy about Hendrick," Yolanda said circling his name with a black marker.

Abigail asked, "Why is Ellington on the list?"

"Because he doesn't like dogs and Yolanda hates that." Brenda giggled.

Yolanda snickered. "Very funny. I didn't put him on the list."

They all turned to me. I shrugged. "I don't know. He was trying to date Fran, right? She rejected him. He's the scorned lover, sort of."

Yolanda picked up the coaster and said, "It can't be Ellington. Brad and Gottlieb told us that last night."

Abigail took the coaster from Yolanda and flung it across the bar, so that it landed close to the other coaster. "I supposed they'd know if the killer was a cop, huh?"

"Why are there only men on your list?" Max asked. "What about the assistant? Cornelia."

"Right," I wrote Cornelia's name on a fresh coaster. "She sent Rachel an e-mail saying she could kill Fran for stealing her ideas."

Brenda shifted uncomfortably in her seat. "I don't think Cornelia did it."

"Why not?" I asked.

"While it's true she was upset with Fran, it doesn't seem like she would seek legal counsel if she was going to murder her," Brenda said. "You know, that's like putting up a billboard sign."

"Yeah," Abigail agreed. "To kill your boss seems like the kind of thing that only happens in movies."

I tapped the pen against the table. I wasn't ready to take Cornelia off my suspect list. I added Darla's name to another coaster. Everyone around the table nodded in agreement.

"If it was her in the van, trying to run you two off the road, then I think we've found the killer," Max said.

Yolanda sprang to her feet. "Let's head right to her house! She's probably got Beepo there!"

At the mention of their friend's name, both Missy and Pee Wee began to howl.

Abigail scooped Missy onto her lap and rubbed her ears, while Brenda patted Pee Wee's head and said, "Hush now, boy. We're going to find him in no time."

"I don't know where Darla lives or I'd agree with you," I said to Yolanda.

"Geraldine might know. She was the one who invited her to start walking with us. Where is Geraldine, by the way?" Abigail asked.

I hadn't included Geraldine on my group text message and there was a very good reason for it. I wrote Geraldine's name on a new coaster. Abigail frowned.

"She's a suspect?" Max asked.

Just as I was about to elaborate, Missy and Pee Wee bolted for the front door. Glancing out the window of the bar, I spotted a familiar figure. Geraldine was making her way across the patio. One hand shielded her face from the sun, as she squinted through the glass. The other hand held fast to a Wine and Bark Day-Glo leash. Secured on the end of the leash was her beautiful show poodle. Next to the poodle was another familiar little fellow.

Yolanda sprang up and rushed to the door. She flung it open, screaming, "Beepo!"

He sniffed at her feet happily and wagged his micro tail. Missy and Pee Wee jumped on Beepo and tackled him to the floor.

Yolanda rescued him from their affection and pressed him to her cheek. "What happened to you, Beep?"

"I found him at the beach wandering around," Geraldine said. "Not far from your house. Did he get loose?"

"More like someone let him out," Yolanda said.

Geraldine frowned, glancing around at us, the coasters, and the pastry box. "What's going on?"

"Emergency meeting," Max said.

"Why didn't anyone call me?" Geraldine huffed. She seated herself immediately, and grabbed a pastry. "I knew something terrible must have happened. I was passing by and I saw the lights on."

Brenda and Abigail both shifted uncomfortably. Max rose and ducked behind the bar to get an extra mug for Geraldine. Her gaze landed on the coaster with her name on it and she pressed her lips together in thought. Max poured her some hot coffee.

I pushed the sugar bowl close to her, but she shook her head at the offer.

"Why is my name on that coaster?" she asked.

Taking a deep breath, I said. "I heard you had a fight with Fran. Can you tell us about it?"

"A fight with Fran?" Geraldine asked. "Where did you hear that? It's a lie. Fran and I were best friends. You know, I've been very upset since she passed away. In fact, this is the first morning I've felt well enough to venture out for a walk on the beach. I had to get out of my apartment. Queenie had to get out."

"I can imagine," I said. "I'm just curious what you fought about."

Geraldine frowned at me. "I told you, we didn't fight." She took a sip of coffee as if punctuating her statement.

"Where were you on the night she died?" I asked.

Geraldine looked as if she'd come out of her skin. "What?" She glanced around at all of us. To their credit, everyone kept still and watched her squirm. "You can't possibly suspect me in my best friend's murder!"

Brenda put out a soothing hand and patted Geraldine's shoulder. "Of course not, dear. We're just simply trying to figure things out. Accounting for everyone's whereabouts and whatnot."

Brenda's soothing tone did little to calm Geraldine. "I had business. I have an alibi, if that's what you're asking."

Yolanda crossed over to the table and slammed a palm against it, making the coffee spill out of Geraldine's cup and splatter onto the table. "It *is* what we're asking! What is your alibi? Where were you?"

Geraldine's face paled, and Yolanda nostrils flared. They stared at each other. Finally Geraldine muttered, "I don't know why my whereabouts are any of your concern."

"Did you take Beepo?" I asked.

Geraldine whipped around to glare at me so quickly, I thought she'd give herself whiplash. "Take Beepo? Of course not! I told you, I found him on the beach!"

"What about this?" I took the note with the loopy writing out of my pocket and shoved it under her nose. "Is this your writing?"

Brenda stood and crossed to stand between us. "Now, Maggie." Her voice was calm and full of reason, but I was beyond that now.

"Stop playing games, Geraldine," I pressed. "Where were you the night Fran was killed?"

"I told you, I had business. About a pet show. I was hired to consult."

Max scratched at the back of his head. "Okay, you were hired. You have a client. Who was it?"

"What difference does that make?" Geraldine demanded.

"Well, if the client is your alibi, it makes a difference," Abigail reasoned. "What if, say Cornelia hired you. And you both were in cahoots to kill off Fran."

"Cornelia? Why, she's a twit! And she doesn't have two pennies to rub together. She couldn't hire anyone," Geraldine said.

Brenda looked miffed. "She hired me."

128 •   Diana Orgain

"What for?" Geraldine said.

"We'll get to that. First, tell us who your client is. We need someone to corroborate your alibi," I said.

Geraldine hesitated, looking out the patio window as if waiting to be rescued. We waited her out in silence. Finally, she said, "There's a shop opening in town. They heard about my success at the Carmel Pet Show. They wondered if I might be able to lend my expertise—"

"A new shop?" Yolanda asked. "Do you mean the Kitty Corner?"

A collective gasp came from the group followed by a stunned silence. Then suddenly everyone burst into, cries of "You're kidding!" and "The Kitty Corner" and "How could you?"

Even the dogs seemed to share in the outrage.

"Traitor!" I said. "Rachel is going to be out of her mind with the Kitty Corner opening up! Are you trying to put us out of business?"

"It won't affect the Wine and Bark. It's a cat adoption place," Geraldine protested. "It's not like it's a cat bar. *Wine Lives*. That would be direct competition . . . Anyway, they were going to open up shop anyway," Geraldine said. "It didn't have anything to do with me. I was only going to help them get into the pet show. I didn't create the lease!" With that final comment, she glared at the one attorney seated at the table.

Brenda!

I groaned and Brenda looked as if she'd rather be swallowed whole by the earth than have to face us.

"It's not my fault," she squeaked. "The landlord for Bradford and Blahnik is the same one as the property where the Kitty Corner wanted to lease. I had to do it or risk a bad relationship with my own landlord. So I wrote in ridiculous terms. I never thought the Kitty Corner would agree to it."

Yolanda let her head bonk on the table and Abigail got up and paced.

"So you didn't kill Fran," I said to Geraldine. "And I hope the news that you and Brenda are helping the the Wine and Bark's competition isn't going to kill Rachel."

Chapter Sixteen

The Roundup Crew dispersed to take their dogs to the beach, leaving Max and me alone at the Wine and Bark.

I loaded some dishwater with the coffee mugs, while he took out the trash. When he returned he said, "If the editor of *Doggie Day* wants a different look for the Wine and Bark why don't we grab the leather sectional from my place and bring it here? It's leather, so the dog hair won't cling so much and it won't cost Rachel a dime."

I perked up. Fixing up the Wine and Bark would take my mind off Fran's murder. "That's so sweet of you to offer, Max. Are you sure you don't mind?"

He shrugged. "I don't mind." He examined the floor. "What about a floor polisher? We can rent one and I can polish up the floor, nice and bright."

"Yeah!" I said, my excitement growing. "She mentioned draperies. I don't know what to do about that."

"I'm not an interior designer." Max glanced at the windows.

"Let's see, she wanted a couch, draperies, sort of like fabrics to soften the place up?"

"Right," I agreed.

"A lady's touch." Max smirked.

"Hey, hey! Watch out, buddy! What are you trying to say? That Rachel and I don't have any taste?"

He laughed. "No. I'm just thinking . . . Wasn't Cornelia trying to hit up Rachel for a job?"

I studied him a moment. "Yes."

Max scratched at his chin. "Maybe we should hire her for the day. See if she has any advice on draperies . . ."

"Grill her about Fran, you mean?" I asked.

He grinned unabashedly at me. "Noooo. Your boyfriend doesn't want you investigating."

"He's not my boyfriend. You know that."

"Good," Max said. "I like the other guy better for you."

I laughed. "You only like Gus because of his culinary talents."

"Guilty as charged," Max confessed. He looked longingly across the patio at DelVecchio's. The closed sign hanging in the window weighed on my heart.

"He made the show," I said. "He's worried about landing in the crisper in the first episode. I promised we'd all call in and save him if that happened. The show airs tomorrow night."

"Let's grab the TV from my place, too, then. We'll turn the Wine and Bark into a trendy viewing lounge. The editor of *Doggie Day* will love that."

"Let's do it," I agreed.

As we walked together to the front door, a plump elderly woman with scads of gray curls shooting out in every direction atop her head hustled over to us.

"Who's that?" I asked Max.

He shook his head. "Beats me. She must be new in town. Never seen her before."

The woman wore a floral housedress and black ballet slippers. She had on bright fuchsia lipstick and large horn-rimmed glasses. In her arms she held a fruit basket. She approached the front door of the Wine and Bark as if on a mission. Although she seemed startled to see Max and me standing there watching her.

I unlocked the door and greeted her.

"I'm looking for the owner, Rachel Patterson," she said.

"I'm her sister, Maggie. Rachel isn't available," I said.

"What a shame!" she said. "I was hoping to introduce myself. I'm Lois, the owner of the new Kitty Corner."

Max and I exchanged a look.

Adrenaline shot through my system. So this innocent-looking nice lady, who reminded me of my grandma, was to be our business rival. I suddenly felt sick.

Lois studied us anxiously. "I was hoping we could be friends. Local businesses getting together and helping each other," she said, shoving the treat-filled basket into my hands. "Even though I encourage cat adoptions and I know you cater to little dogs, it doesn't mean we can't get along." She smiled brightly at Max and me.

Max quirked an eyebrow at me, encouraging me to respond to Lois.

I accepted the basket. "Of course not," I said. "Pacific Cove is a very tough town to make a go of business. We all try to support the local economy."

Lois smiled brightly, then craned her neck to see around us into the Wine and Bark. I moved slightly to block her view. She licked her fuchsia-colored lips and turned around. "I see that DelVecchio's is closed now." She tsked. "So many good places have closed down."

"That's just temporary," I said, but didn't elaborate for her when she turned back around and gave me a curious look.

Max riffled through the gift basket unabashedly and popped a chocolate-covered strawberry into his mouth.

Lois looked pleased. "I hand-dipped those myself."

Max gave her his winning boy-next-door smile. "Delicious!"

Lois pulled out a bundle of knitting yarn from what seemed like a permanently attached handbag, then dug further into the bag until she found flyer, which she handed to me. "I hope you and your sister can stop by and maybe help me get the word out."

"I'll see what we can do," I said noncommittally.

Guilt surged through me as I took the paper from the woman. Rachel wouldn't like my talking to her one bit.

Lois smiled and patted my arm. "Thank you, dear, I hope to see you soon." She pushed up her glasses and smiled at Max and me as she turned to leave.

As soon as she was out of earshot, Max glanced at the flyer she'd handed me. It was for a grand opening happening on Friday. There was an image of a kitten climbing up a scratching post.

Max laughed, but I said seriously, "I suppose we could go to the grand opening."

"Are you kidding?" Max said. "Rachel would kill you if you went. And if Rachel doesn't kill you, then Yolanda, Brenda, or Abigail would."

I made a face. "Not as a patron," I said.

He narrowed his eyes at me. "What then? Like a spy?"

I shrugged. "Why not? What do you think she was doing over here? Being nice? Being neighborly? She was snooping around. Checking out the competition."

Max snorted. "Maggie. Don't go over the deep end. She's, like, someone's grandma. She's not an evil villain just because she's a cat person."

I snatched the fruit basket out of his hands. "Aha!" I said, pointing a finger in his face.

"What?" He laughed.

"You're a cat person, aren't you?"

He shrugged. "Actually, when I was a little boy, I had a kitten named Whiskers. He was a gray puff ball. Cutest thing in the world." He put his finger to lips. "Don't let Brenda know, though. She'd kick me to the curb if she knew I was a cat lover."

I giggled. "Hardly. She's too soft on you."

Max smiled. "Even still, I wouldn't want to risk it."

"Don't worry, your secret's safe with me."

◇◇◇

Max drove us to his place while I poked around on my phone, researching where we could rent a floor polisher.

"There's a place on Oak View Circle. Will that work?" I asked.

Max nodded as he parked his pickup in front of his beach home. "I'm going to need some help lifting the couch. Let me see if my neighbors are home."

"What am I? Chopped liver?"

He shook his head. "I'm not letting you lift a heavy couch. If you throw your back out, the fuzz will be all over me."

"Chicken," I said.

Max indicated the beautiful wraparound porch of his house. There were a few Adirondack chairs sprawled on the deck. "Plus, my TV is really heavy. If you drop it, I'll have to kill you."

"Right," I said, slipping out of the pickup truck, walking over to his porch, and sinking into one of the deck chairs. I slipped off my sandals and tucked my feet under me. "I'll just take a load off here in the hot sun. Pretend that I'm on my cruise after all."

Max waved as he ran down the street to one of the neighboring bungalows. "I'll be right back."

I dialed the hospital to check on Rachel. She picked up immediately.

"How are you feeling?" I asked.

Rachel sighed. "I'm okay. Up and down. I hope they let me out of her soon. I'm going a little stir-crazy."

"I'm sorry. Do you wants some company?" I asked.

"Ronnie is with me. He's taking very good care of me. But I wanted to talk to you about tomorrow," Rachel said. "I'm hoping I can get out of here by then and meet with Vrishali, but I'm going to need some help."

"Don't worry. Max and I are on it. We have a few cards up our sleeves."

"Aww, Mags. I wouldn't be able to survive without you."

"Before you hang up, Rach. Max and I are going to need some help, too. I know Cornelia was looking for a job . . . Is it okay if we hire her temporarily?"

"That's a great idea," Rachel said. "I'll call her right now."

A few minutes later Rachel texted me Cornelia's address, with a little note saying she was in.

In the distance Max came into view with two of his neighbors in tow. They were burly guys, one with a green goatee and the other looked like he'd stepped out of the pages of a surfing magazine. Neither looked particularly happy to be roused so early in the morning to move furniture.

Max gave me the thumbs-up, to which I replied, "Game on."

Once we had the couch and TV loaded onto the back of Max's pickup, we headed toward Cornelia's duplex. She lived on the east side of town. The district was eclectic, with a healthy mix of California natives and a more recent bohemian population of artists and musicians who'd been priced out of the west side.

Cornelia's place was a small pink bungalow with a straggly palm tree in the front. The siding was chipped, and in desperate need of fresh coat of paint. The front porch was also badly sun damaged and creaky.

Max whispered under his breath. "I don't know about having her redecorate the Wine and Bark."

I socked him in the arm and rang the bell. "Don't go weak-kneed on me now."

He smiled and shifted his weight onto his heels, giving me his best aw-shucks look, just as Cornelia came to the door. She was dressed in dark clothes and her frizzy dark hair looked unkempt. Her face was splotchy and red, her eyes swollen and raw.

Have we interrupted a crying bout?

She sniffled as she held the door open for Max and me. "Maggie! Come in. Rachel told me you'd be by. Please come in." She gestured for us to enter the living room.

The living room was haphazard; everything seemed perched an inch close to tumbling off into the next pile. Laundry overflowed onto a shabby couch and Cornelia raced around the room straightening items.

"I'm so sorry," she said. "I wasn't expecting company. Ever since finding out about Fran, I've sort of been zoned out and not up to housework. Can I . . . uh, get you anything? Tea or—"

Max waved a hand around. "No. No. Don't worry about that. Maggie and I just came by to see if you are up for helping us at the Wine and Bark. Rachel said you were looking for a job."

Cornelia perked up. "Oh, yes. Yes, that would be perfect. I can't really be around here anymore. I'm going crazy. That's what I told the police, too."

I quirked an eyebrow. "The police?"

"They were just here," Cornelia said. "Asking questions, always questions."

"I'm so sorry," I said. "This whole ordeal must be really awful for you."

Cornelia pulled a tissue from the pocket of her lumpy sweater and dabbed at her eyes. "You have no idea. It feels like, well," She sniveled into the tissue. "It feels like . . ."

I glanced at Max and he nodded, encouraging me to probe. After all, wasn't that why we were here?

I patted Cornelia's shoulder and waited. After a moment, she said, "It feels like the police don't want to believe my story."

"What story is that?" Max asked.

I frowned at him and he shrugged.

How do men get away with being so direct?

Cornelia blew her nose and cleared her throat. "About Fran being alone in the store that night. She'd gone back after she'd been at the Wine and Bark. She called me all upset and begged me to go pick her up so we could get a drink somewhere in town. But I was mad at her. Upset that she was cutting my hours at Chic Chickie. I didn't feel like being her shoulder to cry on that night. So I told her to stuff it and that I was quitting."

"Wow, 'stuff it,' huh?" asked Max.

I poked him in the ribs. I didn't want him interrupting her confessional flow.

"I told the police I didn't go down there. But they don't seem to believe me."

"Why wouldn't they believe you?" Max prodded.

"It's just a feeling I get. The way they ignore me. Not Ellington, he's fine. I think he buys my story alright. It's the other one. The mean one, Brooks."

My heart clenched.

She thinks Brad is mean?

Well, given that I thought Ellington was the mean one, it occurred to me that maybe they traded off playing good cop/bad cop.

Cornelia looked up from her crumpled tissue. "Could you talk to Brooks for me? I mean, being that he's your boyfriend and all?"

"He's not my boyfriend," I said, fighting the feeling of being put under a microscope.

How could Cornelia possibly know Brad and I had gone on a few dates?

I suddenly missed New York, where everyone was anonymous and strangers had no interest or information about your love life.

She shrugged. "He isn't? I thought that's what Ellington said. A friend anyway, he's certainly sweet on you. Maybe you can put in a good word for me?" Then, Cornelia fixed her eyes on me, her look so determined and cutting, I couldn't help but be reminded that her boss was dead.

Murdered.

Chapter Seventeen

Cornelia and I were tasked with pushing around the tables at the Wine and Bark. We moved a few of them to the back storage area to make room for the couch and TV Max had provided.

It was a good thing Max was so resourceful, he immediately found two men walking down the street and convinced them to help him unload the couch in exchange for a bottle of wine.

"What do we do about drapes?" I asked Cornelia.

She frowned as she looked at the bare windows. "I like them open like that."

"Me, too, but the editor of *Doggie Day* wanted curtains. And I think Rach is committed to doing whatever it takes to get the spread in the magazine, you know?"

Cornelia spun around the room, blinking rapidly, lost in thought. "What if . . ."

"What?"

"It's probably a bad idea . . ."

Max slipped past us looking for a wrench to mount the big screen

TV. "Oh, uh, bad idea, don't tell it to Maggie. She's a sucker for those."

I socked his shoulder.

Cornelia leaned in closer to me, so she wouldn't be overheard by the two men now stuck holding the TV in place while Max faltered around the bar searching for tools.

"Chic Chickie has rod curtains, the kind that are easy to put up and take down . . . we could *borrow* them . . ."

I chewed on the inside of my cheek.

Was it ethical to borrow drapes from a business whose owner had recently been killed?

Well, Chic Chickie wasn't currently open . . . What would it hurt? And it would give me a chance to get back into Chic Chickie and snoop around.

"How do we get in?" I asked.

Cornelia smiled. "I have a key."

Max found a wrench, and he and the two men secured the TV in place. Meanwhile, my mind raced. No one would be there and we might find something that could help with the investigation.

How can I pass up this opportunity?

"I think we should go for it," I said to Max.

Max collapsed onto the couch. "I'm not feeling so hot."

The men frowned, possibly thinking Max was flaking out on his end of the bargain.

"Thank you for helping us," I said, retreating to behind the bar. "I have some nice bottles of Merlot from Verdant Vines I'd like you to have as a token of our appreciation."

I handed them a bottle each. They smiled warmly and disappeared out the front door before they could be assigned any additional work.

Max propped his feet up on the couch and closed his eyes.

"You look a little pale, are you going to be alright?" I asked.

Max mumbled, "Just need to rest my eyes a minute. Got a bit of a headache."

Cornelia and I exchanged glances. "I can drive his truck," she said.

Max dug out his keys and tossed them to me. "I didn't get much sleep last night. I'll take a quick nap here. Hold down the fort."

I patted his head. He grabbed my wrist and pulled me close. "Are you sure you're safe with her?" he whispered.

I shrugged.

"She could be . . . you know . . ."

I nodded. "I'll be careful."

He stood. "I'll go with you guys—" He clasped his hands to his head. "Whoa, I feel a little dizzy."

I pushed him back onto the couch. "You stay here. We'll be back in a flash. Text my cell if you need anything."

He sat back down reluctantly. "Okay, you do the same."

I think he was asleep before we even walked out the door.

<><><>

Returning to Chic Chickie was a bit surreal for me. While the store remained the same, the air seemed charged somehow—as if Fran's ghost was hovering around. I could smell the metallic scent that lingered in the air, and the image of Fran lying in a pool of blood still haunted me.

The overhead bell chimed as we stepped into the shop and I nearly jumped out of my skin. Cornelia, however, didn't seem a bit bothered by any of it as she pranced around the store, ogling the items.

"I can't believe she made a display of these pot holders," Cornelia said. "Look at the colors! They aren't even the right season. It's way too early for olive-green and maroon. Fran was always bit tone-deaf when it came to making the displays. I would have changed this around on Saturday morning if I had been able to open the shop."

I watched Cornelia fingering the hen-and-rooster salt-and-pepper shakers.

"I loved working here," she said. "You know, the whole thing was my idea." She shrugged. "But I didn't have the capital to open the shop." She paused and looked around the store, the wall of mounted colorful birds, the trinkets on every table, and then the bright yellow curtains that hung on brass rods.

"Fran and I used to be good friends," Cornelia continued, "but when she opened the store, she changed. Always telling me what to do, demanding this, demanding that. It was a drag." She sighed. "If she'd been a true friend, I think she'd have let me in on half the business. I talked to a lawyer and apparently you can't sue for that sort of thing."

"What do you mean?" I asked.

"I went to see Brenda and she told me that under copyright protection law I didn't really have a case. Fran was legally able to steal my ideas and make a shop! It was her capital that built the shop. Never mind about my creative capital. Fran wanted to expand. I don't know how far she would have gone, but I thought she was foolish for not joining forces with Yolanda. I love those little handbags, aren't they the cutest thing?"

Oh goodness!

I couldn't believe I had willingly opened myself up to hear chatter about chicken fashion!

"So what was Fran upset about?" I asked. "Earlier you said she was calling you to get a drink."

"Oh, that," Cornelia said. "She didn't like running into Hendrick. Their relationship had ended badly. She thought he was rubbing it in her face how well the winery was doing."

"Is the winery doing well?" I asked.

"Yes! His wine club membership is at all time high. The winery got featured in some kind of wine club circuit or something," Cornelia said.

"I think Yolanda would still like to buy the business," I said. "I don't know how the legal stuff works."

Cornelia perked up. "Would she consider going into business with me? Chicken fashion is my passion!" she singsonged.

"I really wouldn't know, you'd have to talk to her about it." I glanced around the store. "But I can definitely say chicken fashion is her passion, too."

"I created all these designs." She pointed to a row of mugs that were the shape of a chicken and then to a pillow that clucked when pressed.

Instead of sharing my true feelings on the chicken empire everyone seemed so fond of, I looked up at the curtains and said, "We're going to need a step stool."

Cornelia nodded. "There's one in the back."

I hesitated. The back room was where Yolanda and I had come across Fran and, while I knew the crime scene team had probably cleared the area, I still felt a bit squeamish.

Cornelia somehow read my face. "Is that where . . . ?"

I studied her.

Is she pretending?

If she was the killer, then certainly she knew where Fran had been murdered. Cornelia kept her eyes on mine as if truly waiting for an answer.

"Yes," I said.

She made a dramatic show of shuddering. "Would you mind going back there then? I don't want to go."

I nodded, but as I turned, I couldn't help the feeling of being set up. I glanced over my shoulder. Would she follow me into the back room? Then what? Kill me like perhaps she had done to Fran?

No! I was being ridiculous.

If she was the killer, Max knew I was here with her. She wouldn't chance something like that.

I've nothing to worry about.

Regardless, I still shivered as I pulled back the creamy canary-yellow curtain that separated the front of the store from the back.

I was oddly aware of my shoes resounding against wide the wood-planked floors. My heart raced as I faced the narrow passageway. Electricity seemed to crackle in the air and the metallic scent of blood was more pronounced now.

I fought the desire to look for a window to air out the place. The best thing I could do was grab the step stool and get back to the main store, the back rooms were creeping me out!

The door to the small office was open. I scanned the room for a step stool, but didn't see any. There were several file cabinets and I resisted the urge to rummage through them. I didn't want Cornelia to come back here looking for me.

I skipped past the bathroom, figuring if there was a step stool back here, it'd be in the storage room where we'd found Fran. I hurried to the last door on the left and peeked in. The room was still overcrowded with boxes, and I knew it was ridiculous but I half expected Fran to be there crumpled on the floor.

Instead, a chalk outline greeted me, along with a bloodstain. The crime scene team had done a terrible job of cleaning up. The room reeked of death and misfortune. Along the far wall, a step stool hung next to a dustpan and broom. I grabbed the item as quickly as I could and hightailed it back to the main part of the store.

Cornelia waited for me by the window. She said nothing as I raced toward her, toppling over several kitchen spoons as I brushed too close to one of the display tables. She helped me repair the display and then the two of us made fast work of taking down the curtains.

Suddenly, I thought of Brad. Would he be angry to know I'd returned to the scene of the crime? But the curtains were already down here, right? Certainly if Cornelia had a key and she hadn't been instructed not to use it then it seemed like we were safe.

"What will happen to the shop now?" I asked.

Cornelia made a sour face. "The ex gets it. Can you imagine?"

"Hendrick?"

"The one and only."

My heart beat faster.

If Hendrick stands to inherit the business, that gives him a strong motive for murder.

Chapter Eighteen

After we'd pulled the curtains down, I hurried to the back to re-place the step stool. This time, I barely stopped to catch my breath. I wanted to get back to the Wine and Bark so I could talk with Max about Hendrick.

"Ready?" Cornelia asked, as I returned to the front of store. She stood with the curtains bundled in her arms. "These are getting pretty heavy."

"Yup," I said, hurrying to open the front door and lead her over to Max's pickup truck.

She winced as she released the curtains into the bed of the pickup. "We should have brought a blanket to bundle these up."

I hesitated. "I saw a blanket in the storeroom."

We exchanged looks. I got the feeling Cornelia was as ready to leave the store as I was. After a moment, she said, "Do you mind running back in there and grabbing it? We should return the cur-tains when we're done and if they're dirty or whatever Hendrick is sure to say something."

I nodded. "I'll get it."

Racing back into Chic Chickie, I scooted toward the storeroom and grabbed the blanket I'd seen nestled in a corner on top of one of the cardboard boxes. When I grabbed it, something clinked to the ground.

I bent to examine the wood grain floor. A small circular green gem flashed in the light. Picking it up, I turned it over in my hand and rubbed the front and back. The gem wasn't real. The back side was flat and dull.

I had seen something like this before, but where? My breath caught.

It looked like the kind of stone that might have been glued onto a dog collar. Could this have belonged to the killer? If I could match the stone to a dog collar, could I find the murderer?

<><><>

When we returned to the Wine and Bark, I was shocked to find that the front door was unlocked, but Max wasn't there. It wasn't like him to leave the bar unattended.

Where has he gone?

Cornelia helped me hang up the curtains. I marveled at how transformed the bar had become. With a few simple items—the TV, the couch, and curtains—the Wine and Bark looked more like a place to cuddle up with a good book, than with a cocktail. Still, I knew it would please Vrishali, the editor from *Doggie Day*.

I paid Cornelia out of the cash register for her help and we agreed that she would return tomorrow during Yappy Hour to help us serve.

After she left, I quickly dialed Max's cell phone.

He picked up after the fourth ring. His voice sounded muffled, as if I'd woken him.

"Hey! Where are you?" I asked.

"I'm at the Wine and Bark," he said.

I looked around the room. "No. I'm at the Wine and Bark, and I'm sorry to tell you but you're not here."

"I'm in the john. Been puking out my guts."

I rushed toward the restrooms, skidding past the row of famous dog portraits and banged on the men's restroom door. "Let me in!"

"It's not locked," he said.

I pressed on the door and it opened to reveal a pale and drenched Max. He looked as if he dunked his entire head in the sink.

"What can I get you?" I asked.

He shook his head. "I think I'm fine now, just had a wild bout of hurling."

"Let me get you over to the couch." I grabbed his arm and guided him down the short hallway toward the bar.

He collapsed onto the couch and said, "It's passing now. What did I eat? The doughnuts?"

"Did you put milk in your coffee?" I asked.

"Nah. Take mine black."

"Late night, last night?" I asked.

"Not really. Not any later than any other night really." He smiled. "On the bright side, I feel much better now." He looked around the bar. "It's looks great. The only thing left to do is the floors."

Eyeing him, I said, "You had me worried. I thought you were going to end up in the hospital with Rachel."

He shook his head. "I'm better now."

"Are you up for driving me to go pick up the floor polisher?" I asked.

He nodded and stood. "You didn't crash my truck, right?"

I poked him in the ribs on our way out. "Just because I don't own a car doesn't mean I don't know how to drive."

As we rode out to pick up the floor polisher rental, I told Max about Hendrick inheriting Chic Chickie.

"That could be motive to kill Fran," I said.

Max made a face. "Dude owns a vineyard. Would he really want a chicken hat place?"

"Why not?" I asked. "If he's a businessman. Maybe he figured out a way to combine the businesses."

Max raised an eyebrow at me. "The Wine and Cluck? I don't see it."

I shrugged. "Well, we need to pick up the cases of wine for tomorrow from Verdant Vines. Why don't we head up there and ask him ourselves?"

<><><>

The drive to the vineyard with Max seemed shorter compared to the first time when Yolanda and I went there. The vineyard was quiet when we arrived, the wind turbines churning silently.

"Pretty cool," Max said, parking the truck next to a car-charging station.

"Pretty green," I said, getting out of the truck and following Max. We walked together toward the old farmhouse that held the tasting room. "It's a very cute place," I said. "You should bring Brenda out for wine tasting."

"I'd love to. Nice romantic evening out on the porch." He smiled shyly, reminding me how new their romance was. "I think the wine is highly rated, too, but you didn't invite me to the last tasting. So how would I know?"

I laughed. "The wine is excellent. I'm sure Hendrick will give you a sample now, if you want."

We stepped into the tasting room.

"Hendrick?" I called out. "It's me. Maggie. We're here to pick up the cases of wine."

The tasting room was eerily quietly. A chill crept up my spine. I turned to Max. He was tapping his foot and looked about as laid back as one could get.

Maybe I was too jumpy for my own good.

I called out again, "Hendrick?"

"Do you think we should go look for them?" I asked.

"Yeah. He's probably out back," Max said.

We walked through the tasting room and out to the back patio. We had a clear view of the vineyard. Nothing.

This time when I glanced back at Max, he seemed a bit more tense.

"Strange that the place is open and no one is here," Max said.

"Let's get out of here, before we get in trouble. I'll leave him a note. He can deliver the wine for tomorrow night."

We went back inside and I ducked behind the small bar to grab a notepad. The bar was neatly organized with several varieties of wine lining the wall. I found a small tablet with the Verdant Vines logo on top. I grabbed a pen lying next to it and scrawled a note for Hendrick. Tearing off the top page, I placed it on the bar.

Meanwhile, Max wandered down a corridor to the left.

"Where are you going, Max? Let's get out of here."

Max pointed at the floor. "What do you think that is?"

On the floor were a few red drops. They made a trail down the hallway.

My throat went dry, and I found it hard to speak. "Uh . . ."

"Stay here," Max said. He moved quickly down the hallway, but I followed him as if magnetized.

The drops looked sinisterly close to blood. But that couldn't be right, could it?

Perhaps, it was . . . what?

Wine!

Perhaps dregs from a broken wineglass, or simply a small spill from a bottle?

Max stopped in a doorway, holding up a hand to prevent me from following him further.

"What is it?" I asked.

"Hello?" Max said.

I waited, watching Max's body language. He was on high alert, like a panther ready to pounce.

"Max!" I hissed.

"Call the police," he said.

I rushed to his side and peeked into the room. It was a bedroom. There was a still lump on the bed, immobile. Blood trailed from the bedside to the doorway.

I screamed and pushed past Max.

He grabbed my hand. "No! Don't touch anything!"

"He may still be alive!" I said. "Maybe he needs CPR." Propelling myself toward the bed I tore off the bedsheet. Darla lay still before me, her long blond hair matted against her head. There was some sort of wound on her chest, where the blood seemed to be the thickest, but her arms were folded over it and what caught my eye was the large diamond ring on her finger.

I screamed again, panic edging out of my brain any sanity that remained.

Max pulled me away. "Let's call the police. Call them now, Maggie!"

"Yes," I said. "I'll call Brad."

My legs felt wobbly and I leaned against Max, turning away from Darla. Then I saw it.

On her nightstand was something familiar and I gasped to see it.

My journal!

I reached for it, but Max stopped me.

"Maggie, we shouldn't touch anything!"

"It's my journal, Max. She's the one who broke into my apartment."

He chewed his lip. "I think you should leave it. Let Brad admit it into evidence."

I snatched it off the nightstand. "No!"

Max looked shocked. "What are you doing?"

"Do you know the things I've written about him in here?"

Max burst out laughing. "I'm sure he'll be very flattered."

I shoved the journal into my bag. "Don't say anything about it. Promise?"

Max nodded. "I don't know what good it would do now anyway. She's dead."

We hurried out of the room together. Pulling my phone out, I dialed Brad. He picked up immediately.

"Hey, is this about another missing dog?" he joked.

"I wish."

"What's wrong?"

I told him about Darla and he instructed Max and me to leave the building and to wait for him and Ellington in the parking lot.

As Max and I headed out of the winery, we spotted a dark van rumbling up the hill.

Chapter Nineteen

I grabbed Max's arm. "Oh, no, it's Hendrick! What do we do?"

Max's eyes grew wide, both of us thinking the same thing. If Hendrick was the murderer, neither of us wanted to be on his bad side; but if he wasn't, one of us was going to have break the news to him.

I groaned. "Oh God, I don't want to tell him. He just proposed to her."

Hendrick parked in the green parking lot, next to Max's pickup truck. He smiled and waved happily at us as he got out of the van.

Brad and Ellington's police cruiser appeared on the horizon. For the first time in my life I would actually volunteer to keep my mouth shut and hop into the back of the police car.

Max seemed to have the same idea, because he shifted uncomfortably as Hendrick approached.

"Maggie! Sorry to keep you waiting. Did you come to pick up the wine?" He pointed at the van. "I could have delivered it. Or maybe Darla helped you?" He looked around, past us into the tasting room. "Is she here?"

Oh, she is here alright!

Brad's cruiser came to a stop in front of us, and he stepped out. It was all I could do not to jump into his arms.

"Good afternoon," Brad said formally to Hendrick.

Hendrick frowned. Then, when Ellington popped out of the passenger side, Hendrick stiffened.

His shoulders thrust back suddenly, as if expecting the worst. "Officers. What can I do for you? More questions about Fran? Do I need an attorney?"

Ellington glanced from Hendrick to Max and me. I shrugged ineffectually.

"We were alerted that this might be a crime scene," Ellington said.

A white vehicle crested the horizon.

The crime scene team.

I shivered and stood. "I'm sorry, Hendrick," I said simply.

Hendrick looked confused, Brad stepped in. "Hendrick, please come with me." He gestured for Hendrick to step away from the house. Together they walked a short distance, Brad calling over his shoulder. "Maggie and Max, wait for me in the cruiser."

Relieved, Max and I jumped into the backseat.

I leaned my head onto Max's shoulder. "God, this is awful!"

He rubbed the top of my hair playfully. "It could always be worse."

"It doesn't get much worse," I said.

"You're wrong. Brad could have found your journal."

◇◇◇

While Brad talked to Hendrick, Ellington came over to knock on the window of the backseat of the cruiser.

Nervous energy coursed through me as I saw his stern face.

"Oh, no," Max said. "What now?"

Ellington motioned for us to get out.

"We're going to need to escort Hendrick down to the station. Can I count on you two to drive yourselves?" he asked.

"Certainly, Officer," Max said agreeably.

Ellington's eye landed on me. "You're heading out of town, right?"

Resentment enveloped me. Why did Ellington have to push my buttons?

"I'm *not* going out of town," I said. Suddenly I regretted not being on the cruise yesterday. What had I gained? The editorial spread for the Wine and Bark was still undetermined, Rachel was still in the hospital, and now we'd found poor Darla dead.

Sensing the tension between Ellington and me, Max said, "I'll be sure to drive Maggie and myself down to the station."

Ellington took a deep breath. "Head straight there. I'll message Sergeant Gottlieb to make sure he can greet you."

"We'll head straight there," Max agreed.

"Right after we pick up the floor polisher," I said.

Ellington shot daggers at me with his eyes.

I smiled coolly. "It'll only take us a few minutes, and it's on the way."

"No way," Ellington said. "I can't have you two running errands all around town. Report directly to the station, or I'll call another cruiser out here to escort you."

Max held up his hands. "No, no. No problem. We'll head straight there." Max grabbed me and whirled me around in the direction of his truck. "Stop arguing with him, it'll only make matters worse for us."

◇◇◇

We got into Max's truck and tore off down the hill. I offered Brad a wave, but his back was to us and he was still speaking with Hendrick. Max and I rode in a somber silence, each of us lost in thought. Despite the sun casting a warm reflection all around, I shivered. Then a tear slipped down my face.

Max glanced at me. "You okay?"

I wiped away the tear. "I can't believe we found Darla like that. I think I'm in shock."

"Me, too," he admitted.

Suddenly sobs burst out of me and I buried my face and wept for Darla and Fran. Max pulled over and parked the truck, offering me a box of tissues that nested in his side door pocket.

"I'm going to swing by and pick up the floor polisher, but I swear if you let Ellington know, I'll never speak to you again," he said.

I laughed through my tears. "Right. Now you want to play hooky?"

"They're going to take forever up here. If we head straight to the station, they'll eat our whole afternoon," he said. "Plus, I gotta distract you a little, or you'll completely fall apart."

I punched his arm and he smiled. He maneuvered the car toward the freeway and I thought about the black van.

I sniffed and blew my nose. "Why would Darla break into my house?"

Max shrugged. "Well, we don't know that she did, right?"

"She had my journal," I reasoned.

"Or Hendrick did," Max said.

"It doesn't make sense," I admitted.

He smiled. "That's why we're supposed to leave the investigating to the professionals."

We both chuckled, probably more to relieve our stress and nerves than anything else.

"What about Cornelia?" he asked. "She was pretty sketchy when we picked her up earlier."

"What? Do you think she'd just gotten home from murdering Darla?"

"I never can tell with women," Max joked. He exited the freeway and pulled onto our destination street. He parked in front of the floor polisher rental storefront and turned to me. "She had a bone to pick with Fran, right? What if she killed Fran and then Darla somehow figured it out."

"She said she went to see Brenda about her rights to the store. We should probably ask Brenda about it. It makes sense, you know. She could have a really clear motive. I wish Brenda would tell us what exactly she was advising her on."

Max shook his head. "There's no way she'll tell us anything. Attorney-client privileges. She's strict about that," he said.

Suddenly an evil thought struck me. "You don't happen to have a key to Bradford and Blahnik, do you?" I asked.

His eyebrows shot up. "You're a little devil! Are you suggesting I break into my girlfriend's business and peek at her clients files?"

I feigned innocence. "No! Not break in. Use the key, you dolt!"

"I have a key," he confirmed. "But I would never jeopardize the trust of the hottest girl I've ever dated."

I sighed. "Oh, boy. A romantic."

He got out of the pickup truck and glanced over his shoulder. "However, I can't always vouch for the company I keep. If someone were to swipe her key out of my glove box while I was, say, picking up a floor polisher, well, there really wouldn't be anything I could do to stop them. Especially, if I *didn't know* about it."

He rapped on the side of the truck and waved.

As soon as he was in the store and out of sight, I fiddled with the glove compartment. A ring of keys immediately sprang into my lap.

I suddenly felt guilty. I couldn't really break into an attorney's office and riffle through her files, could I?

The image of my apartment being broken into flashed through my mind. Someone had already done that to me, and left me a threatening note to boot. The killer had struck again. I had to do something to stop him or her. I pocketed the key ring and decided to park the guilt along with it.

As soon as Max came out of the store, he heaved the floor polisher into the back of the truck and started up the engine. He said nothing further about Brenda's keys and neither did I.

◇◇◇

At the police station, Max and I waited on hard plastic chairs in the hallway as Brad, Ellington, and Gottlieb had some sort of powwow. Two uniformed officers sat at their computer stations down the hallway, giving us the impression that we were being watched.

"I hope we don't get stuck getting questioned by Gottlieb," Max said under his breath. "He's got eyebrow game."

I chuckled.

"If he looks at me and furrows his brow, I think I might lose it. That will either make me look guilty or like I'm cracking up or something."

Nervous giggles coursed through us. One of the officers from down the hall looked up from his computer screen. Max and I stifled our snickers. The attempt to hold back our laughter only made us want to laugh harder. When the officer lost interest in us, we sagged against each other in fits of snorting.

"We are cracking up," I said. "How can we laugh at a time like this?"

Max nodded his head. "I know. I'm the worst. As soon as anything heavy happens I start laughing like a jackal. Last girlfriend I had, dumped me. When I went into a complete psycho fit of laughter, she thought I was mocking her—but I was really heartbroken. Just couldn't process it, I guess. I must be demented."

I patted his knee. "It's just a way to release the anxiety."

"It's a little cuckoo," he said.

"Well, you are a little bonkers, but we all probably are." We sat in silence for a moment, the severity of the situation descending upon us again.

Max finally asked, "Do you think the same person that killed Darla also killed Fran?"

"I would say. It can't be a coincidence. I think the police think it's Hendrick."

Max shook his head. "I can't believe Hendrick could kill his fiancée and his ex-girlfriend. Seems so wrong."

I shrugged. "Maybe he wasn't in love with Darla at all. Maybe he proposed to make it look like he wasn't the bad guy—"

Max shook his head. "He seemed totally in shock when he saw the police. First he was all happy to see us, and I don't think he'd be that way if he knew she was lying dead in their bedroom. Then, when the cops arrived, dude went into complete shock."

As far as I knew, Brad hadn't let Hendrick inside the house. In fact, my guess was that Hendrick was now sitting in the stark interrogation room with the two-way mirror.

But, what did I know? Maybe he called his attorney.

Which remind me of the keys to Brenda's office burning a hole in my pocket.

"Should we call Brenda and ask her to join us?" I asked Max.

Max shook his head. "She doesn't do criminal stuff. Besides, we don't need an attorney, we're witnesses."

Now, I regretted having driven up to the vineyard. Why hadn't I had the wines delivered?

My phone buzzed. It was a text from Yolanda checking in with me. I discreetly texted her back.

Darla's been murdered!

She immediately fired back.

I told you Hendrick was shady.

I replied to her that Max and I were at the police station and to bring Brenda. Even though I knew Max didn't feel she could be helpful here, I figured it was always better to have legal ears on the team.

While we waited, I ruminated on the motive for Darla's murder and depression weighed me down.

"Why would Hendrick kill his fiancée?" I asked. "It makes no sense." I was sick with the thought of it. "He'd proposed to her. He loved her," I said. "He told me as much."

Max sighed. "Unfortunately, just because someone told you something doesn't make it true."

"But why would he kill her in the bed and leave the winery? Wouldn't he think that someone was bound to show up sooner or later?"

"Maybe he didn't think it through," Max said. "What if he was going to get the van so he could dispose of the body and we just sort of interrupted things? He wasn't expecting you at a certain time, right?"

"I didn't make an appointment. That much is true. But he wouldn't leave the winery wide open like that, right? I mean we just walked in."

Before Max could reply, Brad entered the hallway. The two uniformed officers at their computer stations looked up. One waited expectedly, the other had a bored expression on his face. When Brad bypassed them and approached us, the officers lost interest and returned their attention to their screens.

Brad walked up to us. "Hey. I'm sorry you two had to find Darla."

We all three hung our heads in a moment of silence for her. Then, Brad turned to me and asked, "May I have a word?"

Chapter Twenty

Brad ushered me down the stark corridor and into his office. Despite his desk being covered with paperwork the office appeared tidy. There was a slick laptop and black phone handset that completed the tone of effectiveness. Inside my purse, my phone rang loudly. I ignored it.

Brad said, "Go ahead and check it."

I frowned, but dug out my phone and glanced at the screen to see a text from him. "Why are you texting me when you're standing right next to me?" I asked.

"I wanted to make sure you had my phone number."

Confusion swept through me. "Of course, I have your number."

"Just wanted to be sure, because sometimes it feels like you think you need to stumble over a dead body before you call me."

Something behind my left eye throbbed. "I don't think that," I squeaked.

Brad squared his shoulders. "You didn't go up to Verdant Vines to investigate, did you, Maggie?"

"No, no! I went there to pick up wine I'd ordered for the Wine and Bark."

Brad took a sharp inhale of breath. "Maggie—"

"I swear! I was there to—"

Brad shook his head. "You knew he was a person of interest. I specifically asked you not to go to that winery."

Guilt overwhelmed me, my heart sinking. While it was true I'd needed the wine, I'd really wanted to be the one to figure out what had happened to Fran.

"You could have walked right in on the killer," Brad said, anger reverberating in his voice. "What would you have done then? Did you even think it through?"

"No," I admitted.

"You could have had the wine delivered, right?" Brad insisted.

"Yes," I said. "But if Hendrick was out to kill me, then wouldn't he have killed me when he delivered the wine?"

Brad shook his head and leaned back on his desk, as if overwhelmed by either my stubbornness or stupidity. "I don't think anyone is out to kill you. But if you interrupt a murder, you might get yourself—"

"Well, I wouldn't have gone into the winery if I thought I was interrupting a murder!" I said, although my defense sounded hollow. "Besides, I was with Max."

"Oh, right," Brad said sarcastically. "Like that's supposed to help."

"We didn't see anything that tipped us off—"

"Yeah?" Brad said. "What about the blood in the hallway? Did you stop to think that the murderer might be hiding somewhere in a closet or the bathroom?"

I gasped. "Was someone there?"

"That's not the point," Brad growled. His handsome face was now red with anger.

Distress to see him so upset bubbled up in my chest, and it felt even worse knowing I was the cause of it all.

I reached out for his hand, but his grip was tight around his desk, his knuckles white. I backed off. "I'm so sorry, Brad. We didn't see anything that made us think we were in danger. Max is the one who wandered down the hallway . . ."

Brad stood and retreated behind the desk, putting some distance between us. I resisted the urge to follow him and wrap my arms around his waist.

"Did you see any vehicles leaving the winery on your way in?" he asked. It was an official question now. His tone was serious and formal. He was now just a cop asking a question of a witness. And I was just a witness.

Sadness overwhelmed me.

Have I blown it with him?

"I didn't notice any vehicles," I said. "We can ask Max—"

"No! Damn it!" Brad exploded. "Not *we*, Maggie! I will ask Max. I will ask him because I'm the investigating officer. You will not ask him. I don't want you discussing this death or Fran's murder with anyone."

"I understand," I whimpered. Even as I said it, I fought the compulsion to ask him what he meant by *death*. Was it still unclear whether Darla had been murdered? Could she have killed herself?

Brad turned his back to me and looked out the window. "People think this job is easy," he grumbled.

Unsure if I should go to him, I remained rooted in place. "I don't think your job is easy. I know it must be very difficult to figure out who did this—"

"That's not the hard part, Maggie." He turned back to me. "The hard part is keeping you safe." He gave a small, sad chuckle. "Don't you get that? Figuring out who did this is only one part of my job.

The important part is keeping everyone in Pacific Cove safe. That's my real job."

Before I could reply, he added. "That's why I'm unclear why you seem to want to undermine me at every turn."

My heart felt heavy. "I don't mean to do that. Really. I'm so sorry. You're right. I could have had the wine delivered, but Cornelia told me Hendrick inherited Chic Chickie—"

A look of surprise crossed Brad's face. "You've talked to Cornelia about Hendrick? I didn't think you knew Cornelia."

Uh-oh.

"She asked Rachel for a job. She wanted to quit working for Fran," I said.

Brad nodded and seemed to somewhat relax, then a voice barked from the down the hall, "Brooks!"

Brad straightened his shoulders and took in a deep breath. "I gotta go."

A moment later, Sergeant Gottlieb stuck his bald head into the room. He smiled when he saw me. "Oh, hello, Maggie. Please excuse me."

"No problem," Brad said. "We were just finishing up."

<><><>

I left Brad's office feeling unsettled. He didn't want me to investigate, that much was clear. But was I really in danger?

In the hallway, seated on the hard orange plastic chairs were Yolanda, Max, and Brenda.

Oh, no!

My sixth sense told me Brad would be furious to find Yolanda and Brenda here, but before I could signal them, Gottlieb appeared behind me.

Yolanda sprang from her chair and rushed over to him. He greeted her warmly, put a hand on her elbow and ushered her down the hallway. Yolanda smiled and winked at me as she passed me in the hallway. Then Officer Ellington appeared from the opposite direction and asked Max to follow him.

Brenda stood and said, "As his counsel, I request to be present in the interview."

Ellington shrugged. "That's fine. Follow me."

I found myself alone in the little hallway, with no idea what to do next. I glanced at the two uniformed officers at the front. They seemed completely uninterested in me. I figured I was free to go.

Outside, the sun had burned off the coastal fog. The day was another scorcher.

I walked briskly without direction. Soon I was on the cobblestone path that led to the center of town. I passed the fountain, with the marble statue of a man on a horse. Then I turned and walked past the sundial. In front of me was Brenda's law firm/designer shoe outlet, Bradford and Blahnik.

I shaded my eyes and peered into the window, past the prominently displayed beautiful pairs of strappy sandals in all the summer colors. I was drenched with sweat and it had nothing to do with the heat or the walk.

The lights were out in the shop, as I'd imagined. With Brenda distracted at the station, now was the perfect time to check out what information I could find at her office.

I prayed Brad wouldn't find out about my snooping. I consoled myself with the thought that if I found nothing, no one would be the wiser.

I glanced over my shoulder to see if anyone was in sight. There were a few people scattered about, however, no one seemed to notice me. I tried the front door. It was locked. With another surreptitious look behind me, I pulled the keys from my pocket and unlocked the chrome handle on the door.

If anyone approached me, I was prepared to tell them that Brenda had sent me. But I was relieved to see that no one gave me a second look. I entered the store quickly and was startled to see Brenda's Chihuahua, Pee Wee, charging at me.

He growled and bared his teeth.

My heart raced and my blood pressure skyrocketed.

Good God! Is Pee Wee actually going to attack me?

"Pee Wee! It's me. Maggie," I said.

He snarled at me and gave me his most ferocious bark.

"I only need to take a look around, Pee Wee, calm down!"

His growl turned into a half snort and he sniffed my feet.

Why hadn't I thought to bring any Bark Bites? Pee Wee loved those things.

While Pee Wee circled me, I surveyed the front room. A while back, Brenda had opted to keep her law practice open by bringing in a line of designer shoes in order make the rent on the building. Although the pair of pink pumps by Manolo Blahnik next to the cash register was enough to take my breath away, I figured there'd be plenty of time for shopping when Brenda was here. Now was my time to snoop. If Pee Wee let me that was.

I cautiously stepped around him, then hustled to the back room. Brenda's office was the small adjoining room. The room was dominated by a large glass desk, a metal filing cabinet, and a blue doggie bed tucked in a corner.

Pee Wee followed me into the office. I pointed toward the bed.

"Go back to sleep, Pee Wee."

The dog hesitated for a moment, but when I repeated myself and pointed a bit more emphatically to the bed, he obeyed. He popped into the doggie bed and dropped his head.

"Good boy," I said, stepping toward the filing cabinet.

He lifted his head and kept an eye on me.

"It's fine," I said. "Go to sleep."

I didn't need a witness to the crime. Not even of the canine persuasion.

I fiddled with the key ring. There was a small blue circular key that looked like it opened either a file cabinet or desk drawer. I jammed it into the file cabinet and Pee Wee came unglued. He turned his snout into the air and howled like a banshee.

"Hush now!" I said.

He ignored my command and continued to howl. I decided to ignore him and try the key again. The cabinet came open and I rummaged through the files. It took me about ten minutes to figure out there wasn't any file on Cornelia.

I closed the cabinet and moved over to the desk. Pee Wee didn't seem to mind my presence at the desk so much, he calmed down and took to his doggie bed again.

Brenda's desk only had one main top drawer. I silently eased it open.

My breath caught and I suddenly felt nauseous. The room gave a sickening twirl and I held on to the desk to steady myself.

Inside the drawer was a shiny silver handgun, the Berretta logo stamped plainly in sight.

I slammed the drawer closed, as if that would make the vision disappear. Then, tempted by faith I edged it open again, the gun stared up at me. Teasing me, taunting me.

I swore under my breath and Pee Wee lifted his head, pried an eye open and observed me.

What kind of gun was used to kill Fran and Darla?

This was ridiculous! Brenda couldn't possibly be the killer.

Although she could be safeguarding the gun for a client. Whose gun was that?

I dug my phone out of my pocket and pulled up the camera. I took a few snapshots of the gun and then closed the drawer.

I had to get out of there before Brenda returned.

Chapter Twenty-one

I slept poorly, the image of Darla lifeless in bed haunted me. Brad's lecture also weighed heavily on my mind. I knew he hadn't wanted me to investigate any further and yet, I'd snuck into Brenda's office. That had been a mistake. I resolved to stop poking around and asking questions. After all, what had it gotten me? I'd skipped my cruise and all I had to show for it was more trouble.

I would let Brad and Ellington investigate. Darla's and Fran's murders were none of my business.

I padded into the kitchen to brew a morning cup of tea and fortify my resolve by rooting around and finding some biscuits. As soon as I settled down to enjoy my new favorite tea blend—Maharaja Chai Oolong Tea, infused with cinnamon, ginger, pepper, and cloves—my phone rang. I groaned inwardly.

If it was Yolanda, Brad, or Rachel there was sure to be some talk of the investigation and I'd barely had time to ferment my resolution to stay out of it all.

I peeked at the caller ID with one eye. It was Gus.

I rushed to answer.

"Hey there, gorgeous," Gus's deep voice filled the line and a delicious warmth spread through my belly. Gus was one person I wouldn't have to discuss murder with.

"Hi, Gus! How did your first show go?"

He groaned. "I got put into the crisper."

"Oh, no! What happened?"

"They put out a bunch of envelopes with recipes inside. Only we didn't know what they were, right? I picked a simple quiche—"

"You make a great quiche! I love your quiches," I raved.

"Thanks, but I didn't have any eggs. I couldn't even trade or coerce anyone because no one had eggs. I came up with a vegan variation, and the judges loved it. But in the end, they said it wasn't a quiche."

"If they knew there weren't any eggs available why did they assign you a quiche?"

"Ack, that's the way the show's set up. They want people to fail. They want drama or they wouldn't get ratings," he said.

"I'm so sorry," I said, although a part of me wanted Gus back home so badly I could taste it. "What happens now?"

"Tonight the show will air and the judging part will be live. Do you think you can call in and vote to save me?"

"Absolutely! The Roundup Crew will be at the Wine and Bark tonight. Max brought in his couch and TV. We'll have our own viewing studio. Everyone will call in."

"You're the best, Maggie." His voice dropped an octave and he said, "I miss you."

I took in a deep breath and let Gus's adoration fill me. I needed the boost of confidence.

We were silent for a moment and then Gus asked, "So what's up with you? Anything new?"

I thought about Darla, but refused to get sucked back into mystery mode. "It's been quiet here," I lied.

When I hung up with Gus, a call from Rachel beeped through. "How are you?" I asked. "Any news on the discharge?"

Rachel sighed. "The nurse says she wants my iron levels up before they release me. Right now I'm anemic."

"Oh, Rach!"

"I know. I'm afraid they're going to release me from one ward and admit me right into another one."

I laughed. "Nah, they would have done that years ago, if you were really that crazy."

"You will cover for me tonight, right?" she asked. "With Vrishali."

"Of course," I answered.

"Oh, Mags, what would I ever do without you?"

◇◇◇

Yolanda sat on my couch. Her feet curled up underneath her, while Beepo wandered around my apartment and whined at the glass door that led to the deck. I let him out and admired the view of the Pacific.

"What do you think about Darla?" she asked. "Hendrick did it, right?"

I sighed. I hadn't wanted to be dragged into this conversation, but I knew the minute Yolanda and Beepo showed up on my doorstep that that was exactly what would happen.

"You don't have to answer me," she said smugly. "I know he did and, more importantly, Gottlieb knows it, too."

I shrugged. "Well, then it's settled."

"Tea?" I asked.

She made a face. "You know I don't drink that. It's flavored water."

"Isn't that what coffee is, too?" I asked.

She looked horrified. "It most certainly is not!" She waved a hand around. "Anyway, about tonight. We'll have Max head over early and polish up the floors. I want Vrishali to be über impressed when she sees our transformation. There's no way I'm going to let the Kitty Corner steal our thunder."

"Have you been over there to check out the location yet?" I asked.

Yolanda shook her head. "No, I don't want to go near it."

"She's having a grand opening this weekend. We should go."

"Why?" Yolanda demanded. "She doesn't want us there and—"

"Why do you say that? She's very nice. She came over with a fruit basket and personally invited us."

"Invited *you*!" Yolanda said. "She didn't invite me. I don't have to go. Anyway, you know how I feel about cats."

I snickered. "How do you feel about cats?"

"They eat birds!" Yolanda shrieked.

"Not chickens though, right?"

Yolanda turned her nose up at me and plucked an imaginary hair off her skinny jeans.

"I didn't get a chance to tell you, but Cornelia might be interested in going into business with you. She heard that you made Fran an offer on the business. She said Chic Chickie had been her idea."

Yolanda tapped her long, lacquered nails on my coffee table. "Well, I don't know. Hendrick inherited the business, but with him in jail . . ."

"Wait, he's in jail?"

"Not yet," Yolanda said. "But he will be. Gottlieb just needs some evidence. Anyway, with Hendrick out of the picture, perhaps Cornelia and I could open up a new storefront together."

I refilled my tea and wandered to the back deck. Relief swept over me, if Hendrick was indeed the killer, then I didn't need to worry about investigating or not investigating. I was free to focus on the evening's festivities and to ensure that the Wine and Bark secured the cover of *Doggie Day*.

Finishing my tea and I said, "Let's get cracking, we have work to do at the Wine and Bark."

Yolanda stood. "Oh, yes, you really should head over there and get things straightened out. I'm going to over to Abigail's to get my hair done and then home to change."

"Why is it when there's work to be done, you always have a hair appointment?" I asked.

Yolanda smiled. "I have great timing."

◇◇◇

Max rolled the floor polisher around the terra-cotta, sprucing up old dents and marks that had been on the floor since forever. I had to admit the Wine and Bark was starting to really shape up. I arranged the Verdant Vines wines behind the bar. The Merlots together, the Chardonnays together, and the Syrahs together. It was true, that I had reservations about serving the wine due to the circumstances of the evening before, but I gathered Vrishali wouldn't be any the wiser about Hendrick. And besides, everyone was innocent until proven guilty.

Further, I wasn't convinced that Hendrick was the one who had killed Darla and Fran. It wasn't my place to judge. I opened one of the bottles of Syrah to let it aerate before the crowd showed up. Although I wasn't a wine expert, I knew that allowing the wine to breathe would break down the tannins and lessen its astringency, providing for a smoother flavor.

Max turned the floor polisher off and turned on the TV. "What channel is *Gourmet Games* on?" he asked.

"Our local twenty-two," I said. "I can hardly wait."

"I brought my laptop," Max said. "So I can go ahead and vote for him online and then through my phone, too. Double up the voting, you know?"

"That's a great idea," I said.

Across the patio I could see Brenda approaching. Max lit up like a little boy and ran to the door to greet her. She was dressed in her traditional black outfit with a tight corset and leather pants. She looked so beautiful and curvaceous that she reminded me of a cartoon. In her arms she carried her faithful Chihuahua, Pee Wee.

"The place looks great!" she said. "I can't wait until we make the cover of *Doggie Day*." Approaching the bar, she said, "Do you have a Bark Bite for Pee Wee?"

Pee Wee fixed his big brown eyes on me and licked his chops.

Behind Brenda, Max was drooling over her about as much as Pee Wee was drooling for a Bark Bite. I grabbed a doggie treat from the silver bowl next to me, and handed it to Brenda. She fed it to Pee Wee and released him to the floor. He ran happily toward the window, but lost his footing and slid all the way across the floor.

We all stared, horrified.

"Oh, no!" Max said.

Pee Wee, confused about what was going on, tried to run back to Brenda, but he slipped and slid the whole way. Brenda laughed uncontrollably, then picked up the Chihuahua.

Max asked, "Will the floor be too slippery for the dogs tonight?"

I came around the bar to examine the floor. It seemed fine to me, but I had rubber treads on the bottom of my sneakers.

"I'm not slipping," I said.

Brenda tentatively put Pee Wee down again. He ran over to the front door and skidded all the way there. Pee Wee seemed completely unbothered about slipping and sliding. Although for us it was going to be a huge issue if all the dogs came in and had same experience.

"Geez," I said. "This is going to be a disaster."

Brenda giggled, and Max buried his head.

"What do we do?" I asked Max.

"Do you think this is just a Pee Wee thing?" he asked. "Or will all the dogs have this reaction?"

"Hard to say," Brenda said. She pulled out her phone and sent a quick text to Yolanda. "Let's have someone else come on down and weigh in."

<><><>

Yolanda was not pleased to have been called to the Wine and Bark to test the quality of the floor. She showed up with her hair drenched and stuck to her face. Abigail, on the other hand, seemed fine with interruption. "We were halfway through setting her hair, but I didn't like the way it was looking, so I wet it down and we'll have to start again. It was perfect timing," Abigail said.

Yolanda held Beepo at the door of the Wine and Bark. "What do you want me to do?"

"Just put him down," I said. "Let's see if he can get traction."

She put him down and I tempted him with a Bark Bite. "Come here, Beepo," I called.

He ran to me and, sure enough, he slid across the floor.

Yolanda gasped, horrified. At her side, Abigail giggled. "Let's try with Missy." She put down the Shih Tzu, but Missy never even got started. She flopped immediately onto the floor, looking like a furry mop.

Well, a furry mop with a rhinestone bow on its head.

I laughed, but Yolanda glared at me.

"What were you thinking?" she demanded.

Max ducked behind the bar, hoping to escape culpability. "It was Max's idea," I whined.

Yolanda stepped gingerly into the bar, running the bottom of her foot back and forth along the terra-cotta. "I think even people can slip on this if they're not wearing the right kind of shoe."

Yolanda herself was wearing a pair of Blahnik's. Brenda chirped out, "I'm happy to sell sensible footwear to anyone who needs it."

I laughed. "You don't sell any sensible footwear."

"I can start," she said. "Especially if we're going to enjoy a Mutt-tini. Speaking of which . . ."

"I'll get right on it," Max said, grabbing a bottle of Stoli from behind the bar.

"Isn't it too early to drink?" Abigail asked.

"These are desperate times," Brenda answered.

"Well, in that case, I'll sample some of the latest Verdant Vines specialties," Abigail said.

"No!" Yolanda said. "You have to finish doing my hair."

Abigail waved a hand, dismissively. "Girl, I can still do your hair. I'm not going to go all stupid on one glass of wine."

Max poured her a glass of the newly opened Syrah, and Abigail appreciatively batted her long eyelashes at him.

I approached Yolanda. "What do we do about the floors?"

"I think we should get some small area rugs. There's a discount place, just a little ways out of town." She glanced at her watch. "I don't know that I have time to get there."

"Maybe I can fashion some little designer dog booties, with a grip surface," Brenda offered.

"No time," Yolanda said.

"I love that idea, though," Abigail said. "They'd have to be be-jeweled though. Otherwise, I wouldn't dare put them on my little princess."

Bejeweled.

That reminded me of the gem I'd found in the storeroom of Chic Chickie. I discreetly looked at Missy's collar.

Not even close. Missy wore clear rhinestones. Lots of them, but only rhinestones. I looked over at Pee Wee's collar. He had on a simple collar, no stones, only an identification medallion. Beepo, I knew, didn't wear a jewel collar.

I felt a modicum of relief. At least I knew none of the dogs in my immediate circle had been in the stockroom of Chic Chickie. Then a disturbing thought hit me: *Unless the dogs have multiple collars . . .*

Chapter Twenty-two

That evening, the Wine and Bark exuded a nervous energy—a buzz, really—where it seemed that dogs and humans alike were bouncing off the walls.

Max had run out to return the floor polisher, insisting on a full refund since they hadn't properly warned us not to use it on terracotta flooring. Then, he picked up some colorful area rugs and a movie-theater-style popcorn popper. The place definitely felt like someone's living room. There was a comfort and warmth about it, but I wondered if it would wind up making patrons want to nap instead of indulge.

The Roundup Crew was sprawled on the couch waiting for the beginning of *Gourmet Games*. If I didn't know any better, I would have sworn this was an exclusive Oscars screening. The gang waiting for the editor, Vrishali, with bated breath, but so far she had yet to make her appearance.

Finally, *Gourmet Games* began and Gus's handsome face filled the large-screen TV. My heart sped up to see him, although my reaction was tempered because he looked so worried. The crowd at the Wine and Bark burst into a round of applause for him, with shouts of "Go, Gus!" and "Look at him!" and "I can't believe it!"

Even Beepo barked furiously at the screen as he ran up to it, yapping as if he wanted to lick the screen.

Yolanda said, "Now, Beepo! Stop that. Come sit next to Mama." She patted the seat next to her and Beepo immediately tore across the rugs and settled at her feet comfortably.

We watched the show as Gus picked the card with the quiche and made some trades with another chef. There was a beautiful blond chef that inspired a little jealousy in me, but Gus barely spoke to her.

My brain screamed at me, *What right do I have to be jealous when I am dating Brad at the same time?* But my heart didn't listen, I wanted Gus all to myself.

First Gus traded with one heavyset chef: M&Ms for tofu. Then Gus negotiated with a lanky chef: some spinach in exchange for his bacon. I knew Gus was a pancetta man at heart, but it must have stung to let go of the bacon because he gave a sorrowful look into the camera as he handed it to the lanky chef. However, at this point I knew he'd anything to stay in the competition.

Gus whipped up his vegan quiche, just like he'd told me, and presented it to the judges. Everyone seemed impressed with the quiche, but in the end they put him in the crisper along with two other chefs.

The gang at the Wine and Bark, hooted and howled when Gus was banished to the crisper. Shouts of "No! That can't be! Gus is the best!" filled the bar.

The host of *Gourmet Games* instructed the audience to call in and save our favorite chef. Immediately the crew in the bar whipped out their cell phones and texted the number to save Gus.

Then, through the window of the bar, I spotted a tall man with broad shoulders, in a uniform. As if I already didn't know who it was, my guess was confirmed by his one-of-a-kind gait. Officer Brad Brooks was about to crash my *Gourmet Games* viewing party.

I leapt off the couch to intercept him at the front door, my heart hammering like crazy.

"Hi!" I said, overly cheerful.

He smiled warmly, glancing around the Wine and Bark. "Wow, what a transformation. What's going on? Some kind of fancy shindig?" He looked up at the large-screen TV, which now was currently playing a commercial for a revolutionary type of plastic bag that would seal flavors into your leftovers.

"We had to change things around for the editor of *Doggie Day*. We're trying to snag the cover."

Brad looked around the room. "Which one is she?"

"She's not here yet."

He glanced back at the TV, just as the commercial break was over. Gus's face filled the screen. Brad frowned.

"It's Gus's cooking show," I admitted. "He's in the crisper," I explained the premise of the show to Brad and told him that Gus could be eliminated from the series tonight. "Everyone is dialing like crazy to vote for him."

Brad smiled and pulled out his phone. "Let me get the guys at the station on it."

"On what?" I asked. "Are you going to vote against him?"

"Hell no. I'm going to put out an APB. Everyone needs to vote for DelVecchio, stat."

"You would do that for him?" I asked.

"For him? I'm doing it for me. Anything I can do to keep that guy in New York, away from you, I'm doing."

I smiled, a tingling sensation spreading through my body.

Brad pulled the radio off his shoulder and instructed all Pacific Cove officers to dial the number to vote for Gus to stay on the show.

Meanwhile, Max opened up a fresh bottle of wine and refilled glasses around the room.

In the middle of our celebration, I saw a woman in a beautifully detailed blue and purple sari approaching the Wine and Bark. "Vrishali's here," I said to the crew.

As Vrishali reached the front door, Yolanda sprang to her feet and greeted her.

Vrishali came in and looked around the room, a smile growing on her face.

"Come in, have a seat," Yolanda said, motioning around the room. "We've been expecting you."

Max rushed over with a glass of Malbec from Verdant Vines.

Vrishali gave him a pleased nod as she accepted the wine. "Wow! What a change. It looks nothing like the old place."

Yolanda practically preened. "You wanted atmosphere. We took that note. You wanted something different and we accommodated your wishes."

On the television there was a graphic display of the votes being tallied. The chef next to Gus was tall with a large potbelly. He was bald and wore a very worried expression; so far, he'd received about twenty-six percent of the votes. On the other side of Gus was a pe-tite brunette with a pixie cut, she smiled boldly into the camera and was tied with Gus at thirty-seven percent.

During another commercial break, Vrishali asked Max about the show. While he explained to her, Brad leaned into me.

"I thought you might want to know, Hendrick was arrested this afternoon."

I gasped. "Really? You had enough evidence to charge him?"

"We're working on building our case, but we found the gun in his van."

Reality settled into my bones.

Hendrick had killed Fran and Darla. That was it then, it was settled. Suddenly the beautiful fruity wine turned to vinegar in my mouth and I put the glass the down.

Brad put a hand on my shoulder. "I wanted you to know that you're safe."

"Yes," I said. "Darla must have been the one to break into my apartment."

Brad frowned. "What makes you say that?"

I sighed. I didn't want to tell him about the journal, so instead I said, "The note, it was a woman's handwriting."

He paled a bit. "What note?"

"Whoever broke into my apartment left me a note," I confessed. "Told me to stay out of the investigation."

He made a face. "At least they gave you good advice." Before I could reply he said, "I'll need the note, so I can admit it into evidence. And I wouldn't say it was Darla. Likely, it was Hendrick. Probably trying to figure out what you knew. Darla figured out what he'd done and he killed her."

"Why did he kill Fran?" I asked.

"A winery is an expensive thing to run. Did you know it takes about three hundred thousand dollars to put in new grape vines?"

I shook my head.

Brad shrugged. "At a minimum. Anyway, Fran left him everything."

"Did she have much? Just the shop, right?"

"No, she owned her home and a few other real estate holdings. I think she'd just closed on another property. So overall, Hendrick stood to inherit quite a bit. Plus, he was still listed as the beneficiary on her life insurance."

I frowned. "But if he really did it for the money, wouldn't he have figured out a better way?"

"What do you mean?" Brad asked.

"A way to kill her where he wouldn't get caught."

Brad smiled sadly. "Well, just because he inherited money, doesn't mean that he intended to kill her. It still could have been a crime of passion. He went there to see her. Ask her to take him back, she refused him and then in the heat of the moment . . ." Brad made a gun out of his fingers and pulled the imaginary trigger.

I shifted uncomfortably. "Has he confessed?"

"Of course not."

I thought about that day at the bar. When Hendrick had been given me a private tasting. It seemed like so long ago. He'd been upset when Yolanda and Fran had interrupted us. He'd definitely given me the impression that he had unresolved feelings for Fran. And yet . . .

"Wait, he told me he was with Darla that night."

Brad nodded. "Yes, Darla was his alibi. But now she's dead, too."

Suddenly the gang at the Wine and Bark cheered. I looked up at the television, dismayed that I'd completely lost my attention on the show. Gus was smiling. He'd received more than forty percent of the vote and his place on the show was secure for another week.

Brad smiled. "Well, that's a relief," he joked.

"Do you want something to drink?" I asked.

He shook his head. "I'm still on duty. I have to head back now." He stepped closer to me and cupped my chin in his hand. "Now that you can't investigate anymore, you must have loads of free time on your hands."

"Loads," I agreed.

"Even free time for lunch tomorrow at the Charcoal Corral?"

I smiled. "Yes."

"You can stay out of trouble until then, right?"

I nodded.

He tilted my face toward his and pressed his lips against mine.

A delicious shiver sent goosebumps over my arms. He pulled away smiling and winked at me as he disappeared out the front door.

I retreated behind the bar, feeling like I was on another planet. Yolanda approached the bar, putting her empty wineglass on top of the smooth marble. "Hit me with one more, sister, the night is going great. I think Vrishali is super happy with everything." She put a hand to her mouth and whispered conspiratorially, "She's talking feature story."

Over near the couch, Vrishali was taking selfies with Brenda and Max. They switched positions and took more pictures, including the dogs perched on the couch.

I poured Yolanda a refill, as Vrishali approached us.

"I love the new homey feel," Vrishali said. "I can imagine the cover image now."

Yolanda squealed and grabbed Vrishali's arms. "You mean we're in? We did it!"

Vrishali held up a hand. "Oh, no, no. Not yet. And, honestly, I think I like the look of the bar better the other day."

Yolanda flashed me a look of despair.

"Before the curtains and the couch?" I asked.

Vrishali looked around the bar. "Yes, but without the streamers and complicated décor. I think it will work best on the cover if we go with the simple look. I have to send over the photographer, of course. He'll give me his professional opinion, see if he can get any workable shots. Can someone meet us here tomorrow around noon?"

Yolanda slapped a hand down on the bar. "Absolutely! Maggie—"

"I have a date!" I said.

Vrishali and Yolanda both turned to me as if I was crazy. After all, what was I doing? Dismissing the editor of *Doggie Day* in favor of a burger at the Charcoal Corral?

Yolanda glared at me. "Put him off, darling. A girl never wants to appear too eager."

Vrishali gave a knowing look. "Yolanda is right. Men appreciate a woman who lets them chase her a bit."

I sighed. I wasn't into playing games, but I knew the cover of *Doggie Day* meant so much to Rachel. "I'll see what I can do to re-schedule," I grumbled.

Vrishali smiled. "Oh, that's very good. Now, after the photographer tells me if it's doable, I'll have to reevaluate Kitty Corner. They're having a grand opening this weekend, and that might make a lovely cover, too. Really expand our readership, I think," Vrishali said, seemingly thinking out loud. "If I can draw in the cat people we could grow exponentially."

Yolanda looked worried, but before she said anything, Vrishali wiggled her fingers at us and left.

Chapter Twenty-three

That night I got home exhausted. I'd checked in with Rachel several times and her blood iron was slowly on the rise, but until the lab results confirmed she was out of the anemic condition she wouldn't be released. So when I called to give her the skinny on the *Doggie Day* cover, we made plans for me to visit her the following day.

I expected to sleep better knowing that the police had Fran and Darla's murderer in custody, but somehow sleep eluded me. Could Hendrick really have pulled the trigger? How could anyone kill someone else, especially someone who had been their lover?

Somehow it felt like there was a missing piece to the puzzle. I fretted about having to reschedule my lunch date with Brad. I hated feeling tentative about his feelings toward me. He'd been so upset with me for poking around and asking questions, that I feared I might disappoint him again. Finally, I drifted off into a fitful sleep.

I awoke to the sound of a ringing phone. It was my sister, Rachel, on the line.

"Hey, Maggie," she said. "I'm finally feeling better. I think they're going to discharge me today!"

It wouldn't be the first time she told me this, so I didn't want to get my hopes up, but nevertheless, I said, "I'll call Yolanda and we'll come pick you up."

"Great, see you soon," she said, hanging up.

I dialed Yolanda and gave her the news; before long she and Beepo were in front of my apartment in her red convertible. I opened the passenger-side door and upended Beepo, who growled at me.

"Quiet now, Beep," Yolanda said, as he scrambled into her lap. "You know the drill."

Yolanda gunned it toward the hospital as I fiddled with the radio. "Do you know any more about the case?" I asked.

She shook her head. "After I left the Wine and Bark last night I called Gottlieb, but he was very tight-lipped about what evidence they have. Told me I shouldn't worry my 'pretty little head.'"

Another woman, like myself, would have been offended by that comment, but Yolanda somehow seemed to appreciate it.

When we arrived at the hospital, Rachel was already dressed and out of bed.

I rushed to hug her. "It's so good to see you up and about."

"Yes," she agreed. "I'm so grateful I'm feeling better." She clutched my hands. "Thank you for taking care of everything while I was cooped up in here."

"I'd do anything for you, Rachel." And it was true. Since I could remember, my sister, albeit flaky and completely unpredictable, had always been a top priority in my life.

"I know," Rachel said, hugging me back.

Yolanda sought out the green chair by the window and sank into it. "Me, too, you know! I'd do anything for you."

Rachel rushed over to her. "Of course, you would, darling. Thank you so much."

"It's because of Yolanda that the Wine and Bark will be the feature story in *Doggie Day*. We might even get the cover spread."

Rachel clapped her hands in childish delight and cheered.

Yolanda waved a hand around, dismissing the accolades. "Everyone helped. Maggie and Max did tons: the TV, the couch, the rugs. Everyone pitched in, even Cornelia helped."

"It's not final yet," I cautioned. "We need to actually get the Wine and Bark back to normal."

Rachel quirked an eyebrow. "What do you mean?"

"Vrishali liked the place without the couch, TV, curtains, etc.," I explained. "She's coming back today at noon—"

Rachel squealed. "Oh! So much to do. My head hurts thinking about it." She glanced at the wall clock. "Let's get out of here now. I need to get home and shower, then get ready to meet Vrishali."

Yolanda smiled at me. "Now you can go on your date with Officer Hot Pants, Maggie. You don't need to worry about the Wine and Bark."

<><><>

After Yolanda dropped Rachel and me off, I headed to the local grocery to pick up a few things for Grunkly. I walked along the beach over to his house. In one arm, I held the bag of groceries and in the other, my shoes. I wiggled my toes into the sand as I walked, admiring the sun and surf. In the distance, I saw a couple walking hand-in-hand. They looked familiar and I hurried to see who it was. To my surprise, I made out the tall male figure. It was Officer Ellington.

What with Hendrick being arrested and Fran and Darla's case being closed, apparently he had some free time.

The woman, had light brown hair secured in a ponytail and I realized with a certain degree of pleasure, that it was Cornelia. I was pleased that Ellington had found a potential love interest; he'd seemed so broken up about Fran's death. Maybe Cornelia could soften him up. I smiled. Everyone loves a happy ending.

188 • Diana Orgain

When I arrived at Grunkly's, I rapped on his door and waited. "It's me, Grunkly. Maggie!"

No answer.

I knocked again at the same time pulling my cell phone from my pocket. I knew Grunkly would tell me to use key under the doormat, but I hated the idea of barging in.

He picked up immediately. "Benny?"

Benny was my great-uncle's bookie. "No, it's Maggie. I'm at the front door," I said.

"Magpie! You don't have to call me. I've told you before, just use the key from under the mat. Come in!"

I hung up, dug the key out from under the mat and entered. I beelined for the kitchen to set the groceries down. "Good news," I said. "Rachel is out of the hospital."

Grunkly burst into spontaneous applause. "Thank goodness! I was worried sick!" He followed me into the kitchen and began unpacking the groceries alongside me.

"Yeah, it's good," I agreed. "What are you up to?" I maneuvered around the broken toaster, to put away the bread. Then, I unplugged the toaster and picked it up. "Can we toss this thing?"

Grunkly looked horrified. "The toaster?"

The toaster looked like a relic from the *Titanic*. There was no way it functioned.

"It could start a fire," I said.

Grunkly shook his head. "No, no. It works perfectly fine. I like my toast extra toasty." He pulled it out of my hands and clung to it as if it was a prized possession.

I sighed. I'd never win the declutter game with him.

He plucked out a few cans of Dinty Moore stew from the bottom of the bag and stuck them in a cupboard. "I thought you were Benny calling," he said. "I've been waiting on his call all morning."

"A hot new horse you have to bet on?" I asked.

Just as certainly as I'd never win the declutter game with Grunkly, I'd also never win the "You're wasting your time and money gambling on horses" argument.

"Not a horse. I saw your friend on that cooking show."

I paused. "Gus?"

"Yeah!" he said, his face lighting up. "He's going to win that thing."

"Grunk, he nearly got voted off last night!"

Grunkly laughed. "Not hardly. I heard all about it on my police scanner. The kid has quite a following. Anyway, I know how those shows work. They act like the guy most likely to win is ready to get axed, but nothing could be further from the truth. Anyway, I've sampled his cooking. I know he's going to win."

I couldn't help but be cynical. "Let me guess. The odds are against him."

Grunkly patted my shoulder. "Atta girl!"

I giggled. "Well, I'll let him know you believe in him."

We finished putting away the groceries and made our way out to the living room. Prominently displayed on the coffee table was a fruit basket.

"What's that?" I asked.

"A nice lady named Lois came by earlier. She just opened shop. A cat adoption center."

Unexpectedly, despair clutched at my stomach. "What?" I asked. "Lois came here? Why?"

Grunkly walked over to the coffee table and picked up a card. He handed it me. "She was asking if I would consider leasing to her or selling the property that houses the Wine and Bark. She's having problems with her location and she hasn't even opened her business yet." He showed me the flyer for the Kitty Corner's grand opening. "I told her there was no way, no how, that'd I could sell the property."

Grunkly owned quite a few pieces of real estate around

town. Anytime he'd hit it big with the racehorses, he invested in property.

"And you know, Magpie, I don't ever sell my real estate!" he continued. "That's for you and Rachel when I kick the bucket."

I hugged him. "Thank you, I know."

"Anyway, Lois said if I wouldn't sell then she wanted to rent from me. But I told her Rachel is my niece and she has the lease for as long as she wants it."

So the owner of the Kitty Corner wants to put the Wine and Bark out of business, quite literally.

"That's right, Grunkly. Rachel has no intention of letting the business go. In fact, she's getting a nice spread in *Doggie Day* magazine." I left out the part about the whole breaking our backs redecorating and then un-decorating the Wine and Bark in order to get Vrishali to agree to it.

Grunkly beamed. "You girls have good heads on your shoulders. The business is going to succeed, and I'm delighted to hear Rachel is out of the hospital." He rummaged through the fruit basket and pulled out a handful of chocolate-covered raisins. He offered them to me. When I shook my head, he popped them into his mouth and said, "These are delicious. Such a nice lady."

◇◇◇

I walked along the beach, but instead of heading home, I found myself heading toward the Kitty Corner. If Lois was desperate enough to seek out Grunkly to try and buy his property, I wondered what was wrong with her location.

As I turned onto the street where the Kitty Corner was, I could see there were preparations for the grand opening. A yellow banner was strung across the façade and in the window was an enormous cat tower designed to look like a tree. Kittens were scampering in and out of faux tunnels, hanging on branches, and sliding into each other. A young girl in pigtails pressed her hand against the glass.

Next to her was a man dressed in plaid shorts and blue polo shirt. They stood at the window mesmerized by the cats.

The girl squealed and pointed at the cats as they romped after a pom-pom that rolled into one of the cubbies.

"Daddy, daddy. I've always wanted kitty. Can we get one? Please? Maybe the gray one." She pointed to a kitten as he scored the pom-pom away from another kitten. "Or maybe the tiger-striped one." She pointed to one snoozing in a tunnel. "Or the black-and-white one. Look at him. Isn't he cute? We can call him Whiskers."

Her father smiled. "They're all adorable. But the store's not open yet." He indicated the grand opening banner. "We'll have to come on Saturday and see if we can adopt one."

Inside the store, Lois emerged from the back. She saw me at the window and scurried over to the open the door. We stood in the doorway, the little girl and her father looked on curiously, but soon moved down the street.

Lois said, "Maggie, right? It's good to see you again. We're not open yet, but you'll come to the party on Saturday, won't you?" Her voice lilted upward, her eyes sparkling as she waited for my reply.

"I'll try," I said. "But really, I came to talk to you because my uncle said you approached him about leasing the property where the Wine and Bark is at."

She frowned, a deep crease appearing between her eyes. "Oh." She pushed up her glasses and glanced around nervously. "Yes. It's true. I was considering the locale. It has good foot traffic . . ."

I indicated a couple walking past and then a group of teenagers that were close by. "I don't understand. This location has excellent foot traffic."

Her lips pursed. "Moving wouldn't be my first choice, after all, I haven't even opened shop."

"Then why are you researching other locations?" I asked. "Are you getting evicted?"

Lois folded her arms over her large bosom. "In a matter of speaking. The building's been sold."

"The new owner wants you out?" I asked.

She shrugged. "She did . . . but then . . ."

"What?" I probed.

"She died."

Chapter Twenty-four

Blood rushed into my ears, creating a *whoosh* sound, and my legs felt like they might wobble out from under me.

Another murder in Pacific Cove?

"What do you mean she's dead?" I stuttered.

Lois leaned in confidentially, "Oh, you hadn't heard? That woman. The one who owned that ridiculous shop, Chic Chickie."

Relief flooded me. There hadn't been another murder in our small town; this was just the local gossip making its rounds.

"Fran?" I asked.

Lois nodded. "Yes, Fran! She wanted to expand and tried to get the lease for this property here. But I hired a very savvy attorney. The nice one, lady from Bradford and Blahnik. She has a little dog. She frequents the Wine and Bark, I think."

"Brenda. I know her."

Lois smiled. "Yes, Brenda." She nodded in unison with me. "Well, if it wasn't for her, Fran would have swiped the lease right out from under me! But as it was, Brenda wrote in some terms that really swayed the owners."

I frowned. "So what's the problem?"

"When they rented to me, Fran became furious and she put in an offer to buy the building, with one stipulation, of course."

"That you be evicted?" I asked.

Lois nodded. "She wanted the space. She was ruthless."

"She was murdered," I said, watching Lois's face carefully.

"I know," Lois said, her eyes flicked back toward the shop. "I can't say that I'm exactly brokenhearted about it." An orange kitten darted toward us. Lois picked him up deftly by the scruff of the neck. "No escaping, Little Archie." She stroked the cat between the ears, and he let out a ferocious purr that sounded like a lawn mower. Something on his neck, flashed in the sunlight.

My breath caught.

Little Archie has a bejeweled collar!

"Oh, what a cute little guy," I said. "May I hold him?"

Lois passed me the kitten and I discreetly examined the collar. The jewels were blue, not green. It wasn't a match. Still, I suddenly felt the wild desire to check every collar in the store to see if there was a match.

The kitten squirmed in my hands and Lois took him. She released him back to the floor and he scampered inside to romp it up with his friends.

"I thought the new owner might be more reasonable," Lois said.

"The new owner?" I asked.

She nodded. "That man, Hendrick. He inherited the property from Fran, but he told me he needed to wait for the estate to settle before he could commit to anything."

"So you've spoken with him already?"

"Oh, yes," Lois said. "As soon as I heard about Fran. My attorney told me not to approach him. But I couldn't help it." She wrung her hands as she spoke, and a sense of desperation seemed to waft off of her. "I've put so much into this business already, and we haven't even had our grand opening yet."

I nodded. "I know how much goes into launching a business."

Lois tsked, her face almost a mask of agony. "The best I can hope for is to have a successful launch and try to land another lease, in case Hendrick moves forward with the eviction."

"But Fran wanted the space for her store, right? Maybe Hendrick will let you continue to lease?"

Lois filled her cheeks with air and let it out in a great big huff. "I don't know. It's unfortunate now that he's under arrest. I'm sure that will drag things along even more."

She knows about the arrest. What else does she know?

Lois seemed to have a pulse on the latest Pacific Cove gossip.

"Just out of curiosity," I said. "When did you visit with Hendrick?"

Lois squared her shoulder to me and tilted her chin in defiance. "Monday."

Goosebumps grew on my arms.

Monday was the day Darla was murdered.

"At Verdant Vines?" I asked.

Lois nodded, keeping her eyes on mine. "Yup."

<>◇<>

I hurried home, marveling at how I ran late all the time. I'd had plenty of time to pick up Rachel from the hospital and shop for Grunkly, but stopping at the Kitty Corner had thrown off my entire schedule.

Even though I hated the feeling of rushing, I had newfound energy. Lois had a bone to pick with Fran. She'd been very upset about being evicted. What if they'd had a confrontation at Chic Chickie that ended with Fran's death?

What about the gem I'd found at Chic Chickie? Could it have

come from one of Lois's kittens? The unsettling feeling I'd had while speaking with Lois grew. Something was off. She was distressed about her business, that much was clear.

But how far would she go to ensure success?

Could she have shot Fran in a rage over the eviction?

Once home, I quickly changed into a fresh shirt and khakis. Nothing too fancy for the Charcoal Corral. I reapplied my lipstick and ran a brush through my hair. I was out the door when my phone buzzed.

"Maggie, it's Brad."

"Brad, I'm so sorry I'm late. Hang tight and I'll be there."

He sighed. "Oh, I'm glad you're not there yet. Listen, I'm so sorry, but I'm going to have to postpone. Can you give me a rain check?"

"Of course, I understand," I said, trying to mask the disappointment in my voice. I felt deflated. I'd been looking forward to our lunch and now he was canceling.

"I hate to do this to you, Maggie. It's just that something's come up."

"Is it about the Hendrick case?" I probed.

He chuckled. "You know I can't discuss the case with you."

Still something in his voice gave me a jolt. "Has there been a development?"

He was silent for a moment, then he said, "I heard Rachel is out of the hospital."

Boy, he was smooth at changing the subject.

"Yes. I picked her up this morning."

"I'm happy to hear that. I know you must be relieved."

"I am. We're all happy she's back home. Well, really she's at the Wine and Bark. Looks like we might get the cover of *Doggie Day*, after all."

"Great," said Brad. "Well deserved. I'll talk to you soon, okay, Mags?"

"Yes . . . but wait, before you hang up . . ."

"Hmm?"

"I stopped by Kitty Corner. To talk to the owner, well, it's a long story. But she mentioned to me that she'd been up at Verdant Vines on Monday. That's the day—"

"Maggie! You're not investigating again—"

"No, no. Nothing like that, it's just that—"

There was a break in the line, the kind that comes when another call beeps through.

"Uh. I have to get this one, Maggie. Stay out of trouble!"

◇◇◇

I puttered around the house, looking for something to occupy myself. I fussed around in the kitchen and realized I didn't have many groceries because I'd planned to be on the cruise right about now. While I was making a shopping list for myself my phone rang.

"Hey there, beautiful," Gus's voice filled the line. "I had a break and wanted to give you a call."

I relaxed just hearing his voice. "Hi, Gus! How's the show going?"

"I made the next round."

"I had no doubts," I said. "And I'm sure Grunkly will be happy to hear it. I think he's placed a couple of bets on you."

He laughed. "I'll try not to disappoint."

Suddenly I missed him like crazy. "If you go all the way on the show, when will you be home?" I asked.

He made a little tsking sound. "Couple weeks still. We only tape one show a week and the elimination round is live. Why? You miss me?"

"Of course."

"Especially since you're not dancing your head off in the Mexican Riviera, right?"

"Dancing my head off? More like working another part of my anatomy off. I don't think they let pursers dance."

"You should have applied for cruise director, like Julie McCoy," he said.

I laughed. "No no. There's too much dealing with people in that role. Like I do at the Wine and Bark. It's what drives me crazy. With numbers, there's a right and a wrong. Things balance. With people, there's no telling."

Gus was silent for a moment.

"Are you there?" I asked.

"Yeah. I was just thinking. Why don't you do the books for the Wine and Bark? Rachel hates that sort of thing. Come to think of it, so do Norma from the Meat and Greet, and Camilla from Piece of Cake. If you wanted to, you could run your own bookkeeping service. In fact, once I get back into town and reopen DelVecchio's I'll be your very first client."

His suggestion stunned me. Part of me wanted to travel, but the other part wanted to stay put in Pacific Cove and await his return.

As if he sensing my anxiety, he said, "If you have the travel bug so bad, you can come see me in New York."

"I just left there not too long ago."

"Great," he said, without missing a beat. "You can show me your favorite hangouts."

"Well, smarty-pants. I need funds for that."

"*Pfft*. If money is a problem I'm happy to send you a ticket."

"Of course, money is a problem," I teased. "And not just for the ticket, but for rent. You know. Otherwise, I might have to move in with Grunkly."

Gus burst out laughing. "No! You'd get lost among the boxes, Maggie. We'd never see you again."

I giggled. "I'll tell him you said that."

"No, no! I like being on his good side," Gus said.

"Right. Don't get on his bad side. It might cost you a veal pic-cata or two."

"That's no sweat. You like saltimbocca? I'll make that for you and Grunkly when I get back."

Before I could answer, Gus said, "Ugh. Sorry, Maggie. They're calling us into hair and makeup now."

I giggled. "You're wearing makeup now?"

He chuckled. "Only because they make me, and I want to win this thing. Think about what I told you, okay?"

"I will," I said as we hung up.

◇◇◇

After shopping for myself, with the bit of extra time on my hands, I decided to head over to the Wine and Bark. The bar almost looked like its old self again. The couch and TV were gone, as were the area rugs. Even the curtains we'd borrowed from Chic Chickie were curiously missing.

When I arrived, Rachel and Yolanda were in deep discussion with Vrishali, while a bearded man walked around installing lights. Presumably, he was the photographer. Rachel and Yolanda both wiggled their fingers at me in greeting, but after that more or less ignored me.

I paced around avoiding the photographer and tried not to think about the call I'd had with Brad.

Had there been a development in the case? He hadn't given me a straight answer. My gut told me Hendrick wasn't a murderer, but if not Hendrick then who?

It seemed like Brenda might have some answers, so I headed over to Bradford and Blahnik, pondering how I could ask her about the gun I'd found while snooping around in her office.

Is she holding on to it for a client?

Was it hers? Did she keep it there for protection?

When I arrived at the storefront, I browsed the window display. There were several new pairs of sandals, flats, and boots on display. One pair of low-cut blue suede boots caught my eye.

They were breathtaking.

I'd have to ask Brenda if she had them in my size. I pushed open the front door and scanned the room. She was nowhere in sight.

"Brenda?" I called out.

There was a rustling sound from the back room, followed by hushed voices.

Brenda appeared from the back. "Maggie, I wasn't expecting you. Is there something I can help you with?" she asked.

"I love the new display. I was hoping maybe you have those boots in my size."

Brenda shifted uncomfortably from one foot to the other. "Oh, I can check. But, right now I'm with a client."

Max appeared from the back room, waving cheerfully. "Hey, Maggie."

Brenda looked annoyed. He turned to her. "I can entertain Maggie for a few minutes if you want to finish up with Hendrick," he said.

Brenda frowned and looked distracted.

Max shuffled his feet and looked chagrinned. "Oh. Was I not supposed to say anything?"

Hendrick suddenly appeared from the back. He was red-faced and had dark circles under his eyes. He looked like he hadn't eaten or slept in a week. His clothes were rumpled and he had aged tremendously since the last time I saw him. In short, he looked grief stricken.

My heart ached for him.

Hendrick wailed, "I'm being framed. I know it. This has been the worst week of my life. First, someone murders Fran, then Darla.

And the next thing I know, the police are arresting me. My life is over!" He collapsed to his knees.

"Now, now," Brenda said reassuringly, taking hold of one arm.

Max grabbed his other arm and together they shuffled him over to one of the leather couches clients usually sat on while trying on designer shoes. "We've talked about this," Brenda said. "We mustn't lose hope."

She motioned something to Max, who seemed to understand, because he immediately moved toward the front door and flipped the open sign to closed, then drew the front drapes.

"I can recommend a criminal defense attorney," Brenda said. "He's relatively local. He has an office in Monterey."

Hendrick grimaced. "Criminal defense! I'm not a criminal."

Seeing him protest so furiously, suddenly made me realize why Brenda had a gun in her office. It had to be for self-defense. If Hendrick was a killer, he could easily go off the deep end—and if she'd been alone with him it could have turned dangerous.

Brenda said, "We're going to do what we can to find out who's behind all this." She used a patient tone that made everyone in the room focus.

"I was with Darla the night that Fran was killed," Hendrick said. "When they killed Darla, too, they killed my alibi. It's a setup."

"Why do you think someone would want to frame you?" Brenda asked.

Hendrick shrugged. "I think I seem like an easy target. I inherited all of Fran's property. The police had me down as a person of interest after Fran's murder because they found it suspicious that she never took me off as a beneficiary." He looked around the room as if searching for solace. Max put a hand on his shoulder, which made Hendrick nod and say, "But we'd been together a long time, and frankly, I hadn't taken her off as my beneficiary, either."

"What about Darla?" Brenda asked.

Hendrick's face looked pained. "She was always jealous of Fran. In fact, I'm ashamed to admit that I considered she might've hurt Fran in the first place."

"That's not possible," Max said. "Because somebody killed Darla, right? I mean, it wasn't suicide."

Distress flickered through Hendrick eyes. "She didn't kill herself. She would have never done that. We were going to be married. She was excited. Happy. And I realize now she could have never hurt Fran. I know that. Though, we did have an awful fight about it."

"You fought about it?" I asked.

Hendrick pressed his hands to his forehead in anguish and let out a sorrowful moan.

"Why would you fight about it?" I pressed. "There was no way she could have killed Fran because she was with you that night, correct?" I squinting at him. "She was your alibi . . ."

Hendrick gave an overexaggerated, unconvincing nod. "I know. I wasn't thinking, I was emotional. I can't explain it. It's just that I know I'm being framed. Whoever killed Fran knew that I stood to inherit everything. Someone is after me."

"Or the property," I said.

Everyone turned to me. "What?" Brenda asked.

"Fran wanted to evict Kitty Corner, right?" I said.

Brenda glanced toward Hendrick and waited for him to reply.

He shifted nervously and frowned. "What do you mean? The property on Magnolia Street? Yes, Fran wanted to move Chic Chickie to that location. She thought there was more foot traffic there. She bought the building . . ."

"I know. The business owner, Lois, is frantic. She's wondering if you're going to evict her now that Fran's gone."

Brenda folded her arms and scowled at me. "Maggie, I hardly think this is the time to negotiate a deal for Lois."

"I'm not negotiating for Lois," I protested. "What I'm saying is: She is desperate to keep the lease."

"I'm sure that can be arranged," Hendrick said.

Max gasped, then nodded sagely. "I get it! You think Lois killed Fran in order to keep renting the space for her business."

Chapter Twenty-five

Brenda pounded a hand onto the counter, sending a display of trouser socks careening to the floor. "Lois didn't kill Fran!"

Max scrambled to pick up the display.

"Why do you say that?" I asked. "What makes you so sure?"

Brenda took great interest in the sock display, putting it back together with Max's help. Hendrick and I waited until Brenda shrugged and said, "She's just not the type."

Hendrick sprang up off the couch. "And I am?" he said.

Brenda mumbled something that sounded like, "If the shoe fits."

Max moved to stand in front of Brenda, blocking my view of her. It was a protective move, I realized, as he'd positioned himself between Hendrick and Brenda.

"What was that?" Hendrick demanded.

"She said she's going to get that referral for you," Max said.

Hendrick sagged back onto the couch and Brenda disappeared into the back room. I wanted to tell Max about the jewel I'd found at Chic Chickie, but refrained from saying it in front of

Hendrick. Instead, I asked, "Hendrick, why would Darla break into my house?"

Hendrick looked at me, a puzzled expression on his face. "What do you mean?"

"Yolanda and I were followed the other day, by a dark van. I was pretty sure Darla was driving it. Then my apartment was broken into. My journal—"

Max cleared his throat interrupting me.

I glanced over at him and he gave me a definite don't-go-there warning with a firm shake of his head.

He was right. It probably wouldn't be smart to mention I had tampered with evidence at Hendrick's house. Instead, I said, "The intruder left me a note."

Hendrick sat up straighter. "What kind of note?"

"It said: 'Stop asking questions or you'll end up like Fran.'"

"I don't understand. Why do you think it was Darla that left the note?"

Max glared at me, another warning wafting my way. This time I ignored it. "She took something from my apartment and I saw it at the vineyard."

Hendrick grumbled. "The killer must have planted it. Just like they planted the gun."

Brenda emerged from the back room. "Alright, Hendrick, I found an attorney who can help you." She handed him a business card.

Hendrick slumped back on the couch and sighed.

<><><>

Once Hendrick left, I told Max and Brenda about the jewel I'd found at Chic Chickie.

"I'm glad you didn't say anything to Hendrick about that," Brenda said. "Lois is my client, you know."

"Well, if she's guilty of murder—"

Max held up a hand. "I think we're in over our heads here. You should take the jewel, along with your journal, and give them to the police."

Brenda looked alarmed. "Your journal?" I opened my mouth to speak but Brenda clapped both hands over her ears. "Lalalalala!" she shouted. "Don't tell me. I don't want to know."

Max laughed.

With her hands still covering her ears, Brenda yelled, "Did you want me to check to see if I have those boots in your size?"

I nodded and she disappeared into the stockroom.

"Seriously, you need to take all the evidence to Brad," Max said.

I sighed. There was no way I wanted to confess about taking my journal back from the scene of the crime, but what choice did I have? It could help Brad take down a killer.

"He canceled lunch plans with me. I thought maybe there was a new development in the case and that's why he canceled."

Max shrugged. "Maybe. I hope so. I don't think Hendrick did it."

Anxiety squeezed at the base of my neck. I didn't necessarily think Hendrick was guilty, either; but could Lois really have murdered two people over a store that hadn't opened yet?

It felt like a stretch, but who really knew what motivated people to kill?

Brenda reappeared with a shoebox in her hand. I sat on the couch Hendrick had just vacated and tried on the boots. They felt like they hugged my feet and I found myself relaxing. I suppose nothing quells stress better than retail therapy.

◇◇◇

At home, I paced around in my new boots waiting for Brad to call. I'd left him several messages, but had yet to hear back from him.

When the phone finally buzzed, I dove for it.

Yolanda's voice filled the line. "Sugar. Where are you? We're all at Yappy Hour and you're not."

"I'm waiting around for Brad to call me," I whined.

"You can wait for him to call while you down a couple of Mutt-tinis. *Doggie Day* took some great photos this afternoon. I think we definitely scored the cover. Come down and celebrate with us."

"Alright. But before you hang up, have you spoken to Gottlieb today?"

"No, why?"

"I just want to know if there have been any developments on the case," I said.

"What do you mean? I thought Hendrick did it," Yolanda said.

Pacing around my apartment, I said, "I ran into him over at Bradford and Blahnik. He says he's been framed—"

"Of course he says that!" Yolanda shrieked. "You didn't think he was going to come out and confess, did you?"

"I don't know. I guess I hadn't expected to believe him. He's grief stricken."

"*Pfft,*" Yolanda said. "It's all an act. Come down to the Wine and Bark and let's talk. Cornelia is here. I think she's hot with Ellington right now. You can ask her if she knows anything."

◇◇◇

On my way down to the Wine and Bark, I took a small detour to Magnolia Street. I couldn't stop myself from walking over and peeking in again at Kitty Corner.

There was a tuxedo kitten sharpening her claws on one of the posts in the window. She wore a pink diamante collar.

Not a match.

I peered into the window, to search out more kittens. Then something unexpected caught my eye. On the far side wall were shelves of cat carriers, strollers, slings, beds, collars, toys, posts, and clothes. Lots of items sparkled, and I strained to get a better look.

I had to get inside.

The grand opening was still a few days away, but surely Lois would be on-site tomorrow toiling. I'd come back in the morning and examine every single jewel that sparkled until I had a match.

Turning to walk the rest of the way to the Wine and Bark, I spotted a familiar face across the street. Brad was inside an unmarked sedan. But instead of waving at me, he lowered the car shade and seemed to try to hide.

What is he doing here?

Next to him in the passenger seat was another man.

Ellington.

Officer Ellington sat with a hand pressed to his ear, as if listening to some kind of headset.

Oh goodness!

They are on a stakeout.

Did they have a bug or a wiretap or something in Kitty Corner, so they could monitor Lois?

I frantically glanced over my shoulder, obsessing over the fact that I'd just interrupted official police business. I tried to hide myself by pressing against the glass of the Kitty Corner window display.

It was ludicrous! I felt so foolish I wanted to shrink right into the earth, finally I just turned and hustled toward the Wine and Bark.

When I arrived, I yanked open the door to the bar and bumped into Yolanda.

"Maggie," she said. "I was about to send out a search party!"

"Well, I did sort of interrupt one," I said, laughing as she pulled me up to the bar. Rachel was behind the counter, mixing up a pitcher of Salty Dogs. The Roundup Crew was piled around several cocktail tables that had been squeezed together, while the dogs tore around chasing each other.

"It's nice to have the place back to normal," I said.

"Well, we completed the photo shoot. We'll have to keep our fingers crossed that we get the cover, but right now our work is done." Everyone raised their glasses and cheered.

"We have to get the curtains back before they're ruined," Cornelia said.

I turned to her. "We can take them back tomorrow." I glanced around the room. "Where are they?" I asked.

Rachel made a face. "We had to move them to the back room. I'm so sorry," she said to Cornelia.

When Cornelia didn't respond, Rachel poured her a glass of wine. "But don't worry. Yolanda and I took great care to lay them out right. I'm sure they're fine. Thank you so much for lending the curtains to us."

Cornelia winked at Rachel. "It was my pleasure. I need them back because I'm hoping to reopen the shop."

I nearly spit out my cocktail. "You're going to reopen Chic Chickie?"

She nodded excitedly. "Now that Hendrick's been arrested for murder, I called Fran's brother in Michigan. He gave me permission to reopen."

My mind reeled. I glanced over at Brenda and Max, but they were caught up in another conversation across the room.

"Hendrick was released," I said.

Several emotions crossed Cornelia's face: incredulity, shock, dismay, then alarm. "What do you mean, he's been released?"

I shrugged. "I thought you might know. Has Officer Ellington told you anything about the investigation?"

Like the fact that he's on a stakeout right now with Brad.

"No," Cornelia said. "I can't believe it. It must be some sort of mistake!"

"I guess they don't have enough evidence," I said.

"They have the gun! Ellington told me as much," Cornelia said.

Then why would the police be staked out in front of Kitty Corner? They had to think Lois was the one. Yes, I could feel it in my bones. Lois was guilty.

Next to me, Yolanda shrugged. "Do you think if Hendrick's not in jail, he won't let you run Chic Chickie?"

Cornelia bristled. "I don't know what to think." She pressed a hand to her forehead and sighed. "I only just negotiated everything with Fran's brother. Now I'll have to talk to Hendrick. And what if . . ." Her voice trailed off.

Rachel dumped a bucket of ice into the ice well. "What if he's a murderer? You can't negotiate with a murderer."

Cornelia slid her empty cocktail glass closer to Rachel.

Rachel refilled it and sighed. "I know it's tough, honey. Everyone wants their business to be successful, but you can't take unnecessary chances."

"It's not Hendrick. He didn't do it," I said.

Cornelia gave me a sidelong glance. "What makes you say that?"

I thought about Brad begging me to stop probing at the investigation and my reply died on my lips.

Chapter Twenty-six

It was a restless night. I dreamt about Brad and Ellington's stake-out, only, in my dream, I ran over and banged on the car window, screaming for them to let me in on the action. Obviously, I had too much time on my hands!

In the morning, I busied myself with calling my supervisor, Jan, over at Soleado Cruise Line, to inquire when the next cruise was leaving. Unfortunately, my call went straight to her voice mail. So I cleaned the house, took out the garbage, paid bills, and did laundry—all in the name of not thinking about what Brad and Ellington could have been doing parked in front of Kitty Corner.

Finally, I put on my running shoes and filled a water bottle. It had been a while since I had had time to run and I felt anxious for some physical exertion. The sea air would calm my nerves. I set out to run on the beach. The sun was low in the sky still, only begin-ning to warm up our ocean-side property. I zipped up my jacket to protect me from the light breeze that buffeted me as I ran.

The repetitive action of putting one foot in front of the other actually seemed to increase my brain function. I suddenly found myself reviewing the case again.

What did I know?

Someone had killed Fran and Darla. Lois had been to Verdant Vines on Monday the day Darla had been killed. Lois'd been upset with Fran . . . And the police were staking out her location . . .

Before I could really decide anything, I found myself on the path toward Magnolia Street and Kitty Corner. I perused the street, but the unmarked car I'd seen Brad and Ellington in yesterday was nowhere to be seen. Despite the early hour, I'd have bet Lois was at the store, prepping for her grand opening.

I marched purposefully toward the front door, although I was full of doubt, I pushed my shoulders back and tried to give myself an air of confidence.

What the heck did I think I was doing?

Was I actually planning to accuse Lois of murder?

I peered into the front window and every hesitation I had vanished. In the middle of the room, Lois stood over a man who was seated in a chair. The man's back was to me, but Lois was in plain sight. She was ranting; her hands flying around, her face angry.

Shock jolted my system as I recognized the man in the chair.

Oh, no!

It was Grunkly.

I was right! Lois killed Fran and Darla and now she was going to kill Grunkly if I don't stop her!

Fear struck me immediately, propelling me into action. I pounded on the window like a crazy woman, pumping a fist into the Plexiglas repeatedly. Inside, the kittens on the tree tower scampered away, frightened. On the outside, the yellow grand opening banner, which had been strung across the façade, came loose and rained down upon me. I batted it away, swinging at it furiously.

Lois ran to the doorway, Grunkly swiveled around in the chair.

In his hand was a chocolate-covered strawberry that he dropped to the floor. From his lap, a gray kitten bolted toward the back of the shop. Both Grunkly's and Lois's faces mirrored my own fear and shock.

The chocolate-covered strawberry . . . from the fruit basket!

Max had eaten one and had gotten sick. And then there was Rachel's salmonella. Had Lois given her a fruit basket and poisoned her?

Brad's voice echoed in my head about salmonella being a terrible way to try and kill someone, but I couldn't ignore Lois. What if she was trying to poison my Grunkly!

Lois opened the door and ripped the banner away from me. "Maggie! Maggie! Are you alright?"

She grabbed at me, but I pushed her away. "Let me go!" Rushing inside ahead of her, I screamed, "Grunkly!"

"Maggie! Is everything all right?" Lois scanned the street. "Are you in danger? Who are you running from?"

My heart pounded so ferociously, it felt as if would explode through my chest. I rushed toward my great uncle. "I'm here now. Everything is going to be fine."

"What's wrong?" he asked, looking confused. "Has something happened?"

"Should we call the police?" Lois asked. Her face looked panicked and she pressed a hand to her heart.

"Yes! Call the police!" I screamed. "In fact, they're probably listening in now."

Lois frowned and glanced nervously around the room. "Listening in?"

Grunkly looked as confused. "What's going on, Maggie?" He got up from the chair and came over to me. He placed a soothing hand on my arm.

Adrenaline coursed through me causing me to shake.

Grunkly patted my hand. "There, there, honey. Calm down."

"Lois is a murderer! She's already killed two people. I won't let her hurt you. You didn't eat any strawberries, did you?"

"What are you talking about?" Lois asked, puzzled. "I've never hurt anyone." Again, she glanced around the room. "Why would the police be listening in? What did you mean by that?"

I pointed an accusing finger at her. "You wanted Fran out of the way after she bought this building and wanted to have you evicted. You went to see her that night at her shop. Maybe you tried to bargain with her, but she refused you and you killed her. I know because while you were there you left a piece of evidence." I fumbled for my bag and realized I didn't have it. I searched the far wall of carriers and collars, but didn't immediately see a match to the gem I'd found.

It doesn't matter. The match is here somewhere, I know it.

"A jewel from a collar or one of those carriers," I motioned toward the display shelf.

Lois shook her head. "No, Maggie. It isn't true. I never hurt Fran. Why, I never even stepped foot into that shop. That woman was toxic. I never would have confronted her."

I ignored Lois's denial. "Then, it was you that almost ran Yolanda and me off the road."

Lois looked to Grunkly for support. "Ernest, honestly, I don't know what she's on about."

Grunkly pushed the chair he'd been sitting in, toward me. "Maggie? Do you need to sit down? You look very flushed."

"Why did you do it, Lois?" I pressed

"Do what?" Lois asked.

"Kill Darla. You went up to the vineyard on Monday, the same day Darla was killed."

"Maggie," Grunkly said, grabbing ahold of my arm. "Maybe you should sit down." He flashed an apologetic look to Lois.

Lois pressed her lips together and nodded, as if accepting my great uncle's apology.

They think I'm insane.

Discomfort swept through me, either I'd gotten everything terribly wrong or Lois was a better actress than I'd bargain for.

Then, out of the corner of my eye, I saw a car pull into a parking spot across the street.

"You're a killer!" I shouted at Lois. "And the police know it, too! They've been staking you out!"

"What?" Lois exclaimed.

From the vehicle across the street, Brad and Ellington emerged. I raced to the front door and swung it open. "Help! Help!" I screamed. "Lois kidnapped my great uncle! She was trying to poison him."

"Kidnapped?" Grunkly asked.

Brad and Ellington jogged over. An orange kitten darted through my feet and out the open door. Lois squealed and ran after the cat. "She's getting away!" I called.

Brad hesitated, torn between chasing after Lois and getting to me. Ellington turned on his heel and chased after Lois.

"What's happened?" Brad asked.

I grabbed his arm. "She did it! Lois is the one."

Brad shook his head, looking from Grunkly to me. "What?"

"I came by here and she was screaming at my great uncle. Her face was angry, twisted. I had to stop her."

"No, no," Grunkly said. "She wasn't doing anything to me. I came to adopt a cat."

"What?" I asked.

Grunkly looked around the shop, but all the kittens seemed be to hiding. "Where is she? The little gray. Have you seen her? She's darling."

"Lois was standing over you. She was gesticulating wildly. I thought she was going to kill you!"

Grunkly laughed. "Oh, no. She was telling me a story. She's a hoot! She's a wonderful storyteller. She was telling my how Fran behaved when Lois told her she wanted to do whatever possible to keep the store lease. That woman Fran sounds like a piece of work."

"Well, what about the strawberry?" I demanded. "She was making you eat it."

"Making me? No. She wasn't making me. She offered me one. She brought a fruit basket to the house the other day, you remember?"

I shook my head. Frustration was boiling up in me, making me fidgety and angry. "Max ate one of her strawberries and got sick."

Brad reached out to me. "Maybe he's allergic. Lois dropped off one of her baskets at the station the other day. Everything got swallowed up in nothing flat."

I grabbed Brad's hand for support. "You must think she's guilty. I saw you and Ellington yesterday, staking out the place."

Brad frowned. "Staking out the place?"

I pointed across the street. "You were both there in the car. Ellington had on a headset. I assumed he was listening in on some kind of wiretap or something."

He shook his head. "We weren't staking it out. Ellington had dry cleaning to drop off. He was on his cell phone, talking to Cornelia. I had to wait while they made a date."

A rock formed in my stomach as, I glanced across the street to the dry cleaner. "Uh . . ." I stuttered. "The gem."

"Hmm?" Brad asked, leaning in closer to me.

"I found a gemstone at Chic Chickie, I thought it might have come from one of these collars."

Brad glanced around the room. "I don't get it," he said. "What does a gem have to do with this?"

"The other day, I saw that a lot of the cats here had on bejeweled collars. I thought the gem might have come off one of them. That maybe Lois had one in her bag or something, and it fell out." My reason sounded off even to my ears.

Brad frowned and blinked at me. "So what if it did?"

The rock in my stomach grew. He was right. Even if the jewel had come from Lois or one of her cats' collars, what did it prove? That she'd been inside Chic Chickie. Yes, but it didn't mean she'd pulled the trigger.

The rock inside my stomach turned to nausea and I gripped the chair Grunkly had offered me earlier.

Lois bustled back into the shop, cradling the runaway cat in her arms. "Thought we lost Little Archie for good this time! He's an escape artist."

Ellington stood outside the shop in the doorway and sneezed.

Brad gave me a sad look.

He thinks I'm crazy or pathetic or both.

He stepped closer to me and put a hand on shoulder. "Can I give you a ride home?"

I nodded, turning to Grunkly. "Do you need a ride also?"

He shook his head. "No, I want to finalize the deal for the cat." He looked hopefully to Lois.

She smiled wickedly. "Oh! I was going to hold off on all adoptions until our opening tomorrow. But who can resist you?"

"I'll need a carrier," he said. "And a litter box, too. Maggie, do you want to help me pick something up?"

I shook my head. "Stay away from the bejeweled stuff," was all I could mutter.

Ellington stayed behind to patrol the neighborhood, but I knew that was just an excuse to give Brad and me a chance to talk.

My skin prickled as I got into the police cruiser. I felt great disappointment building inside me. I'd accused a nice woman of a double homicide because I'd found a green gem in a store. What kind of logic was that?

I'd built a finance career in New York. Things used to add up in my world, and now I'd made a complete mess of things.

Brad drove me home in silence.

When he pulled into a parking spot across the street from my apartment house, I asked, "Do you want to come up for a few minutes? Have a cup of tea or something?"

He didn't answer but got out of the car and followed me up the stairs. A chill was overcoming me, either from still being in my sweaty running clothes or from the Brad's silent treatment.

Once inside my apartment, he said, "Please give me the gem, Maggie."

"The one from Chic Chickie?" I asked.

He nodded. "I'll admit it into evidence."

I frowned. "But you told me it was nothing. That it meant nothing,"

"It doesn't prove anything by itself. But it's my duty to admit it into evidence, even if it doesn't amount to anything."

"I understand," I said, but for some reason my feet remained rooted to the ground. Finally, I asked, "What about our rain check for lunch at the Charcoal Corral? Can you break away today for lunch?"

Brad bit his lip and glanced at his watch. His body language was not in my favor.

"Are you mad at me, Brad?" I asked.

He looked down at his feet and sighed. "I'm being considered for a promotion."

"That's fantastic!" I said.

He shifted, rocking his weight to his heels, slowly distancing himself from me. "It's a big deal, yeah. It's something I've been working toward for a long time." His eyes remained on mine as if he was trying to communicate something to me without actually having to say it.

"And?" I asked.

"It doesn't reflect well on an investigating officer when there's a private citizen running around town accusing people of murder."

"I'm sorry, Brad. I'm so sorry. Let me get the jewel." By the expression on his face, there was more he wanted to say now that he'd warmed up to the topic, but I suddenly felt the heat and I wanted anything but to hear whatever he had to say next.

"It especially doesn't look good for the officer if he's dating said citizen."

I flinched.

He said it out loud. There is no unhearing it now.

My heart cramped up and it felt like the wind had just been knocked out me, replaced by a searing pain.

I left him in my living room and retreated down the hallway. In my bedroom on my nightstand table was the green gem. It rested on my journal. I hesitated, then picked up both items.

When I returned to the living I handed them to Brad.

He examined the journal, turning it over it in his hands. "What's this?"

I felt hollowed out, but I had nothing left to lose. "It's my journal. It was taken the day someone broke into my apartment. I found it at the vineyard, when Max and I found Darla."

Brad stiffened. "You found this where, exactly?"

"It was in the bedroom where we found Darla."

Brad's eyes bore into mine. "You took this from the scene of the crime?"

My mouth went dry and I had no words.

"I thought you wanted to help us find the killer, Maggie. Why would you take a crucial piece of evidence?"

"I . . . I don't know. I . . ."

Brad exploded. "You don't know? Tampering with evidence is a criminal offense! It's actively interfering with an investigation."

"I didn't do it to interfere—"

"What other possible explanation can you have?" he demanded. "Sergeant Gottlieb is going to go through the roof. Do you know we arrested a man—"

"Hendrick, yes, I know."

"He can sue us. But that's not the worst case. Now a killer is free to strike again."

A suffocating sensation tightened my throat. It was my fault. All my fault. "It was stupid," I whimpered. "I didn't think. I just wanted my journal back."

I couldn't say all the rest of it. That I hadn't wanted to be embarrassed with him reading my innermost thoughts. It seemed so shallow now in comparison to catching a criminal.

Brad spun on his heel. "I have to get this over to the lab immediately. See what prints they can pull off of this besides yours and mine."

Chapter Twenty-seven

After Brad left with my journal, the gem, and a piece of my broken heart, I wallowed in self pity, serving myself an enormous bowl of mint chocolate chip ice cream topped with chocolate sauce and a heaping pile of unsalted peanuts.

How could I have been so stupid?

Lois? A killer?

The same nice lady who could have been my grandmother? What was I thinking?

I laid down to take a nap and ignored the fact that my phone kept ringing. I wasn't in the mood to talk to anyone about anything.

When I awoke, my mood was only slightly better. How could I have messed up the relationship I was building with Brad? Why hadn't I been able to see that my poking around would inevitably cause problems for him?

I recalled my talk with Ellington on the beach. He'd inferred that I was selfish. He'd been right. I'd dismissed Brad's requests to stay out of things for my own selfish motives.

My door buzzed and I fought the urge to ignore it. I slumped down the hallway to open the door for Yolanda and Beepo.

"Maggie! Why aren't you answering your phone? Is the battery dead?"

Before I could answer, she said, "You look awful! What's happened?"

I collapsed onto the couch and tucked my feet under myself as Yolanda took the seat next to me. I told her about my morning, about accusing Lois, about mistaking that Grunkly was under a threat, and, worst of all, about Brad cutting ties with me.

She frowned. "I can't believe it! He doesn't know what he's talking about. He's crazy about you. It'll only take a couple days, you'll see. He'll come around here, checking up on you, and before you know it you two will be holding hands and splitting a milkshake over at the Charcoal Corral."

I shrugged. "I don't know. I think I really messed this one up," I said.

She poked my ribs trying to get me to smile, but I wasn't ready to be cheered up out of my funk.

"Just wait until he's promoted, then he'll be over here soon enough. You'll see," Yolanda said. "But play the game a little differently next time."

"I'm not playing games."

"Well, that the problem," she said. "You have to play it a little. When relationships start out, one person is the pursuer and the other is the distancer. He got nervous that you were pursuing him too hard and now he's put some distance between you."

"That's ridiculous. What? Did you read it on some dating site or something?"

She grinned. "Of course. They all say that!"

I sighed and waved away her cheeriness. "I wasn't pursuing him anyway," I lied.

Beepo sniffed at my hand, waiting for me to stroke him between the ears. When I didn't move, Yolanda said, "He knows you're upset. He's not going to have it."

I stroked his triangle-shaped ears and he jumped up to settle into my lap.

I warmed to him, hugging him to me. "I never thought I'd appreciate a little canine affection."

Yolanda nodded. "They know how to cheer a girl up. And he won't walk out on you."

"I guess you don't have to worry about that sort of thing with Gottlieb, huh?"

"What? Him walking out? Sure, a girl always has to be on the lookout for that."

"I mean, he won't dump you for investigating. Or say that he's trying to get a promotion or whatever."

"Do you think he's the one who told Brad to end it?" Yolanda asked.

I shrugged.

"I'll talk to him," Yolanda said.

"No, don't. Brad's a grown man. It was his decision no matter what pressure came from above."

Yolanda shrugged. "Well, the good news is, you always have the hot chef."

"He's in New York," I complained, hating that it sounded like I was whining.

Yolanda patted my knee. "Let's get over to the Wine and Bark. I'm sure it will cheer you up. Plus, Rachel wants you to return those curtains."

I sighed. "No rest for the wicked."

<><><>

Yappy Hour was going strong when Yolanda and I arrived at the Wine and Bark. The Roundup Crew was already there and celebrating.

Cornelia, dressed in an oversize sweatshirt and jeans, leaned against the bar, chatting with Rachel.

"Hey, Maggie! I was hoping you could help Cornelia return the curtains." She turned to Cornelia. "I really appreciate you lending them to us."

Cornelia shrugged. "No problem. I know you'll keep my kindness in mind when I need a referral." She winked and turned to Yolanda. "Have you thought about my offer?"

"Yes," Yolanda said, "I've given it a little bit of thought." But before Yolanda could answer, Cornelia reached for a manila file folder that was on the bar. "Look at this," she said, flipping through some pages as Yolanda looked on.

Yolanda oohed and aahed, her enthusiasm growing with each turn of the page.

"What is it?" I asked, peering over her shoulder. They flipped the pages rapidly, but I could make out at least a few designs for purses. Yolanda suddenly grabbed the folder possessively.

"What's wrong?" I asked.

She looked at Cornelia. "Nothing, I . . . These seem . . ." She stuttered, which wasn't like her. "These designs seem a little familiar, is all," Yolanda said.

Cornelia beamed. "Great minds think alike. I also thought of a new name for your business. Cluckety Clutches," she said.

Rachel roared with laughter. "That's a great name."

"Well, you keep thinking about my offer," Cornelia said. She turned to me. "Maggie, are you ready to get the curtains?"

"One second," I said. "Let me see if we can borrow Max's truck."

Cornelia nodded, and I approached Max and Brenda. They were seated at a table in front of the window. A pitcher of Mutt-tinis between them and Pee Wee nestled at Brenda's feet. I noticed that Brenda, as usual, had on a new pair of shoes: silver flats that glimmered in the light. I tried to hold my shoe envy in check.

When Brenda saw me move toward them, she pulled over a chair for me. "What's up, honey? You look a little down."

I sat in the chair, and Max sprang up. "Where are you going?" I asked.

"To get you a glass." He went to the bar and grabbed a martini glass for me. When he returned to the table he poured me a cocktail.

"Not too much," I cautioned. "I need to borrow your truck to return the curtains."

He nodded and stopped short on the pour. "Why do you look so depressed?" he asked.

I filled them in on my morning, both of them listening intently. When I got to the part where I accused Lois of kidnapping my great uncle, Brenda laughed so hard she startled Pee Wee and nearly fell out of her chair.

"What were you thinking?" she said, through her fit of giggles.

I shrugged.

I told Max about turning my journal over to Brad. He bit his lip as he listened to me. "Are we in trouble?" he asked.

"We?"

"I was there with you. I knew you were taking it. I'm as much responsible for that as you are."

I patted his knee. "Aren't you sweet. It wasn't you, Max. It was me. Brad knows that. I'm the one responsible. Anyway, I don't think he's going to press charges, if that's what you're asking."

Brenda made a clucking sound with her tongue. "I guess it all depends on what they find in the journal."

"'In the journal'?" I asked, worried. What were they going to find in the journal? While I might have daydreamed a bit about Brad, I certainly hadn't recorded any thoughts that would help them solve the crime. Who would read it? I envisioned the entire police department snickering over my entries.

"I mean, *on* the journal," Brenda clarified. "If they find some prints that can lead them to the murderer."

I shrugged. "I hope I haven't messed that part up. Smudged them or whatever."

Brenda picked up Pee Wee and placed him in her lap. "Don't worry so much, Maggie. Maybe it's a dead end. The killer could have been wearing gloves when they handled it."

I turned to Max. "Are you allergic to strawberries?"

He frowned. "What do you mean?"

"You got sick when you ate a chocolate-covered strawberry from the basket Lois brought over."

Max laughed. "I hadn't thought of that. When I was kid I would break out in hives if I ate one. Then it just kind of went away in college. Maybe it's back?"

Brenda rubbed his back soothingly. "Oh, sweetie, did you get sick?"

They began to make cooing noises at each and I figured three was a crowd. As I stood, Max passed me the keys to his truck. Pee Wee must have figured the same thing because he followed me over to the bar, looking forlorn that Brenda preferred Max's attention to his at the moment.

From behind the bar, Rachel tossed Pee Wee a Bark Bite and he immediately forgot his woes.

Rachel wagged a finger at Max. "You have to be careful what you eat. The hospital called and the lab results finally came in. I got sick from peanut butter!"

"What?" Brenda said. "Are you allergic to peanuts?"

"No," Rachel said, "but I guess there was some kind of contamination at the factory. There was a recall, but I never saw the notice."

"Good grief!" I said. "Well, at least that's one mystery solved!"

I tapped Cornelia on the shoulder. "I'm ready to take back the curtains when you are."

As Cornelia got up, Rachel asked. "Are you all going to the grand opening?"

My mouth twitched in annoyance. "You mean at Kitty Corner?"

"Yeah," Rachel said, overly cheerful for my taste.

"You're supporting the opening? I thought we were in competition with them!"

Rachel's delicate features crumpled in confusion. "Competition?"

"The *Doggie Day* spread!" I said, hardly able to keep the harsh tone out of my voice.

Rachel held up a hand to soothe me. "Right, right. Well the cover decision is up to Vrishali, but Lois asked me to cater the event. Make it really pet friendly. All the cats and dogs in the neighborhood getting along." She shot a meaningful glance at Yolanda, who in turn pursed her lips. "We're serving wine and a few little appetizers . . ."

Yolanda harrumphed. "I told her it was a bad idea."

From across the bar, Abigail came over to join us. "I pulled a fabulous recipe from online: Kitty Litter Cake."

"Stop it!" Yolanda cried.

"No seriously," Abigail said. "You use Tootsie Rolls to—"

"Ewww. That sounds disgusting!" Rachel screamed.

Abigail scrolled on her phone. "How about Hairball Cookies?"

"No!" Rachel said.

"It sounds purrfect," Yolanda sneered. "Or should I say pawsome!" She gave a fake little cheer by swinging her hands in the air.

"We better get on those curtains," I said to Cornelia. "It's about to get ugly in here."

Rachel grabbed my hand. "Before you go, can you call Gus tonight? Please!"

"What for?" I asked.

"Ask him if he has any ideas. I can't serve the Arf d'oeuvres at a cat-themed party. There has to be something else I can make." She pointed a silencing finger in Abigail's direction. "Something other than Hairball Cookies and Kitty Litter Cake." She batted her eyelashes at me. "I'm sure Gus can think of something. And remind him, it has to be easy. You know my culinary talents are limited."

Chapter Twenty-eight

Cornelia and I carried out the curtains in short order, and piled them in the back of Max's truck. I revved up the engine, and together we took off toward Chic Chickie.

"Are you gonna be able to run the store?" I asked.

She shrugged. "Well, I talked to Fran's brother again. He said I should carry on with what we agreed. He's going to talk to Hendrick for me."

"That's a good plan," I said. "Hendrick's pretty torn up about everything. I doubt he'll stand in your way if you want to continue to run the shop."

Cornelia made a strange noncommittal grunt, which made me turn away from the road and look at her.

"It must be really hard for you to figure out which direction to go in now after Fran's death," I said.

She waved a hand in the air. "I'll land on my feet. I always do."

I maneuvered the truck into a parking spot outside of Chic Chickie. The storefront looked sad now without its bright curtains.

It seemed strangely vulnerable, as if it had been unwittingly stripped naked. Cornelia and I climbed out of the truck and circled around the bed to unload the curtains.

Her phone rang from inside her sweatshirt pocket and she pulled it out to look at the display. Without preamble, she pressed a button to silence the call.

"How are things going with Ellington?" I asked, as we unloaded the curtains.

She shrugged. "He's a very nice man. I don't know how long it'll last, though. But I'll enjoy it while it does. How about you and Brad?"

I felt something sour inside me. Being that I was dating both Gus and Brad at the same time, I wouldn't have thought I'd taken it so hard that Brad didn't want to date me. But I still felt terrible about it. Cornelia must have read something in my face because she patted my shoulder.

"Is something the matter?" Cornelia asked.

My eyes suddenly teared up, but I avoided her gaze. "Not really," I mumbled. I didn't know Cornelia all that well, and I didn't want to tell her about the fiasco with Lois the day before, and especially not about things with Brad.

She dug out the key for the store and unlocked the front door. Together, we stepped inside and put the curtains down in front of the windows.

Cornelia said, "I'll get the step stool."

She left me alone in the front, looking out the window. She didn't seem to have the heebie-jeebies about going into the back room any longer, which I supposed was good, if she was planning on running the shop while the business with Hendrick was straightened out.

After a moment, she returned with the step stool and reached to put up the left side of the curtains.

"Don't worry about Brad," she said, as if reading my mind. "Men sometimes need to be told what's good for them." She gave me a glance and I simply continued to stare out the window.

"He's angry with me. He didn't want me to interfere with the business about Fran," I said. Cornelia looked down at me.

Cornelia paused hanging the curtains and came down from the step stool. "What do you mean 'interfere'?"

I shrugged, trying to avoid the growing discomfort I felt in my belly. "I was holding back evidence."

Cornelia staggered back, lost her footing, and ended up sitting on the step stool. "What were you holding back?" she whispered.

"My house had been broken into," I said. "Someone took my journal. I found it the day I found Darla at the vineyard. My journal was there. On her nightstand."

Cornelia put a hand over her mouth and gasped. "Oh my gosh. So you think Hendrick broke into your place and took your journal. That's so creepy!"

Thinking about people riffling through my journal made my skin crawl. I shivered. "I know. It is pretty creepy."

Cornelia scratched at her chin. "I don't get it, though. What did Brad think the journal could prove?"

I shrugged. "I think he's hoping to lift some fingerprints off of it."

Cornelia eyes shifted in a way that made a chill zip up my spine. Perhaps I shouldn't have said anything about the journal.

She suddenly stood and took off her sweatshirt.

"I'm so hot in this. I can't continue to work." She threw it to the floor. When she took off the sweatshirt, she revealed a huge western belt that had the head of a rooster at her belly. The rooster looked suspiciously like Ronnie's prize chicken, and I had to stifle a laugh. "Do you like it?" she said, noticing my eyes stopping on it.

"Oh, yes," I said. "It's amazing."

She climbed back on the step stool and finished hanging the

curtains. When she turned to me, I noticed something that made my breath catch. The belt was bejeweled, and in the middle of one of the belt loops, where a belt loop ended, there was a missing spot. A million thoughts rushed into my head at the same time.

Could it be?

The gem that I had found had come from Cornelia's belt.

It made perfect sense. She worked here. So it had fallen while she was at the shop. There was nothing sinister about that.

And yet . . .

My knees felt weak.

I glanced around the store at all the chicken knickknacks. Cornelia had told me what a passion she'd had for it all. That'd been her idea. Her stolen idea. With no legal recourse . . .

Could Cornelia have killed Fran and Darla?

It all started to make sense.

I remembered Cornelia showing up early at the store the morning Yolanda and I found Fran dead. What had she been doing here? Coming to get rid of the body? Or maybe to scour the place for some forgotten evidence, like the gemstone?

Then what about my journal? She'd stolen it probably to see what I knew about the investigation. Then she'd left it at Hendrick's in order to frame him.

The room began to spin and I grabbed for the wall.

Cornelia gave me a sidelong glance. "Is something the matter?"

I needed to get out.

"I need air," I mumbled.

My phone buzzed from within my purse and I fumbled for it. Cornelia watched me as she moved the step stool toward the other window and began to put up the other curtain.

I answered my phone.

Yolanda practically shrieked in my ear. "Maggie! Maggie, are you all right?" she asked.

"Yes," I said, my eyes on Cornelia.

"Are you at Chic Chickie?" she asked.

"Uh-huh."

"It's her." Yolanda said. "Get out of there right now. I think Cornelia did it."

"Yes," I agreed.

Cornelia stopped working on the curtains and glanced at me.

Could she hear Yolanda through my phone? I began to back away.

"Shying away from the work?" Cornelia asked.

Through the phone, Yolanda said, "The designs that she gave me, that folder, I've been studying it since you guys left. I think the writing is just like the note you found in your apartment. And another thing, there's no way she came up with these designs on her own. I think she copied some of the designs that she saw when she broke into my house."

My blood seemed to drain to my feet.

"Maggie, are you there?" Yolanda asked.

"Yes," I said. "I should be over at the Wine and Bark in just a minute. We're finishing up here."

"She's with you?" Yolanda asked.

"Uh-huh," I said.

"Get out of there," Yolanda said. "I called Gottlieb. He sent Brad and Ellington. They're on their way there now."

I glanced out the window. Brad and Ellington were nowhere in sight.

"Okay," I said. "I'll be right there." I hung up.

Cornelia turned away from the curtains and loomed above me, narrowing her eyes at me. "What's going on, Maggie?" she asked. Her voice was suddenly deeper, with a menacing quality I'd never heard.

Adrenaline shot through my system, and my body tensed.

"There's been an emergency at the Wine and Bark. I have to get going."

I yanked the truck keys from my purse with trembling hands. Cornelia saw the fear on my face and seized the moment, she leapt off the stool and tackled me.

"What did Yolanda tell you?" she screamed.

I gasped for air and tried to squirm out from under her. "Are you crazy?" I squeaked.

She punched me in the stomach. "Answer me! What did she tell you?"

Some survival instinct deep inside me surged through the pain of her punch and I swiveled myself out from under her. "You killed Fran because she stole the shop from you!"

Cornelia went to land another punch, but I was quicker. I blocked her arm and kicked frantically, desperately trying to recall any self-defense maneuvers I could from a class I'd taken long ago in New York.

Eyes and throat are the most vulnerable.

She lunged for me and I swiped her leg out from under her. She staggered but caught her balance. We faced off against each other.

"Then you killed Darla," I said. My eyes darted around the shop searching for a weapon.

She gave a cynical laugh. "You're so naïve."

"Why did you do it? Why did you kill Darla?" I asked.

"I didn't want to kill Darla," she said. "She was in my way is all. I went up there to plant the evidence to frame Hendrick. Darla had figured it out, though. She was smarter than you. She figured it out from the beginning. You're a bit slow on the uptake, aren't you, Maggie? Doesn't matter that you have a New York pedigree. You're the same as us after all."

She circled me, forcing my back to the window.

She gave a snide smirk. "Fran stole all my ideas and started this business. Do you know how much money this business was bringing in? And she'd mock me every day, telling me I was just a stupid little fool for trusting her. I couldn't take it anymore."

She dove for me, but my hand shot out landing a blow to her throat. She fell back hard, toppling into the step stool, gasping for air. I scrambled for the front door, but Cornelia grabbed the step stool with both hands and swung it at me.

I ducked.

The step stool went flying into a display of chicken crockery that shattered to the floor. Cornelia rushed to grab a jagged edge of a broken spoon rest.

Suddenly there was a loud bang from outside the store. I looked up in time to see Brad and Ellington pop their cruiser onto the curb.

They stormed out of the car and rushed through the front door.

"Freeze!" Ellington said. He drew his gun and squarely aimed it at Cornelia.

She pointed toward me. "She attacked me in my own store! The woman's crazy!" she screamed.

"It's not true," I said. "She killed Fran."

Ellington seemed to shift his gun, so we were both in his range.

Was he mad? He couldn't possible think she was telling the truth!

"She did it!" I screamed. "Yolanda just told Gottlieb!" I said. "Cornelia stole the designs from Yolanda. Her handwriting is the same—"

"Let's just calm down here," Brad said. He put his hands out and motioned for Cornelia to drop the jagged piece of crockery she held in her hand.

The moment was suspended in time. All of us watching each other.

Cornelia dropped the crockery to the floor. It shattered into a dozen small pieces. Ellington quickly advanced, and put her into a police hold where he was able to swiftly handcuff her.

"What are you doing?" she demanded.

"We just need to ask you a couple questions. I'm sorry about this. You have the right to remain silent."

"Well, you don't need to handcuff me," Cornelia protested.

Brad moved toward me and took my arm.

"Handcuff her! Why don't you handcuff her?" Cornelia shouted to Brad.

"Let's go outside," Brad said to me. Together we stepped into the street while Ellington read the Miranda rights to Cornelia.

The sun had set during the short time I'd been in the store with Cornelia, and suddenly it felt like ages. I took a deep breath of evening air and sighed.

"Are you hurt?" Brad asked.

I rubbed at my stomach where Cornelia had punched me. "No. I think I'm okay. Shook up is all."

Brad grimaced "You couldn't stay out of it, huh?" There was a sad note in his voice that hurt me worse than the punch Cornelia had landed.

I stiffened. "I was returning the curtains from the Wine and Bark. I wasn't going to talk about investigations with her. It's just that, she's wearing the belt that has a missing jewel—" Before I could finish, Brad wrapped his arms around me and pulled me into his chest.

"I know," he said. "You were right about this one, Maggie. You knew it wasn't Hendrick all along."

"You didn't?" I asked.

"The evidence looked pretty compelling, but I realize now it was just Cornelia framing him."

Relief swept through me, so much so that I sagged into him.

"I'm so happy to hear it," I said, leaning into the hug and squeezing him.

He disentangled himself from me and regret immediately settled onto my chest.

My throat suddenly burned from holding back my tears.

Suddenly there was an awkwardness between us.

"You have to come to the station and give us your statement."

I nodded.

"You want me call the EMTs first?" Brad asked. "You should get checked out."

I waved a hand. "No, no. I'm fine."

And I was surprised to find that I actually was.

Chapter Twenty-nine

That evening I slept peacefully for the first time, it seemed, in weeks. I awoke to a series of text messages from Gus with various cat-themed concoctions: Cat Eye Cheese Balls, Cat Tea Sandwiches, and Pretty Kitty Cat Cake Pops.

Glancing at the images he'd sent along I was fairly sure Rachel could handle them. I forwarded his messages to her and rolled out of bed.

I'd stumbled into the kitchen to prepare a cup of tea and to mull over the events of the day before. I walked out onto my patio and gazed out at the mighty Pacific. The repeated sound of the surf lapping onto the beach lulled me into a peaceful stupor until my phone buzzed in my pocket.

I dug it out and answered the call.

"Got the recipes. Thanks," Rachel said. "I think I can manage tea sandwiches."

"I'm glad."

"I need you to help me serve at the party, though. I'd asked Cornelia . . . but . . . uh . . . well, you know."

After the showdown at Chic Chickie, I'd gone with Brad to the police station to give my official statement. And although I hadn't returned to the Wine and Bark last night, word had spread pretty quickly.

"I don't have any plans today. I can help you serve."

"Nice!" Rachel said. "Wear black pants and a white button-down top. I want us to look professional. Vrishali will be there."

I got dressed in short order and, headed out to Magnolia Street, to Kitty Corner. The banner for the grand opening had been restored and now there were several bunches of colorful balloons around the door.

Lots of families with children were lined up in front of the windows, gawking at the cute kittens. As I was about to enter the store, Rachel and Ronnie came into view. She had a tight hold on his arm and it brought a smile to my face. At least someone had ended up happily ever after.

Ronnie reached me first. "Congratulations. I heard you took down a killer," Ronnie said.

I shrugged. "Well, I don't know that I took her down. Brad and Ellington did that."

He laughed. "Ah, that's not the way I heard it."

"Well, who'd you hear it from?" I asked.

Ronnie motioned to the window. Inside, I could see Brad chatting with Lois and my heart constricted. I turned away abruptly.

"I'll swing by the Wine and Bark and get the wine," I said.

Rachel grabbed my arm. "No need. Max brought the wine over for us last night. And Brenda's bringing over the food. All we have to do is go in and set up."

My stomach seemed to flip over itself as we walked into the shop.

Fortunately, my sister steadied me, and I realized that I leaned on her for support almost as often as she leaned on me. Ronnie followed close behind us. I spotted Yolanda in a corner, looking like she was trying to disappear.

"I'm surprised you made it," I said. "Aren't you allergic?"

She wrinkled her nose. "Well, I wanted to do the good, neighborly thing, but honestly, I can't wait to get out of here. These cats are making my teeth itch," she said.

I giggled. "Beepo won't forgive you. He'll be able to smell cat on you, for sure," I said.

Yolanda glanced nervously at a kitten scampering by. "Anyway, I really just wanted to see you. Make sure you're alright after last night."

Before I could reply, Max and Brenda bustled in. Max held several trays of tea sandwiches, shaped like kittens and Brenda brought in the trays of cat cheese balls.

"You did it!" I said to Rachel.

She nodded. "Brenda and Max were lifesavers, though."

Together we organized the appetizers table, while Yolanda stood guard shooing the cats away from the food. I did my best to avoid Brad, who was now talking with Ronnie. Nervous energy raced through me every time he shot a look in my direction.

Max opened a few bottles of wine from Verdant Vines and handed one to me. "As soon as the doors open, we can mingle with the guests and serve wine to whoever would like some. We have some sparkling apple cider for the kids."

Lois rushed over to us. "It looks wonderful!" she said. "I'm so nervous. The new owner will be here. I have to impress him or my lease could be in jeopardy."

Brenda squeezed her elbow. "We're here for you, Lois. I'm sure Hendrick will be very reasonable."

Lois turned to me. "I heard you found the real killer."

Remorse weighed down on me. "I'm sorry I thought it was you."

Lois laughed and patted my hand. "Don't worry, dear. All's well that ends well." She took a quick look around. "Everyone ready?"

Rachel gave her the go-ahead, and with a flourish Lois opened the door to the crowd of families that were awaiting entry.

Soon the Kitty Corner was filled with noise. Kitties who were either eagerly awaiting attention and rubbing themselves against our ankles, or darting out of reach into the hiding cubbies of the tree tower.

Vrishali showed up, dressed as usual, in a breathtakingly colorful sari. She had the same bearded photographer in tow. She smiled happily when she spotted us providing the catering.

"Kitty Cake Pops, how clever!" she said with delight. She poked the photographer and he took a close-up shot of the cake pop.

Rachel flashed me a grateful look. I'd have to remember to tell Gus his ideas had been a success.

Vrishali leaned into Rachel and began to discuss something urgently with her. I tried to eavesdrop, but conversation ceased when Hendrick stepped through the front door.

He looked around the group awkwardly, then made a beeline toward me.

"Maggie, I can't thank you enough," he said.

Brenda and Max stepped close to us.

"We knew you didn't do it," Brenda said.

"It was just a matter of proving it," Yolanda said, joining us.

Brad reached our small group in two strides. He clapped Hendrick on the back. "I'm glad you decided to come out this evening. It must be a relief to know we have Cornelia behind bars."

Hendrick sighed. "I'm glad that everyone knows the truth, yes."

Brenda offered Hendrick a cheese ball, while Max filled his glass with wine.

Brad pulled me out of earshot. "I got promoted," he said.

My heart fluttered a bit. "Congratulations," I said.

Brad scratched his chin. "I was hoping you were free for lunch tomorrow."

Anxiety rippled through me. "Actually, I'm sorry. I have to work."

A look of disappointment clouded his face. "Oh. I see. I didn't know . . . Is there another cruise leaving . . . ? Or . . . do you mean you'll be working at the Wine and Bark?"

I loved that he was floundering, trying to figure me out. Maybe Yolanda had been right about the pursuer and distancer. Good, let him sweat.

"Sort of," I answered. "I'm going to start up my own bookkeeping service. I already have two clients. The Wine and Bark and DelVecchio's."

Brad looked worried for a moment. "DelVecchio's? Oh. Is that guy back already?"

"Not yet. But as soon as he's back in town. He'll open shop again."

Suddenly, Rachael held up her glass.

"Well, everyone, it's been quite a week. We've lost some good friends." Her eyes landed on Hendrick, and his eyes teared up. "And made some new ones." She squeezed first Ronnie's arm, then Lois's.

Everyone cheered.

She held up a hand to silence the crowd. "We have other news. The Wine and Bark will be featured in *Doggie Day* and will be the cover spread." Cheers erupted from the crowd.

Virshali applauded, then said, "And Kitty Corner will also have a special feature."

The photographer snapped shots of the group.

"We have to celebrate all the lovely animals and humans that we see here in this gathering," Vrisahli said. "Not to mention, all the love."

Lois picked up the orange kitten she called Little Archie and said, "That's so delightful. I can't thank you all enough. I also want to announce that Hendrick has agreed to let me stay in the building."

The crowd erupted in applause.

Lois handed Hendrick the kitten. "I know you've had a very trying time these last few days, Hendrick. But sometimes, a new little heart to love can make all the difference."

Hendrick wiped the tears that were streaming down his cheeks, and accepted the kitten. "I've already adopted Darla's little Maltipoo, but . . ." He gave Little Archie a squeeze. "I supposed one small kitten added to the family couldn't upset him too much." The crowd laughed and Little Archie let out such an enormous purr that Yolanda whispered in my ear. "Aw. Purrfect!"

Acknowledgments

Thanks to my wonderful agent, Jill Marsal, this series would not have been possible without your enthusiasm and persistence. Thanks to the editorial team at St. Martin's Press, specifically Jennifer Letwack and Cameron Jones, for your hard work, support, and patience! Special thanks to my dear friend Chrystal Carver, for all the brainstorming, chats, and critiques.

Thanks to Marla Cooper, my early reader, for your notes and support. Also, a special shout-out to my wonderful friend Marina Adair who keeps me laughing.

Lots of love and hugs to my Carmen, Tommy, Bobby, and Tom Sr., you all are simply the best personal cheering crew anyone could ever want.

Finally, thank you to all you dear readers who have written to me, your kind words keep me motivated to write the next story.